Ramon Pons
Count of Toulouse

Michael A. Ponzio

ACKNOWLEDGMENTS

Special thanks to John Horner Jacobs who created the cover.

This novel was enhanced by my wife – Anne Davis Ponzio.

Thank you Nancy Oberst Soesbee for proofing.
Thank you Suzannah Ponzio for help with the cover.

Ramon Pons: Count of Toulouse is the first novel of the
medieval series: Warriors and Monks

Other novels by Michael A. Ponzio
The ancient Rome series, Lover of the Sea:
Pontius Aquila: Eagle of the Republic
Pontius Pilatus: Dark Passage to Heaven
Saint Pontianus: Bishop of Rome

MICHAEL A. PONZIO

CONTENTS

The Historical Basis of this Novel

Raymond Pons (Ramon Pons in Occitan or French) was the Count of Toulouse, France from 924 to 966. Below are excerpts from historical sources.

924 A.D.: "The Hungarians led by Szalard launched an expedition into western Europe. They burned the city of Pavia, Italy, then pillaged Provence, southern France, and Gothia. Near Toulouse, France, they were defeated by Count Raymond III Pons of Toulouse. Raymond Pons's forces cut their army to pieces, as there were few survivors."
Source: View of the State of Europe During the Middle Ages, Vol. 1, Henry Hallam, 1866.

932 A.D.: "Raymond Pons with his uncle, Count Ermengol of Rouergue, and the Duke of Gascony, Sancho IV, travelled north to Paris to pay homage to Rudolph, King of France."
Source: Les Annales de Flodoard, 1905.

936 A.D.: "Raimundus Pontius . . .comes Tolosanus, primarchio et dux Aquitanorum et uxor mea Garsindis . . . —Ramon Pons, the Count of Toulouse, military commander and Duke of Aquitaine, and my wife Garsinda donated property to the Abbey of Saint Pons de Thomieres for the souls of our father Ramon and my mother."
Source: Projects MedLands-Toulouse, 2017.

"The Benedictine abbey of Saint Pons de Tomieres was dedicated to Saint Pons de Cimiez, who was Saint Pontius, martyred in 257 A.D. near Nice, France. Saint Pontius's relics were transferred to the abbey by Count Ramon Pons. Ramon proclaimed a nominal and affinitive identity between himself and the patron saint (Saint Pons)."
Source: Remembering Kings Past: Monastic Foundation Legends in Medieval Southern France, Amy Goodrich Remensnyder, 1995.

Author's Note

In *Ramon Pons: Count of Toulouse*, I did not use the term 'lateen', the triangular sail which may have been invented by the Arabs, because the word was not created until centuries after the historical events of this novel.

I also avoided the word gunwale, the uppermost edge of a ship's side. Originally the word was defined 'as a platform on the deck of a ship to support the mounted guns' and the term is currently used for ships with or without guns. This novel takes place well before the mid-fifteenth century, when the word originated. (and before guns were invented and mounted on ships). Instead I have used terms as: 'the side rail of the ship' or the 'side beam.' It's more cumbersome, but I do not want to disturb the reader with modern terms.

Literature sources dated 1650 to 1903, spelled the name of the site where the Saint Pons monastery was founded as Tomieres. The modern spelling of the town is Thomieres. Because *Ramon Pons* occurs in 924 A.D., the original name of the village, Tomieres, was used.

I have also tried to use words from the Occitan language, which was the most prevalent vernacular of southern France during the time period of the novel. Ramon Pons is Occitan for the main character more commonly written as Raymond Pons. Other words in the novel that the reader may think are mispelled French, Spanish, or Italian words are likely Occitan.

Western Europe 924 A.D.

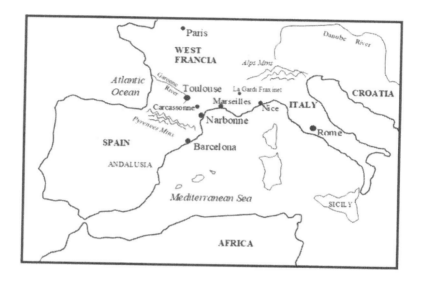

MICHAEL A. PONZIO

Political Divisions of West Francia 924 A.D.

England

Duchy of Normandy

Duchy of Brittany

●Paris

Royal Domain

County of Anjou

County of Poitou

Marche

C. Angouleme

C. Auvergne

Atlantic
Ocean

Limousin

Perigord

Quercy

Duchy of
Gascony

Toulouse●

C. Rouergue

Kingdom of
Provencal

County of
Toulouse

Gothia

Kingdom
of Navarre

C. of Barcelona

Mediterranean Sea

Andalusia

Muslim Spain

MICHAEL A. PONZIO

CHAPTER ONE

Ramon rode his warhorse at a gallop across the sun-drenched meadow and returned to his knights. There would be no more negotiations. He had been challenged by the Marquis of Lodeve, who now waited on the opposite side of the field. The marquis's army was in battle formation outside his castle. Ramon struggled to keep focus, but he was distracted by an overpowering scent that evoked recent events.

The lavender is bursting with beauty—my mother fancied lavender. I mourn her passing; it was only a few days ago, and even sadder for me because I was away. But I must secure the fealty of the allied counties before I return to home. It is critical and now I must concentrate on this duel. The marquis is rebelling against my father's realm, trying to break away. I cannot let this happen. Lodeve is an important holding in County Gothia, a territory belonging to our family and as large as Toulouse. I must win this challenge.

He reined in his mount and joined the second in command, his cousin Hugh. "Ramon, I can tell by the look on your face it's not good news."

"The marquis has challenged me to single combat."

"What! Most of the other nobles have submitted through negotiations. Up to now, we have had a few skirmishes, but no real battles. Now this? Ramon, we have more knights and we are much better trained. The men are ready to fight. Let us take care of this."

Ramon scanned his army. He had learned from his father to field a balanced force, comprised of mounted knights, infantry, and archers. The foot soldiers were *milites*, professionals who were highly-trained and well-equipped. The knights, chevaliers in the local French-Occitan dialect, were minor nobles and also vassals of the Count of Toulouse. Most of them owned manors that generated enough income for them to own specially trained warhorses. These steeds, which were trained to trample their adversaries and bite and kick upon command of their rider, could cost as much as half the annual income of a common laborer. The formation, archers in the front, infantry in the next line, and cavalry on the wings and behind, waivered little in the late morning sun, defying the building heat. Ramon sensed the tension and pressure mounting, anticipating combat.

"Hugh, I have not consented to the duel because of my pride. I learned that the Saracen Arabs have attacked Marseilles again. These Arabs have a fortress at La Gardi Fraxinet and bands of their horse archers have been sighted north of Narbonne. I agreed to have this match with the marquis to avoid weakening our joint defense against the Arabs. If the marquis wins, his prize is independence for Lodeve. And if I lose, I order you to take the men back to Toulouse. There will be no battle today."

Ramon turned and urged his steed to a trot toward the marquis. In his right hand, he gripped a heavy wing spear, its name derived from the metal protrusions at the base of the point. The wings prevented the spear head from penetrating too far into the target. He reached behind with his left hand and grasped a round shield which had been slung across his back. As did most of his knights, he wore a chain mail shirt, which consisted of numerous interlocked metal rings, made with detailed labor and at great expense. As the son of the Count of Toulouse, he could afford the highest quality armor. A one-handed sword and a dagger were secured in his belt. Equally equipped with a shield and wing spear, the marquis surged forward to meet the challenge. Both armies erupted in cheers.

Ramon was not conscious of his men's encouragement, but his blood raced with the pounding of his steed's hooves and its heavy breathing. They charged forward. He focused on the tip of the marquis's spear and as they closed, Ramon deflected the marquis's spear with his own. Ramon slid his spear along his opponent's weapon and smashed the marquis's hand, causing him to drop his own spear. As they passed, Ramon reached back and entangled the wings of his spear in the marquis's chain mail, pulling him off his horse.

Ramon sprang from his mount and pressed his spear point on his challenger's throat.

"Now do you pledge loyalty to my father?"

The marquis answered with his axe. In the blink of an eye, he chopped off the spear head and hurled the axe at Ramon. It glanced off Ramon's shield and struck his right elbow, causing the arm to go numb. Ramon pulled his sword from the scabbard but dropped it. He looked at his arm and there was no blood, but he could not hold his sword when he tried to pick it up. The marquis grinned as he drew his sword and came to his feet. He raised the blade high and charged Ramon.

Ramon counter-charged and crashed his shield into the marquis's sword. He continued to push forward, bowling the marquis over onto his back. His right arm now useless, Ramon discarded his shield and retrieved his sword with his left hand. The marquis, back on his feet, circled Ramon and tested his defense with cautious feints. Satisfied that his opponent's feeble and clumsy left-handed moves would be easy to penetrate, the marquis attacked with rash confidence.

Ramon parried a strong downward slash as he moved to the side and delivered a deep cut to his adversary's arm. The marquis dropped to his knees, trying to stop the bleeding.

"Sir, you could have cut off my hand, but you showed mercy," said the marquis. "You have won. I am in your debt! You can tell your father that Gothia is faithful to the Count of Toulouse!"

Ramon tore off part of his tunic to help the marquis stem the flow of blood. He signaled to his men, and then helped the military governor of Lodeve back to his soldiers.

Ramon was determined to know the location of the Saracens, and later that afternoon he dispatched scouts along the old Roman road to Narbonne. The road was an important link between the port city of Narbonne and Toulouse. It had been built using the highest standards, and had stood up to four centuries of wear. As they rode home to Toulouse, Hugh commented, "Ramon, you are a good and honorable man. You won the duel left handed. So I find it odd that the left hand is considered evil."

Ramon was quiet for a few seconds, then said, *"Those on the right inherit the kingdom of God while those on the left depart into everlasting fire.* This is from the Bible."

"Hmm. Well, the evil hand did good today, cousin! Does anyone know your story?"

"It's not much of a story, Hugh."

"But you keep it secret. I am the only man you spar using your left hand. Now the whole militia saw how well you fought left-handed."

"It is no matter. I am twenty-four. The marquis is ten years older. He's past his prime. A left-handed swordsman could have confused him. Besides, the knights will think I got lucky."

"I saw how you set him up, faking clumsiness. And the story. When you were little . . . how old? Three? Your father was traveling often, governing Toulouse, and never witnessed you playing wooden swords with your left hand. Then one day he saw you and shouted, 'Raimundus! Do not fight with your left hand.' He ordered the smith to make a small sword for you that day and started your training right-handed. What a great story! But it is a strength for you to fight equally well from both sides."

Ramon laughed, temporarily released from the melancholy thoughts of his mother's death, the threat from the Arabs, and his ailing father.

###

The massive walls of Toulouse always revitalized Ramon upon his return from travels. Since he had been an adolescent, Ramon had accompanied his Uncle Odo and his father, Ramon II, making the rounds to the various counties under their Toulousean governance. In the last couple of years, however, his father had become too ill. The younger Ramon, sometimes referred to as Ramon Pons or Ramon III, now took on these duties. But his father was still the count and major decisions were his.

Ramon led his knights into the city through the main gates, which were flanked by two barbicans, huge stone towers. The walls had been rebuilt a century earlier atop the original Roman walls and included more than thirty watchtowers. As they entered the east gate, Ramon glanced southward across the Garonne River. One of the original Roman bridges was still intact and in use, over five hundred years after its construction. Ramon and Hugh, accompanied by their squires, entered the courtyard of the seigniorial castle known as the Chateau Narbonne, the family residence. The knights disbanded and went to the stables where their squires would unsaddle and groom their horses. Hugh had the means to equip himself as a knight, and although he was a noble from the County of Rouergue, he had not yet proved himself in battle to be promoted to knighthood. He lived with Ramon's family in the chateau, which provided a secondary defense as a citadel within the city walls.

"I am indeed ready to be back at our chateau. The camp food does not compare with the royal cooks' fare!" said Hugh.

As their horses plodded across the courtyard, Ramon, his head lowered, wished he had seen his mother one last time before her death. Hugh noticed.

"Oh. I am sorry, Cousin. That should not have been my first thought at our return. Forgive me for being inconsiderate. Of course, we have returned to face the loss of your mother. She treated me as a son, as you have treated me as your brother. My older brother always tormented me when I lived in the Rouergue Castle. It is good I left. I thank your family."

"And I, having no siblings, the Good Lord has rewarded me with the love of a brother, Hugh. Thank you!"

The squires took charge of the mounts as Hugh and Ramon hurried to Count Ramon's chambers. When they entered his study, he was reading. He stood with difficulty and stumbled as he stepped forward to embrace Ramon. His son caught him.

"Father, I am sorry about Mother. You should sit, we have much to report."

"Not before I welcome home my other son. Hugh!" After pounding Hugh on the back, the senior Ramon sat, breathing hard, the simple task being a major exertion. "The reports can wait; let's go immediately to the Monastery of Saint Sernin, where she is buried. Son, I see you have brought her a bouquet of lavender. And the scent . . . the scent . . ." A tear rolled down his cheek. "She cherished those flowers." He gathered himself and continued, "I regret that we could not delay the burial, but your duties might have detained you further."

Servants carried Ramon's father to a litter waiting in the courtyard. They entered the city streets accompanied by Hugh and Ramon on foot. As they made their way toward the middle of the city, the count said, "Hugh, you grew up in Rouergue. Are you familiar with the first bishop of Toulouse?"

"No, sir, I am not."

"In the ancient times of the Romans, the Pope sent a missionary named Saturninus to Gaul. Saturninus: that was Saint Sernin's name in Latin. He became a leading citizen of Toulouse, preaching Jesus's word, and he was the city's first bishop. One day pagans were in the forum preparing for the sacrifice of a bull, and they insisted he take part in their ritual. He refused. They tied him to the animal as punishment, and the bull dragged him along the street and out of the north gate of the city. Thus, the bishop was martyred. The Christians of Toulouse built the Monastery of Saint Sernin in honor of the bishop. That is where my wife now lies, beside my father Odo and mother Gersende. When I die, I will be interred within a sarcophagus next to my wife."

They arrived and entered the graveyard, a grassy area with shade trees and rose bushes located alongside the monastery. It was well-tended by the monks–the roses climbed the walls and the hedges were clipped and manicured. He stood silently for several minutes with his father. Then Ramon, with head bowed, prayed aloud:

"Lord, those who die still live in Your presence, their lives do not end. I pray in hope for my family and friends, and for all the dead known to You alone. In company with Christ, Who died and now lives, may they rejoice in Your kingdom, where all our tears are wiped away. Unite us together again in one family, to sing Your praise forever and ever. Amen."

"Son, the priest said that same prayer several days ago. Your mother wanted a private ceremony, so there were only a few people here. You know your Bible and Scripture well. That is an important attribute for a leader of the people."

Ramon placed the lavender blooms on her sarcophagus. The stone carver's expert work was sharp and deep enough to last for centuries: Anno Domini 923, Guinidilda Pontius, Comitissa Tolosanus, uxorem di Raimundi Pontii, Comes Tolosanus.

"Your mother was a determined and strong woman, starting with the arduous journey across the Pyrenees to marry me. She sacrificed her life of ease in Barcelona to be with me. Then much of the time she raised you herself, which required stamina and discipline. You were always challenging her authority," he finished with a laugh.

Ramon laughed as well. "Yes, Father. I remember when she punished me by swatting me with a wooden spoon. Then she decided my bad behavior could be better tempered by exertion, so she let me have a spoon and we sparred with the spoons, but . . . she did not correct me when I used my left hand, which was natural for me."

After another moment's reflection on happier times, he sought an answer to a question. "Father, explain the engraving on her tomb. It is written with Pontius as a surname. I have heard you addressed only as Ramon."

"We are descended from a noble line of counts. The King of the Franks, Charles the Bald, appointed the first Count of Toulouse. Son, do you know the count's name? The name of your great-grandfather's brother?"

"Yes, it was Fredelo."

"And your great-grandfather's name, who became count when Fredelo passed?"

"Ramon."

"In that time, King Charles wanted to strengthen the loyalty of Toulouse. He could have chosen Frankish counts, but he wanted leaders the people would see as familiar, ones they respected and did not consider foreigners. Do you know the origin of the names Fredelo and Pontius?"

"They are Latin, Gallo-Roman names, names of the descendants of the Celtic Gauls and Romans together."

"That is correct, and when Fredelo was count there were more descendants of the Gallo-Romans than Franks or Visigoths living in Toulouse, just as it is today. We speak Occitan, from the Latin, not from the German.

"We are Toulouseans, a mixture of these nations. Our people might know they are descendants of the Visigoths, or the Franks, or Gallo-Romans, but we speak the same language and follow the same religion. You have read Caesar's *Gallic Wars*, Cicero, and Vegetius, and know that the ancient Romans always had at least two or three names, including a family name. The surname Pontius has come across the centuries. When you were born, I revived the ancient name, the surname we inherited. In Latin, your name is Raimundus Pontius, Ramon Pons in our language."

"Thank you, Father. I always felt honored to be named after you and your grandfather. Now I feel an even deeper connection, knowing of our surname Pontius."

On their way back to the chateau, Ramon could see his father was tired. He ceased their conversation. He would wait until the next day to recount his expedition.

Waiting until the third hour the following morning, Ramon and Hugh met with the count to report on the inspections they had made at the vassal counties. Two of the count's senior knights, Vermundo and Odulf, were present. A maidservant soon brought fresh bread, grapes, and wine for breakfast as they continued their discussion. Ramon had no messages yet from his scouts, but he finished the reports of his expedition to the outlying areas where vassals had confirmed their fealty. He was about to discuss the threat of the Saracens when his father said, "Ramon, you forgot to mention Gothia. Are they still our major ally, or are the rumors true? Have they turned against us?"

"Well, the Marquis of Lodeve agreed to affirm his loyalty to you after a . . . minor disagreement."

"I can see in your face and in Hugh's expression that there was something more than a minor disagreement. My legs may be weak but my heart can take grave news. I know you would not lie and risk our security by withholding information from me. I leave it to you to decide if I need to know more."

"When we arrived at Lodeve, the military governor had mustered his men and declared his city independent of not only Gothia, but from the County of Toulouse. Then he . . ."

The count and his veteran knights harrumphed in unison.

Ramon's father said, "Bello? It was Marquis Bello who did this?"

Ramon was uncomfortable recounting the event and said, "Yes, Father. Hugh, you can tell this story better than I."

Hugh described the single-handed combat, creating an enlivened story that the men followed with interest. When Hugh finished, spirits were high.

"Huh! I am proud of you, Son," Ramon's father said, "and Bello's family, like the Visigoths they are, must always prove their prowess. So, now he respects your bravery.

"Do you remember me telling you that Bello's grandfather had arranged the assassination of your great-uncle?"

"Yes."

"You could have taken revenge, but instead you cemented the marquis's loyalty, and refrained from killing him. That was the better way. There would be much turmoil in Gothia now if Lodeve had been forced to replace its governor. Now let's talk of the Arabs, but we have run out of wine."

Before he finished his sentence, Alda, his late wife's lady-in-waiting and the daughter of the Count of Quercy, brought in a pitcher of wine. The count sniffed the air and his eyes watered. "I am getting old and sensitive. I could swear that wine is blackberry vintage, my sweet Guinidilda's favorite."

The young woman, her blonde hair braided under a white and blue linen cap, said, "It is, Sire. I remember Lady Guinidilda sipping the wine as she offered her wise advice. Perhaps you can reminisce by enjoying this wine. It is first press from your own manor."

The count smiled and held out his chalice. "Guinidilda trained you well, Alda. I am hoping you will continue to stay and direct the household servants, but your skill at writing is something I appreciate even more. Please take your time with your answer."

"Sire, you may have my answer now; I would be honored to stay. I will send a message to my mother and father by way of the next courier."

She curtsied and looked down, but Ramon met her eyes for a fleeting moment as she stood to leave. *I am glad she wore a cap instead of a scarf which would have hidden her beautiful hair. And the blue headband matches her eyes! I wonder what thoughts she has behind those lovely eyes?* He caught himself, realizing his thoughts were elsewhere, then stood and pointed to the map etched into a wooden plank mounted on the wall.

"Umm . . . the marquis reported his men sighted raiders, horse archers, on the Roman road north of Narbonne. They raided isolated farms and manors in Gothia, burning what they could not carry away. Our scouts discovered from traders that Marseilles was sacked and burned! And God help us, they pillaged the Saint Victor Abbey. Two days ago, I sent a mounted troop south to scout along the road to Narbonne. None of them have yet returned.

"We must attack the Saracens, or they will destroy the crops before the harvest. Do not forget just three years ago when Abd al-Rahman's Moorish army crossed the Pyrenees. Yes, they did not try to scale our walls, but the manors and countryside were devastated. God surely saved us when they returned to Spain without any apparent reason. We also have our obligations to defend Gothia and the eastern counties."

The count added, "We must send out a strong force. I have heard the Saracens attack in bands of tens and twenties; then when you do not expect it, the small groups coalesce into an army."

Ramon continued as he traced his finger on the map, "And they will come through this area of flat grasslands and rolling hills, between the Causses highlands and the Pyrenees Mountains. Not only is that the easiest route, but they will want the open areas to maneuver their cavalry."

Vermundo, who wore his hair and beard long and untrimmed expressing his Visigoth heritage, said, "It will be difficult to catch them with our heavy cavalry. We will have to lure them into a small area, and we will need archers."

Odulf, with his neat Frankish beard in stark contrast to Vermundo, added, "There are few archers in the infantry."

The elderly count swallowed the blackberry wine, then burst out, "Guinidilda brought it!"

The men looked puzzled and confused.

"Father, what do you mean? Are you well?"

The count shouted at the door, "Alda!"

She entered, "Yes, sire?"

"Go to the library and bring Vegetius's book."

The young woman departed, and the count continued, "Caesar's book on the conquest of Gaul does not help. His primary force consisted of trained and disciplined heavy infantry. Their equipment and armor were more advanced than the foot soldiers of our militia. But I remember something in Vegetius's writing on tactics against mobile, light cavalry, which describes the way the Saracens fight."

Hugh asked, "Where did you get Vegetius's book?"

"Guinidilda brought me a copy from Barcelona. The Muslims in Spain have well-stocked libraries open to the public in their cities. They keep many documents that our Catholic faith does not think worthy of copying by the monastery scribes. The Count of Barcelona paid a large sum to a Muslim to smuggle a copy out of Toledo, and that Arab was very well-educated. He translated the book into Latin. My wife, thinking it could be useful, brought me a copy, quite a valuable wedding gift."

Alda arrived with the codex. She handed it to the count, who scanned the pages and then said, "Alda, read, starting here. Read aloud to us and translate to Occitan."

"The Roman general . . ."

Vermundo blurted out, "Romans? But they chiefly used infantry."

The count explained, "No, the Romans of the east, of Constantinople. They primarily use heavy cavalry, to this day."

She continued, "The Roman general is advised to deploy his infantry archers in the front line. Their larger bows must have greater range than those of the horsemen and could so keep them at a distance. Once the Turks, harassed by the arrows of the

Roman infantry archers, try to close into range of their own bows, the Roman heavy cavalry is to ride them down. When pike infantrymen are joined with foot-archers in one mixed unit, arrange to have one or two ranks of archers in front of and behind the body of pikemen: about three archers for every seven pikemen."

The men looked at each other in paused silence. Then Ramon said, "A large part of our militia are pikemen, and they are effective against mounted knights, but not horse archers."

"We have archers trained to shoot from the battlements of the city wall," Odulf added, "but we have not trained them as infantry on the battlefield. Besides, who would protect the city if we lost in battle and became besieged?"

The count said, "Although the range of a foot-archer's bow exceeds a horse archer's, it takes years for a man to master such a bow." He nodded toward the crossbow hanging on the wall. "Do any of you hunt? My son and I have rarely had time. The last time I shot that crossbow my father was still alive, but . . ."

"Yes," said Odulf, "I hunt with a crossbow like many other knights and squires. The crossbow takes longer to reload, but a person can be trained in a week to use the weapon."

"Collect all the crossbows we can find and train the militia to use them. And we will need to craft more bows as well," Ramon added. "Only maintain the number of pikemen needed to protect the infantry and use the other pikemen to hold shields while the crossbows are reloaded." He surveyed the group, "Will a crossbow out-shoot the bow of the horse archer?"

"I believe so," answered Odulf. Others nodded.

The count said, "Soldiers, we have a good plan."

Within a few weeks the Saracens invaded Gothia and ravaged hamlets and manors. Ramon organized his knights. He had collected three score knights and several hundred infantrymen. He marched south on the road to Narbonne and confronted a band of Saracens. The twenty or so horse archers approached the vanguard of mounted knights, let loose flights of arrows, then fled. Ramon pursued but kept his force in close order, suspecting an ambush. He was not surprised that within several minutes, as they passed copses of trees and small hills, the enemy force had grown to hundreds of Saracens. Then in clusters of ten to twenty horse archers, they harassed and probed Ramon's lines. Ramon ordered the infantry into a defensive wall composed of shieldmen, who were equipped with pikes and rectangular shields, to protect the forty crossbowmen. Dispersed among the crossbowmen was a smaller number of foot archers. Hugh directed the archers, while Vermundo and Odulf waited on the wings of the infantry line, each leading twenty knights. Ramon commanded the reserves in the rear with a troop of mounted knights to prevent the enemy from getting behind, and to reinforce the line when needed.

The Saracen horse archers dashed toward the infantry, released their arrows, and retreated. The large shields prevented any fatalities to Ramon's militia. Hugh judged the range of the Saracens' bows. As a second wave of Saracens charged, Ramon saw Hugh's signal flag being waved side to side atop a long pike. When the horse archers were still beyond the range of their own bows, Ramon heard a chorus of zips from his soldiers' crossbows.

The count lay in his bed, his steward standing by with a bowl of water as Alda pressed a damp cloth to the elderly man's forehead. The family's doctor had finished bleeding the count and was wrapping a bandage around his wrist. The physician handed a bowl of blood to a servant for disposal. Ramon and Hugh stood before the bed, sullen, and still dressed in their armor. Their hair and clothes were full of dust, and both were in disarray. Ramon's father opened his eyes.

"You look terrible! Did our strategy fail? Are the Saracens at the gates of Toulouse?"

Both men shifted from foot to foot and neither man answered.

"One of you say something. Were we foolish to apply the Roman's instruction?"

"Father, we came as soon as we heard you were sick."

"Ramon, if I die today, that's God's choice. Don't waste my last hours being sentimental. Tell me about the battle!"

Ramon glanced at Hugh. "Hugh will tell you, he was commander of the archers."

"The crossbows worked! We let them charge once without loosing our arrows in order to measure their range. Then at their next charge, our crossbowmen unhorsed at least twenty of their men. The unmounted horses created havoc and interfered with their retreat. That enabled our cavalry to envelop them. The survivors fled, but I believe they lost half of their force and will not soon return!"

The count forced out a loud, "Outstanding!" A coughing fit seized him and he spit out blood. Once he recovered, he motioned for Ramon to come closer. He whispered, "Son, I had wanted both Guinidilda and me to be buried at Saint Pons Abbey, but the Arabs destroyed it a decade before you were born. Remember, your most important duties are to God, the family, and the people's welfare. Rebuild Saint Pons and you will fulfill all these obligations."

"Yes, Father, you have my promise."

The count coughed up blood again and said, "And remember, hundreds of years ago the King of the West Franks entrusted the county to our ancestors. It is our duty to protect the people and be loyal to that ancient covenant. The king has not sent military aid in our lifetimes but has let us govern ourselves. There are many principalities, Barcelona, Provence, and others, that have cut ties to Charlemagne's former empire, but you must carry on the loyalty to the Frankish crown. That was our family's oath."

"Of course, Father. Please try not to talk now, you . . ."

"Son! Yes, I will talk! These are my last breaths!

"Ramon, get married. You need a successor."

The Count of Toulouse, Ramon II, then closed his eyes and slept.

Ramon stood and addressed everyone in the room. "Thank you for your care. Alda, please have blankets brought to the room. I will sleep tonight in my father's chair and I will call if I need help."

Ramon awoke during the night and checked on his father, who was still breathing. The house cat, a calico named Aylmer, had arrived after completing her nightly duty patrolling the chateau for rodents. The cat jumped on the bed and nested to sleep at the count's feet. As the morning light came in the window, Aylmer leaped from the bed to Ramon's lap, which alerted him that his father had passed away.

MICHAEL A. PONZIO

CHAPTER TWO

Three days after his father's death, Ramon stood before the sarcophagi where his mother and father were interred. Carved side by side upon the top of the stone tombs were life-size figures of Ramon's mother, Guinidilda, and his father, Count Ramon. The detailed image of Guinidilda held a Bible clutched to her chest. The sculptured relief of Count Ramon II depicted him in armor, a sword at his side, and his hands clasped in prayer. Thousands of mourners had joined in the funeral procession. After prayers by the Abbot of Saint Sernin, the citizens paid their respects at the tomb and departed. Many would later continue to the Notre Dame de la Daurade Basilica across the city to watch the accession of Ramon Pons to the position of Count of Toulouse.

Remaining with Ramon were his cousin Hugh; Sancho, the Duke of Gascony; Hugh's father, Ermengol, the Count of Rouergue; and Maiol, the Viscount of Narbonne. A few devoted friends and staff from the chateau stayed to pay their respects and offer their support. As Odulf and Vermundo departed, they each slapped Ramon and Hugh on the back. Vermundo said, "We loved your father. Have no worries, you have our loyalty, Count Ramon!"

The senior knights departed, and Ramon recalled the busy last few days conferring with his allies and confirming their loyalties. *Uncle Ermengol also recommended I get married so I will in good time have a successor. Until then he advised I*

*appoint Hugh as my heir, at least until the birth of my first child.
I sense his continued loyalty is contingent upon taking his
advice. Then the Viscount of Narbonne, Maiol, recommended I
marry his daughter to strengthen our alliance. My father died
just three days ago and the politics are already beginning. I
agreed to marry her. It is my duty, but it is also important
because Narbonne has been quite rebellious. Loss of their
loyalty would close the only port on the Mediterranean available
to Toulouse. I do not know when this marriage can take place,
considering my responsibilities. And the one bit of advice I will
take from Uncle Ermengol is to hold a public accession without
delay. At least Uncle respects Father and my inheritance of the
county. King Rudolf could appoint someone else as count if I do
not act quickly.*

The entourage of family and nobles proceeded to the
Basilica of Notre Dame de la Daurade on the Garonne River, a
few blocks south of the Saint Sernin Monastery. After passing
through the forum, they arrived at the church, a dodecagon
topped by a dome. Monks were walking in silence between the
basilica and the adjacent Benedictine monastery, alternating
between their prayers and studies.

Ramon had attended Mass with his family at the cathedral
throughout his life, and he had memories of being there with his
parents. The count had refused to sit and had always stood
during Mass, as did the citizens. To honor the people's wishes,
the count had conceded to stand in front. It also allowed the
young Ramon Pons to see the activities of Mass. His father had
told him that when Toulouse had been the capital of the
Visigothic Kingdom hundreds of years earlier, their kings had
attended the same basilica.

They paused now at the entrance before they pressed through
the crowd into the narthex. The fluted Roman columns lining
the front of the building reminded Ramon of what he had once
been told. The original use of the building had been as a temple
to Apollo. They walked down the nave toward the apse and
entered the seven-sided sanctuary. His gaze fell on the niches
contained in the ornamented columns, then his eyes drifted
upward to the brilliant golden mosaics.

"Count Ramon, it is truly stunning, no? The basilica's name in Latin, 'Our Lady of Gold,' was inspired by these mosaics." Armandus, the Bishop of Toulouse, had come in behind them and was supported by an attendant monk. The bishop had grayed and had difficulty walking, but his eyes were lively and intelligent. "Again, please accept my condolences for your father. He was a deeply pious man and has joined his faithful wife in Heaven."

Ramon genuflected and kissed the bishop's ring. As he stood he said, "Thank you, Bishop. He loved his people and was a devoted father."

"So, we will have a simple ceremony for the people?" said Armandus. "All of you will assemble with me near the altar. I will kiss you to show acceptance. Secular approval will be shown by the presence of your uncle, the Count of Rouergue, as well as the Duke of Gascony, and also the Viscount of Narbonne. Then, to indicate your successor, you will read the document you have prepared. Yes? Then let us proceed."

Sancho left soon after the funeral. He was required at home, west of Toulouse in Gascony, to defend against the constant threat from Vikings. These raiders had been known to row quickly up the rivers and attack at any time. Ramon's uncle, Ermengol, and Maiol, Ramon's future father-in-law, both departed the next day. Their presence was needed in their own realms. The Marquis of Gothia had chosen not to attend the funeral and the subsequent accession because the Saracen raiders were a constant threat on the eastern frontier. He dared not leave his lands unprotected.

The next morning Ramon finished breakfast with his cousin. He seemed distracted, picking only at some grapes and tearing off chunks of bread, but leaving them and his wine. "Hugh, return with me to the Daurade Basilica. I made a pledge to my father to rebuild the Saint Pons monastery. The Abbot advised me to talk to Bishop Armandus, who may know some history of the monastery."

"Cousin, perhaps you should allow time to grieve for your father. Can this wait until later?"

"No, Hugh. It is not necessary. My father and I had a deep, supportive relationship. I have mourned for him over the last two years as he declined. Besides, doing this duty is a way for me to grieve."

Hugh shrugged and agreed to go with Ramon. As they passed the forum, Ramon looked down the Artisans' Lane off to the right. *When I was a child, I remember strolling in this area, watching all the craftsmen working in their open stalls, and I recall Father taking me to sermons at the church at the end of that street. The church had an odd name, Saint Pierre des Cuisines, and I found out the reason. After each sermon, the congregation cooked together and served hearty food. That is where I saw for the first time the Christian pilgrims, who were passing through Toulouse on their way to the Kingdom of Leon. They were on lengthy journeys from northern Europe to the Cathedral de Santiago de Compostela to revere the holy relics of Saint James and to find blessings and miracles.*

Father set a good example; he always went out into the city to be with his people. He never paraded his royalty. El diable! I forgot to employ the woodworkers to craft new crossbows. Tomorrow I will return to the Artisans' Lane with a model.

Ramon felt a tug on his sleeve. Hugh pulled him into a tavern and he nearly tripped. A cat napped on the door step, oblivious about the foot traffic. Many shops in Toulouse had their own cats, and people were used to them lounging on the steps and in the doorways.

"Cousin, let's have a quick drink. It will cheer you. Remember the Bible says, 'Wine makes the heart glad.'"

"Psalms. Hugh, quoting the Good Book!"

Ramon's father had visited taverns to socialize amongst the townsfolk. He had brought young Ramon, who was served very diluted wine. Today's short excursion marginally improved Ramon's mood. After one drink, they continued to the basilica.

They were welcomed into the bishop's study, which overlooked the Garonne River, its flow steady and swift during the early spring. They sat on wooden benches and shared bread, hard cheese, and wine. A shelf along the wall contained a collection of books and scrolls.

"Count, please forgive our simple wine and austere furniture. I am sure you are used to a more comfortable lifestyle."

"Yes and no. When I travel to nearby counties I often camp, sleeping on the ground or in a tent. But when I am invited to the castles of our allies, they occasionally treat us splendidly, with spiced wine and sumptuous quarters.

"Bishop Armandus, my father said there was a monastery called Saint Pontius or Saint Pons. The Abbot of Saint Sernin said you might know of the abbey."

"Yes, I am likely the oldest bishop in Toulouse and Gothia, so you came to the best source. Count Ramon, uh, Count Ramon Pons, are you interested in Saint Pontius due to your namesake? When you were an infant, I baptized you as Raimundus Pontius."

"Yes, Bishop, but only partly. My father told me this was a surname of our ancestors, but it's primarily because I made a promise to him that I would rebuild Saint Pons monastery."

"Rebuild Saint Pons? What!" He took a moment to compose himself. "No, no, forgive me, Count. I should have not burst out like that. But did he tell you where Saint Pons was located? It's hundreds of miles away. The Saint Pons abbey is in Cimiez, a village on a hill overlooking Nice. But before we discuss the abbey, do you know the story of the monastery's patron saint, Pontius?"

"No, Your Excellency, please continue."

"Pontius was a senator who lived in Rome during the third century. He gave up his belongings to the poor and devoted himself to good works, including the conversion of Emperor Philippus to Christianity. After Philippus died, his successor Decius renewed the persecutions of Christians. Pontius escaped from Rome and hid in the foothills of Provence. Remorseful for hiding, he returned to preaching and was martyred in Cimiez. Many years later, Siacre, the Bishop of Nice, founded the Saint Pontius monastery where the relics of Saint Pontius were interred. Then, sadly, the Arabs destroyed the abbey."

"When did this happen?"

"Hmm. Let me figure. The monastery lasted over one hundred years. The Arabs plundered the abbey as well as the city of Nice thirty or forty years ago." Then the bishop choked and leaned over as tears flowed. "Oh, Lord, what have we done to deserve this! The cities of the coast have been terrorized by the Arabs, Saracens, Moors, whatever they are called, they are all Muslim disbelievers!"

"Your Excellency, would you prefer we come back at another time?"

"No, young man, I just grieve over the suffering of the people. Christ said that we will suffer, but we will prevail. As in the gospel of Matthew, 'You will be hated by all because of My name, but it is the one who has endured to the end who will be saved.'"

Ramon added, "For I consider that the sufferings of this present time are not worth comparing with the glory that is to be revealed to us."

"Ah, ha! You read your Bible! That is from the Book of Romans, sir! I am now with good cheer! Let's continue. May I make a few suggestions on your mission, Count Ramon?"

"Yes, of course, Your Excellency."

"There are several reasons why it is not possible to revive the monastery at Cimiez. The monasteries along the coast have been destroyed or have been moved inland, away from the Saracen pirates. Besides, being that far away, the land is part of Provence, land where you do not have jurisdiction. Toulouse already has two monasteries. I suggest you build one in another town on your own land holdings. Your people would benefit from the monastery."

"Yes, good advice, Your Excellency."

"And to sanctify the new Saint Pons monastery, the relics of Saint Pontius should be retrieved."

"Yes."

"The journey to Nice will be long and dangerous. Because the Arabs control the sea, the expedition must be overland through Provence. If you donate the land and acquire the relics, I will help build the monastery and assign monks to staff the property."

"Agreed, Your Excellency. I will ask the Count of Provence for his consent to travel to Nice. Do you have the name of any clergy who may know the whereabouts of the relics of Saint Pons?"

The bishop addressed his aide, "Please bring me the codex on the dioceses." The aide removed a book from the shelf. Bishop Armandus turned a few pages, frowned, pointed, and asked his attendant, "Is this correct?" His aide nodded.

"Count Ramon, Nice has not had a bishop since 791. That is over a hundred years! It must be due to the Arab raids on the coast."

`"What is the next closest diocese?"

"Toulon. Let us see. No, the list also shows the bishop's position is vacant. The closest bishop is Honoratus II in Marseilles, but the Saracens burned the city months ago."

Ramon spent the next several days reviewing the management of the family's manors that were outside the city. At the chateau, Alda helped Ramon understand the roles of the staff and the organization of the household. Several times he lost concentration as they sat close to one another. He was stirred when by chance their hands made contact while she pointed out items in the account books. *Why didn't I pay more attention to her these last few years? But I have accepted Maiol's offer to marry his daughter. Too late, I must simply enjoy her company, which is a very pleasant diversion.*

Ramon worked long hours the next day to balance expenditures and determine the salaries for his professional soldiers, the milites. He estimated the costs to repair weapons, fabricate new armor, and maintain the chateau and the city walls. *There are enough extra funds to make 200 crossbows. The weapons take skill to make and are expensive. But I have no choice. It requires years to train a man to use a hand-drawn bow. Hmm, or the money could be used instead to send an expedition to retrieve Saint Pontius's relics. It will be difficult to get the relics. Cimiez is hundreds of miles away. The Saracens control most of the coast, have built strategic castles, and take hostages for ransom. The countryside is swarming with these Arab raiders.*

Hugh entered his study, "Count, four men have arrived from Marseilles with a prisoner. They claim he has important information for you."

"Marseilles? Bring him to the study. Feed his companions, but make sure we have our men watching them."

Within minutes Ramon could hear footsteps approaching his study. He hid his dagger behind his back and sat. Hugh entered the room, followed by two of Ramon's milites guarding the prisoner, who had his wrists tied behind his back. The guards remained behind him. Two more soldiers stood just outside the open door. The stranger had the dark complexion of a man who worked outside as a farmer or fisherman. His brown eyes were so dark they looked black. He bowed to Ramon.

"How did the men capture you?"

"Count, I will be truthful with you. I am their leader. My name is Abd al-Samad, the captain of the Andalusians at the Massif des Maures."

Ramon blinked. Weapons clinked as the milites placed their hands on their swords, ready to draw them. Hugh said, "I checked, he is unarmed."

Ramon glared at the visitor, "Explain."

"I want your help, and in turn I can help you against an impending danger."

"What threat is that?"

"There is a tribe of nomads called Hungarians. From their homeland east of Croatia, their swift, mounted armies have raided and plundered towns in Germany and Italy. The wealthy city of Pavia was recently burned and sacked. A large force of their horse archers then attempted to invade Francia through the Alps. Count Rudolph of Burgundy led his forces and tried to surround them in the mountain passes, but the Hungarians escaped. They turned south and returned to Italy. I have been informed they are moving west and are raiding Provence.

"Do you know how many Hungarians are in their army?"

"It is hard to determine their numbers because they travel in small raiding parties of between fifty and a hundred. Based on the reports of my scouts, there may well be over 3,000 moving toward Gothia. That was the number of Hungarians that attacked Pavia."

"You say you lead the men that travel with you. They are Europeans. Why do they follow you?"

"Do not become angry when I tell you, respected Count. I convinced them to bring me here under the guise that I was their prisoner. They are Christians, and their families in Marseilles are my hostages. When I safely return, their families will be freed."

Ramon said, "Hugh, talk to his companions and ask them about his claim."

"Captain Samad, you are from Massif des Maures. You mean the Saracens' stronghold at La Gardi Fraxinet?"

"Yes, that is the place. I have Saraceni blood, but my family has lived for generations in Andalusia, which you call Spain. So, you see, I am European as well. Now I live in La Gardi Fraxinet."

"Why are you warning me about the nomads? Do you propose an alliance against the Hungarians?"

"An alliance in sharing information, rather than on the battlefield. I am afraid your soldiers and mine may have bad blood between them."

"Untie him," Ramon said to the guards.

"Samad, would you like wine?"

"No, but I will have water."

Ramon poured water from a pitcher and handed it to Samad.

Samad raised his cup, "To your health!"

Ramon saluted with his wine. "Are you sure you wouldn't like wine? Um, Samad?"

"No, I am a religious man, as I have heard you are a devout man, and Muslims, at least sincere Muslims, do not drink wine. So I will just imagine this water is sweet like the juice of oranges!"

"What is an orange?"

"A sweet fruit grown in Andalusia."

"Like grapes? Would you like grapes?"

"Yes, of course."

Ramon nodded to the men at the door and then said, "Tell me how you can help us, Captain Samad."

A servant brought a plate of grapes, and Ramon offered them to the Andalusian. "You are a fine host and a gentleman, Count Ramon. First, I must say, I am allying with you so we can both carry on as we have in the past. That is, the Andalusians will keep control of the Provence coast. The local nobles and Christian religious leaders in the Provence towns, however, may stay self-governing on the condition they pay a tribute to us."

"I propose that we coordinate to expel the Hungarians. They are coming, you can be certain of that. We want to keep our holdings and you wish to retain your lands."

Hugh returned, stood in the doorway, and said, "The men say he is telling the truth. Their families are hostages in Marseilles."

Ramon could see that Hugh was fuming. Ramon said, "Tell us what you are thinking, Cousin."

"They also told me it was Samad who led the attack against us several weeks ago."

"Yes, that is why I am here. I have seen your tactics and can help you against the Hungarian horse archers. I will improve your strategies."

Ramon rose from his chair and whispered to Hugh, "Brother, hold your anger. He is our guest and we can benefit from his information."

Hugh said, "I will be silent, Brother."

Ramon returned to sit with Samad. "How do I know the men with you are not lying. They may be your soldiers."

Samad said, "You don't, but I have a more valuable hostage that might convince you."

"Who is that?"

"The Bishop of Marseilles."

"I was told you burned Marseille."

"Only a small part of the city. And not the bishop's church."

Ramon paused, then said, "Then tell me, what is the bishop's name?"

Samad, without hesitation, said, "Honorius, of course."

The count leaned back in his chair and said, "Tell me your plan, Captain Samad."

The Arab focused on Hugh. "You have my highest respect. I remember during our battle how you directed your archers and tricked us. You measured our bow range on our first charge. I would recommend you also use that tactic with the Hungarians. The Hungarian bows and the Saracen bows are similar. You already know their range."

Ramon stayed quiet for several long seconds. "Is that all you have to say? Are you also going to fight them?"

"Yes, in our own way and not to cross paths with you," said Samad. "And if you can choose, fight them in the rain. Their bow strings must be dry. Also, each Hungarian soldier has three or four horses, riding them in turn so as not to overwork any of them. Do not pursue the Hungarian horse archers. Ever! It is always a trap. They can shoot backwards as well as they can forward. And they can hang on the side of their horse, unseen, and shoot from under the horse's neck. Their leader is named Szalard. Do not trust him. He promised the leaders of a town in Italy that their citizens could leave unharmed if they surrendered, but he slaughtered everyone once they opened the gates.

"Sir, if you do not want our help, then I will negotiate with the Hungarians."

Ramon forced himself to stay calm. *I hope Hugh doesn't lose control!* Hugh scowled, but remained quiet. Then the count said, "I will be your ally against the Hungarians if you will promise not to enter any of my domains again." He stood and pointed to the map on the wall and continued, "That includes the counties of Rouergue, Quercy, Gothia, and Toulouse."

Samad smiled, "Agreed. And you must promise not to give military aid to the Count of Provence."

"Agreed. Are you willing to sign a document to that effect? Err, you speak Occitan well. Do you read Latin?"

"Of course, sir. I read Latin and Arabic."

Ramon smiled and said, "There is one more condition I ask."

Ramon sent Odulf with a troop of knights to escort the Andalusian captain and his men to Narbonne, where they headed east to return to Provence. He showed Hugh the agreement written and authenticated by the city scabini, the Judge of Toulouse, and signed by Armandus, the Bishop of Toulouse. After Hugh read the short document he said, "I see the scabini wrote that the Saracens will not enter our territories and we will not help Provence. Hmm. Yes, I see, you are rather shrewd. That will still allow us to maintain our loyalty to King Rudolph because Provence has denied fealty to the king. And that means the Arabs will not help the invaders, at least in our territory. They did not agree to fight alongside us. And I see the Andalusians will 'give safe passage to Cimiez for representatives of the Count of Toulouse to retrieve the relics of Saint Pons.' That was a good addition, Ramon.

"I also see that Bishop Armandus insisted we add to the agreement that the Arabs must let the Bishop of Marseilles reopen the city's cathedral."

"Samad agreed and told me the citizens of Marseilles have their rights protected under Saracen laws, but they are required to pay a tributary levy, which he called the *jizya* tax. He referred to non-Muslims living under his rule as *the people of the dhimma*."

"Hm, *people of the dhimma*, repeated Hugh. "I am surprised of the impartial treatment they give the Christians, but then the Arabs want a productive city, not ruins." He retrieved the crossbow mounted on the wall and headed out the door. "It is a good agreement. And now I am going to Artisans' Lane."

CHAPTER THREE

Ramon dispatched riders to notify his vassals of the impending invasion and to recruit more knights and archers for his army. He placed scouts on the eastern Gothia frontier in the towns of Rodez, Millau, and Nimes. More tales reached Toulouse of the horrific devastation in Pavia. As one of the largest towns in Italy, it had been populated by more than ten thousand citizens before the Hungarian attack. Over forty churches had been burned. Only several hundred survivors had made it alive to the nearby city of Milan, the rest killed or sold into slavery.

Ramon, Hugh, Vermundo, and Odulf sat in conference in the chateau. It had been two months since the Andalusian's visit. Ramon's army had swelled from under a thousand to over 1,500 with the addition of milites from the surrounding counties. No sightings of Hungarians had yet been reported.

Ramon addressed his leaders. "What other changes do you recommend, considering Samad's advice? Remember, he said each Hungarian soldier has three or four horses."

Odulf said, "Their strategy of constant hit and run depends on a supply of fresh horses. The reserve herd is probably lightly guarded. I would find a way to scatter their supporting herds. The squires can do that. This a chance for the squires to show their training."

"Good."

"We know their horse archers are inferior to our heavy cavalry in hand-to-hand combat. We must engage them, but not chase them or they will shoot us full of arrows. They have less armor and will try to keep their distance while they rain arrows down on our knights."

"Vermundo?"

"Engage them only when our crossbows can support us."

"Good, stick to this strategy and make sure all your men understand the plan. Stay together, remain patient, and do not pursue the horse archers!

"Hugh, what about the crossbow training?"

"We have 300 crossbows. The men can shoot accurately."

"The Hungarians are very confident when they are in open ground," Ramon said. "They were stopped in the confined passes of the Alps where they could not use their superior mobility. I expect their horse archers will attack, then retreat and try to get us to chase them. When our ranks breakup, they will be able to surround and pick us off in our isolated groups. Hugh, tell us your plans for the archers."

"The large rectangular shields will provide good cover for our crossbowmen. Because of the slower reloading time for the crossbows, the standing archers are dispersed among the crossbowmen. They will shoot when the crossbows are loading. As Vermundo mentioned, our knights should stay within range of our own archers for support. Our cavalry will charge if we are able to find a way to interfere with their retreat."

"Our tactics worked against a few hundred Saracens," said Ramon, "because we surrounded them in their confusion. But thousands of Hungarians could outflank us, putting our knights under threat from their arrows. They want our knights to chase them. We must resist that trap. Their horse archers are faster and can shoot backwards as they ride."

"We can protect the knights by forming our infantry in a crescent, the bulge toward the enemy and the knights staged on each end," Hugh said. "The enemy archers will have to pass through the firing range of our crossbows to reach our knights if we are not in a wide open plain. Thus our best hope is to fight in a valley or on the edge of a wooded area."

Ramon said, "I hope to get that choice. You are brave men, as are your soldiers. But we must remain patient. Timing is everything."

Ramon did not have long to wait. Three days later, messengers arrived in Toulouse with news that the Hungarians had set fire to the outskirts of the city of Nimes and had pillaged the surrounding areas near the eastern border of Gothia. Ramon estimated they would engage them within one or two days, based on the Hungarians' westerly movement. After all the preparation and waiting, Ramon was eager to fight. He led his army to camp near Carcassonne, halfway between Toulouse and Narbonne, where he chose to confront the advancing Hungarians. The ancient fortifications and city had been constructed half a millennium before by the Romans. There were scores of towers built into the walls with overhangs to drop hot oil and objects onto the enemy and to catch them in crossfire from archers. Situated on a hill, the fortifications afforded visibility for several miles in all directions. In the event of failure on the battlefield, the Toulouseans would retreat to Carcassonne. Within the walls the city had wells to supply water, and sufficient gardens and supplies in the event of a siege.

On the morning of June 10, 924, after the dew had evaporated from the grass, the signal came from the city towers that the Hungarians were approaching. Ramon directed his army to assemble in formation across a large meadow bounded by the Aude River on the left and woods to the right. He considered this an ideal location. The infantry ranks, consisting of over 1,000 men, were placed in the center. Their lines formed a crescent, bowed outward in the direction of the enemy. Hundreds of pikemen and shieldmen protected three hundred men equipped with crossbows. Troops of mounted knights were positioned on the flanks at each end of the crescent. Odulf and Vermundo, with reinforcements from Toulouse's vassal counties, now each commanded nearly 100 heavily armored knights. The infantry was half hidden in the long grass of the meadow, but armor glinted in the sun on either end of the crescent. Ramon was satisfied — one flank touched the Aude and the other the woods. There were no gaps.

Other than the clanging of metal weapons and the creaking of saddle leather, the field was relatively quiet. The soldiers had orders not to carry on any unnecessary conversations so they would hear their officers' orders. A redolence of horse scent was prevalent, but in this open meadow the cool winds blew down the Aude Valley from the mountains, carrying the scent of vineyards, pine shrubs, and sweet flowers, which masked the steeds' aroma. On a less stressful day, Ramon would have acknowledged and enjoyed the fragrance of the south of Francia, but today he was obsessed with battle. The allied troops displayed an array of colorful tunics and banners. The majority wore the bright red color of Toulouse emblazoned with the gold Occitan cross. The knights from Carcassonne wore their sky-colored tunics upon which was an image of the castle walls, the symbol of their city. Snapping in the breeze was the banner of his uncle's soldiers from Rouergue, red with a figure of a lion. The Marquis of Lodeve was present with his soldiers, wearing their dark blue tunics covered with icons of stars and crescent moons. And Ramon observed the unique banner of Auch, capital of the Duchy of Gascony. The red and white coat of arms was ornamented with a lion and a paschal lamb, representing the influential Jewish population of the city.

Ramon, commanding the reserve troop of knights, inspected his militia. *The perfect force would include our own contingent of horse archers as well. I wish Samad had agreed to fight with us. But I am concerned. Is this the whole Hungarian army? Samad said we should expect two to three thousand horse archers. I estimate half that many on the battlefield. Where is the rest of their army? Are they trying to outflank us and get behind us?*

Ramon sent out groups of scouts in all directions to determine if there was another Hungarian force. Then as expected, the Hungarians began their attacks in small groups of ten to twenty warriors. They galloped within one hundred yards, shot their arrows trying to break up the Toulousean infantry, then withdrew, tempting the knights to chase them. The crossbowmen held their fire while the standing archers delivered a meager response. The shields of the infantry minimized injuries. With little resistance to their first probes, larger groups of Hungarian horse archers began approaching the stalwart line of foot soldiers. Hugh's signalman was ready. He held the flag of Toulouse attached to the end of a long pike. Before the battle, Hugh had given a selected fifty crossbowmen special instructions to shoot the first volley. He shouted up and down the lines, "Shoot low!"

A shower of bolts from fifty crossbowmen plunged into the ground, short of the enemy horse archers. Laughter could be heard from the Hungarian cavalrymen. Encouraged by the lack of range from the crossbows, a large troop of the horse archers charged.

At Hugh's command, the signalman raised the flag upright and waved it back and forth. Hugh shouted, "Loose!"

Two hundred and fifty crossbows fired. Although advancing, the Hungarians were still beyond the range of their own bows. A mass of Hungarian horses and archers were impaled by the volley. The field of chaos was set for the charge of the knights, yet Ramon signaled to Odulf and Vermundo to wait. *I see them looking hard at me and wondering why I have not signaled an attack. I still do not know if their whole army is here. And unlike our battle with the Saracens, only a tenth of the enemy force in front of us has been committed.*

The Hungarians regrouped after taking large losses and returned to their first tactics. Again, small groups began their ride toward the Toulousean lines to shoot and harass the infantry, but now many were hit by bolts from the crossbows before they got within range. The exchanges between the horse archers and crossbow men continued. The Hungarians' losses were greater during the skirmishes and they became exasperated, and again committed a larger group to charge the infantry. Many riders were shot off their horses during the charge, but their sheer numbers allowed them to get within range to shower arrows into the Toulousean infantry ranks, killing scores. Meeting with success, the Hungarians repeated their mass charge and retreat.

Ramon observed from the rear. *This has become a battle of attrition. We are losing too many infantrymen. To our advantage, however, the crescent formation has prevented their horse archers from getting within range of the knights. How many bolts do we have left?* One of Ramon's knights rode to his side and said, "Count Ramon, the gates of Carcassonne have just been closed."

"Send a scout to the city to tell Count Acfred to keep the gates opened as he agreed."

Has he closed the gates because the result of the battle is uncertain or is this a sign of more rebellion? Does he want to see both armies weakened?

Several scouts finally returned. Ramon asked, "Did you find signs of any other Hungarian troops?"

"Yes, Count Ramon, but . . ."

"Speak out, man! We are in the middle of a battle!"

"Sir, we discovered hundreds of horse archers about five miles down the valley. They were dismounted, leaning against trees or lying on the ground. They appeared sick and disoriented. Only a few acknowledged they even saw us. They were so weak, not one drew a bow against us. We returned right away to tell you they are not a threat!"

Ramon was suddenly distracted by a change of events on the battlefield, and he did not have time to question the scouts any further. The disorder on the battlefield increased when Ramon saw a mass of riderless horses galloping behind the Hungarians. *They brought up their reserve horses. Does this mean they are preparing an all-out attack? But why are they bringing them in so close? It will impede their mobility. No, I see now! Those horses are stampeding! The squires did it! They deserve to be knighted! This is our chance!*

Ramon sent a messenger to Hugh ordering him to move the infantry forward, staying in formation. Leaving a small group of knights at each flank with the infantry, Ramon gathered the rest of the knights and formed a wedge of riders galloping ahead of the crescent. Ramon, Odulf, and Vermundo took the point of the wedge and led the formation as they rushed across the battlefield. The Hungarians were trapped between their own horse herd and the knights.

Ramon and his knights charged through a hail of arrows and smashed into the Hungarian cavalry. He reached the Hungarians first and thrust his wing spear into the back of a fleeing archer.

The wings prevented the point from being stuck, enabling Ramon to extract the weapon and impale another horseman swinging a scimitar. The greater weight of the armored knights and larger horses continued to roll over the Hungarian light cavalry.

The field was scattered with fallen horses and men. Ramon's horse stumbled, throwing him headfirst onto the ground. Odulf turned and galloped back, followed by a handful of knights. Ramon picked up his shield, slung it over his back, and drew his sword. He screamed, "Vermundo lays over there, but he is still alive! Odulf, reorganize the iron wedge and continue to sweep the field! Leave these knights here, but go, go, go, now!"

An arrow slammed into the shield on Ramon's back. Odulf hesitated, not wanting to leave his count, but the wildness in Ramon's eyes and the blood splattered across his face and auburn beard assured Odulf of his leader's command. He urged his horse to race and join the knights.

Ramon clambered over fallen men and horses to reach Vermundo. An injured horse archer lay prone on the ground and drew his bow. Before he could shoot, Ramon jumped over a dead horse and chopped the weapon down, then thrust his sword into the Hungarian. Arrows bounced off his chest armor and shield as he reached Vermundo, who lay on his back clutching his sword to his chest. The main battle had moved fifty paces across the plain where Odulf was leading the Toulousean cavalry; however, stray enemy soldiers still moved about the immediate area. The mounted knights guarding Ramon watched for threats. Ramon kneeled over Vermundo's body. "Vermundo! Old friend and loyal knight!"

But his father's closest friend was dead. Ramon detected movement in the corner of his eye and grabbed Vermundo's sword. A Hungarian lying among the wounded and inside the guards' perimeter had revived. He charged as he swung his scimitar at Ramon. The count simultaneously blocked with his sword and thrust his friend's sword into the enemy soldier. Then, like ghosts rising from a cemetery, a troop of enemy soldiers coalesced nearby. A few had recovered from being knocked unconscious, several had lost their horses and had minor wounds, and others had dragged themselves out from under dead horses. They picked up swords and spears and charged at Ramon's guards.

The knights trampled several of the Hungarians, but more broke through to reach Ramon. Initially surrounded, he purposefully cut off the path of the circling enemy soldiers to avoid combat with multiple opponents at the same time. Ramon kept spinning and slashing, a sword in each hand, and slew most of his adversaries. The knights speared the remaining attackers. Hugh's infantry arrived and his cousin shouted, "Ramon! Look!"

The Toulousean cavalry had swept across the battlefield several more times, destroying the Hungarian army. Few escaped. The fighting stopped and Ramon's milites searched the battlefield to rescue wounded Toulouseans. The knights inspected the battleground and were finishing off the wounded enemy. One of the knights shouted for Hugh and Ramon. He pointed at a dead Hungarian. "We have found several enemy soldiers like this, with swollen faces and necks, as if they have a plague!"

Ramon and Hugh surveyed the battlefield and saw a few more of the disfigured dead. He ordered there would be no contact with the fallen Hungarians, including no pillaging their possessions or weapons. Other than recovering their own wounded, all his soldiers were ordered to evacuate the battleground.

"Hugh, that explains why their army was smaller than we expected. During the battle, scouts had reported seeing bodies down the valley that also looked like they were diseased."

"Count, we were lucky this plague weakened them."

"The bishop would say that God delivered us," answered Ramon.

CHAPTER FOUR

Ramon sent riders ahead to Toulouse to announce their victory. He also dispatched scouts to the east to be certain the Hungarian threat had ended. A contingent of his knights monitored the Hungarians who had been too sick to reach the battle. They soon succumbed to the disease and died. The morning after the battle, Ramon and his men once again walked the Aude plain and completed the somber task of burying their comrades. After the gloomy work, Ramon rode to Carcassonne escorted by a troop of knights. The walled city was atop a hill and was ringed with a moat and numerous towers and battlements. Ramon arrived at the main city gate which was flanked by two massive towers built by the Romans. He shouted at a guard peering through a crenellation atop one of the battlements.

"Tell Acfred that Count Ramon demands to talk to him!"

The guard moved to the side and Acfred appeared. "I am here, Count Ramon."

"Why did you close the gates?" the count shouted. "Your knights were fighting alongside us. In the event of our defeat, you would have sacrificed your own men."

"Carcassonne has declared its independence from Toulouse. The people of Carcassonne support me."

Ramon answered, "We have common enemies. The Saracens and the Hungarians are still major threats. We need to stay united. Open your gates so we can talk."

"My people identify with the Catalonians. We will rely on the protection of the Count of Barcelona."

Disgusted and fatigued from battle, and weary from interring his dead, Ramon led his men back toward Toulouse.

Ramon did not hurry the troops as they journeyed back along the Roman road. Knights and milites from allied counties split off from the army and returned to their homes. The rest of the army continued north with Ramon and Hugh. "I thought Carcassonne would have remained loyal," said Hugh.

"There may be several reasons Carcassonne wants independence from Toulouse," Ramon answered. "Acfred, the Count of Barcelona, and the nobles of Carcassonne are descendants of the Visigoths, so they identify with Barcelona more closely than with Toulouse. The people of our city are mostly of Gallo-Roman heritage blended with the Frankish and Visigoth cultures. In addition, Acfred has married a woman of the Bernard House of Auvergne. The County of Auvergne has always been a threat to us. Toulouse has been buffered from Auvergne because your father Ermengol governs Rouergue. The House of Bernard would have to go through Rouergue to invade Toulouse."

"That means we have enemies to the north, enemies within at Carcassonne, and enemies to the south," said Hugh.

"My mother was from Barcelona, but we didn't keep contact across the Pyrenees," Ramon added. "So it does not help us with any allegiances. And yes, Auvergne and Poitou, two counties to the north, oppose us. But years ago, Uncle Odo and my father drove a wedge between these two opponents when they strengthened ties with Quercy and disposed of the Count of Limousin. Although they were not able to take control of Limousin, the region is now a patchwork of manors that owe allegiance only to their local lords. Some of these lords are loyal to Toulouse and others are opposed to us. If we continue to support and pay visits to our allies in Limousin, we will keep our enemies divided.

"And instead of thinking we are surrounded, you can imagine that the House of Toulouse controls territory which separates and divides our northern enemies in Auvergne and Poitou from our discontented southern neighbors in Carcassonne and Barcelona. Our fathers did as Caesar wrote, 'Divide and conquer.'"

###

Ramon sat alone in the Chateau Narbonne, looking over the city and the River Garonne, enjoying a rare moment of quiet. Julius, the orange and white cat, purred in his lap. Across the river the ruins of the Roman aqueducts rose above the trees. He sipped the rich Auxerrois red wine, one of his favorite varieties. The taste brought Alda into his thoughts. *This is the dark wine from the town of Cahors, north of Toulouse. The grapes are grown in Quercy, the county where Alda was born.*

There was a knock on the door.

"Come."

Alda entered. She was wearing a long linen dress with a surcoat over it. The dress was a dull rouge, and the coarse wool surcoat was gray. Instead of her more formal headdress, she had draped a rouge scarf over her blonde hair, sans braids. The scarf fell before and behind, surrounding her neck. Her dress being less formal than usual, Ramon laughed, "Alda, you look ready to travel. Are you joining the pilgrims on *The Way of Saint James*?"

She frowned. Ramon added, "Oh, I mean, you make those ordinary clothes look grand!"

Alda's expression flashed to joy but was immediately serious again. She said, "Count Ramon, don't you remember, we are going to one of your manors today to do inventory and discuss the husbandry and farming."

"Oh, yes, yes. What would I do without you, my Lady!"

Alda's expression was sunny once more. Ramon notified Hugh that he would be at the manor overnight. Four milites rode with Ramon and Alda as escorts. Although a noble, Alda did not want to ride a carriage. She remained within social convention, riding sidesaddle along the city streets and keeping her hair and neck covered by her scarf. They passed through the north city gate and coaxed their steeds into a trot towards the country manor. As they rode, Ramon noticed Alda did not bother to tighten the scarf as it shifted and blew in the wind, exposing her long blond hair. He gazed at her beauty and chuckled, wondering if the display would be a subject of conversation in his guards' barracks.

Just before they arrived at the manor grounds, Alda tightened her scarf to cover her hair. They rode on a beaten dirt lane which cut through cultivated fields of wheat. Groups of men, women, and children worked strips of land that each family had leased from Ramon's estates. Beyond the fields, the stone houses of the serfs were clustered around a knoll topped by a castle. The south-facing slope of the hill was covered with vineyards. The rest of the hamlet consisted of stables, barns, and outbuildings. Meadows on the slopes were used in common to graze the serfs' livestock. Forests surrounded the entire manor.

The manor grounds were secure, so Ramon dismissed his men to rest and eat. The steward of the manor joined them and they spent several hours in the mild autumn sun inspecting the fields and buildings. At midday, the workers returned to their homes to eat, leaving the fields empty. The steward departed and said their meal would be ready in the castle in about an hour. Alda continued to make her way across a fallow field at the edge of the woods and reached a rock-strewn creek. She nimbly jumped from stone to stone to the other side. Then she turned to face Ramon and loosened her scarf, let her hair fall and said, "Count Ramon, we should inspect this stand of timber."

Alda disappeared into the woods around a bend in the trail, and Ramon duplicated her footsteps across the stream. He entered a secluded clearing in the forest. Alda had removed her surcoat and sat on a layer of bright green moss spread across the forest floor. Ramon said, "That looks more comfortable than a bed." He joined her and felt her shivering as they kissed. Ramon drew back and said, "But I have already promised I will marry Garsinda."

Alda whispered, "It does not matter. I will be leaving Toulouse soon, but I want to be with you once in my life."

He looked puzzled, but she stood and pulled her tunic over her head. She tugged on his leggings as she said, "Hurry, we don't have long before they expect us at the castle!"

He did not need any more encouragement. A short while later, they lay exhausted on the soft moss. *Never have I been with a woman for other than mere sensual pleasure and never has it been this pleasurable!*

The next morning Ramon and Alda departed the manor and rode to Toulouse in silence. Ramon was preoccupied as he relived their time together. Halfway to the city, Alda said, "Ramon, I can guess what you are thinking."

"Yes. I was thinking about us."

She beamed. "I will never forget yesterday."

"Nor I."

"Alda, is that why you were working so hard to teach me about managing the household and the manor? You knew you were leaving?"

"Yes. My father knows you will marry Garsinda. He is getting old, and he has run out of sons to manage his lands. He has confidence in me and wants me to be the Lord, um, it would be Lady, of one of his manors in Limousin."

"I am pleased! I mean, not pleased you are leaving, but pleased you will use your capabilities. You have managed the manor better than most of my foremen and lords."

"And I will no longer be a 'lady-in-waiting' although my advancement is not conventional for a Lady." She smiled and laughed.

Over the following year Ramon and Alda, both knowing their futures were to follow different paths, talked very little and only on subjects related to their work managing the city and manors. During that time, Hugh excused himself from several of

47

nights of socializing at the taverns that Ramon occasioned to keep in touch with the people of Toulouse.

The battle with the Hungarians was almost forgotten and the city had been at peace throughout the spring and summer. Ramon stood in the courtyard watching his cousin, who was kneeling on the steps of the chateau chapel. *Hugh has served me exceptionally well and deserves to be knighted especially after his contributions in the battles against the Saracens and the Hungarians. I wonder if Alda timed her departure for tomorrow so she could be here when he is knighted. They have always had a warm relationship. Well, he will be happy we will start the ceremony soon. He has disciplined himself and has been kneeling on the stone steps for hours.*

A collection of knights and milites assembled in the chapel. The priest sermonized on the responsibilities of a knight, all familiar to Hugh, having been trained in all the duties of a knight. The priest and Ramon stood beside Hugh, who kneeled before them.

Hugh said, "In the name of the Father, Son, and Holy Spirit, I pledge my fealty to Count Ramon Pons."

"Continue with the Knights' Code," the priest added.

"I will never traffic with traitors to the count nor to the king.

"I will never give evil advice to a lady. I will defend her and treat her with respect.

"I will live with self-restraints, attend Mass, and donate to the Church."

The priest nodded. Ramon drew his sword and with the flat side struck Hugh on each shoulder. "I dub thee Sir Hugh."

Odulf was the first to slap Hugh on the back, "Sir Hugh! Yes, I like the sound of that!"

More tables and benches had been set up in the courtyard outside the chapel. A celebration began with food and music. The ladies of Toulouse, the knights' wives, joined the men for the festivities.

After many congratulations from the knights, Alda drew near Hugh. "Sir Hugh. You definitely deserve to be a Knight!"

"And Lady Alda, no longer a dame or lady-in-waiting. Congratulations to you!"

They embraced.

Ramon noticed. *Hmm. Well, they are caught up in the excitement. Does anyone else notice?*

Ramon was distracted from his thoughts once the music began. A man played a lively tune on a wooden flute accompanied by a woman strumming a lute. Ramon sipped his Cahors wine and relaxed, watching many of the townspeople dance. He enjoyed the friendship and celebration, but the rest of the evening was a blur.

###

Ramon woke the next day, his dry mouth reminding him instantly that he had consumed too much wine. *I cannot remember the last time I did that! But it was Hugh's knighthood celebration.* He sat up abruptly. *Alda has planned to leave this morning. I must say goodbye.* Ramon splashed water on his face, dressed, and hurried down to the courtyard. Visions from the previous night flooded his thoughts as he rushed down the stairs. *What? I dreamed Hugh was leaving with Alda! Yes, it must have been due to seeing them embrace one another and dance.*

In the courtyard was an enclosed carriage. Behind the carriage was a wagon for Alda's belongings, mostly clothes. Her horses were tied to the back of the wagon. A band of milites sent by her father for escort waited nearby. When Ramon approached, Alda exited the carriage and said, "I did not want to wake you, so I waited to say goodbye." She curtsied.

Ramon drew close and whispered, "Alda, I wish it could have been different."

She became teary. Ramon, known for his strong character as a leader of men and as a fearless warrior, came close to adding his own tears, when he noticed one of the horses tied to her carriage belonged to Hugh. *It was not a dream! Is he a coward? He is hiding in the carriage!* Ramon started toward the carriage and stopped when he heard a familiar voice behind him.

"Cousin, I thought you would never wake up! We have been waiting to say goodbye."

His face full of anger, Ramon turned to face Hugh.

"Ramon! You look terrible! You really plied the wine last night!" Hugh laughed and said, "I can't remember you drinking that much since we were young squires!"

Ramon stood dumbfounded and disoriented, a combination of disbelief and too much wine. Hugh embraced him and pounded his back. "Ramon, I apologize again for waiting to tell you until last night about going to Limousin. I kept delaying telling you. It was the most difficult thing I have ever done, but you received it so well last night and toasted us a long and prosperous life, and I am grateful."

Hugh pulled back from his cousin and rested his hands upon Ramon's shoulders. He looked into his cousin's eyes and said, "My God! Ramon . . . Brother! You don't remember any of it, do you!"

Alda motioned for Hugh to guide Ramon to the carriage. He led Ramon to sit inside with them so they could have privacy. Ramon sat opposite Alda and Hugh. Hugh said, "Ramon, I stayed here so I could be knighted by you, my cousin, brother, hero, best friend, and liege. You will soon be married, and I must find my own way."

Ramon's face softened as Hugh continued, "You always said, 'Timing is everything.' This is my chance to become a Lord, and more. Alda and I have plans. We will unite the manors in Limousin and once again create County Limousin. I will be loyal to you, of course, and make Limousin a strong ally of Toulouse."

Ramon was silent. *I want to be mad, I have all the right in the world to be mad! But be still. Like in battle, clear the mind. Consider what is the most important goal. Alda and Hugh are sitting before you!*

Ramon placed Alda's hand on his knee, then put Hugh's hand on hers and added his own atop Hugh's hand. He then said, "I love you both."

Ramon exited the coach, closed the door, and raised his arm in farewell. As the wagons and escorts began to move toward the gate, two mounted scouts entered at a gallop and blocked their way. They jumped from their horses and addressed Ramon.

"Sire, we have just come from the south. Armed forces from Narbonne and Carcassonne are pillaging villages in County Toulouse."

Hugh left the carriage and joined them. A third rider hurried into the courtyard and sprang from his mount.

"Count Ramon, I have a message from Count Ermengol. There is an uprising in Rodez. The count's men have captured a few of the rebels, who confessed that the timing of the revolts in Rodez, Carcassonne, and Narbonne were coordinated."

Hugh shouted back to the milites, "Untie my horse and unload my armor and weapons."

He went to the carriage window and leaned in for several minutes as Ramon returned to the chateau. Alda's party departed and Hugh ran to join Ramon.

Within two days, Ramon, Hugh, and Odulf had organized their milites and knights. They formed three mounted companies, each consisting of twenty knights and about fifty milites. The milites were of two-man teams, a shield man and a crossbowman. The knights' role would be to chase down, capture, or kill if necessary, the enemy groups discovered in the countryside. Crossbowmen and shieldmen teams would support the knights if they entered the cities. Hugh led his company to Rodez to reinforce his father and Odulf marched to Narbonne. Ramon would revisit Carcassonne, and with his renewed energy would deal with the rebels.

Ramon and his company had ridden east along the Roman road toward Carcassonne for a full day, camped, and were halfway through the second day's ride when a scout returned from reconnaissance. He addressed Ramon and pointed down the road from where he had just come. A mass of people could barely be seen in the distance.

"Count Ramon, soldiers from Carcassonne have occupied the next village about five miles down the road."

"Is that them in the distance, soldier? The enemy?"

"No, no. They are villagers fleeing to Toulouse for protection . . . those that weren't killed or captured."

They reached the villagers, who informed Ramon that about fifty men had attacked their village. Most of the raiders were armed with swords, and ten or twenty of the men were mounted knights. The raiders were plundering their houses. A scout was sent to reconnoiter the village.

Ramon signaled his company to spur their horses into a trot. After half an hour, he halted the men for a rest next to an old Roman milestone, needing to know his location. He read the inscription aloud, "Eboromagnus. Unum mille passuum."

His second in command, a knight named Pere, asked, "Count Ramon, what does it say?"

"It reads, 'Brom is one mile.'"

"It sounded like you said, 'Big Eboro was a thousand paces.'"

"I will explain later. Take ten knights and half the archers and gallop through the village. Ignore the enemy, do not engage them. Just race through and stop at the next mile marker. It is in a wooded area, so you will be out of sight. I will enter the village and flush out the enemy. When they flee toward you, try to capture rather than kill them."

"Yes, Count Ramon. It may be a trap. What if they stay and fight? How long should we wait before returning?"

"Hmm. Perhaps I am too confident. You are right. After you get to the milepost, if you do not see anyone, return to the village in the time, let's see . . . the time you spend nursing one of your glasses of wine at the tavern."

He laughed, "Count, you know me, I sip my wine slowly to savor every drop."

It took a week of skirmishing for Ramon to end the rebels' raids on the Toulousean villages. He then marched to the gates of Carcassonne and was denied entrance. Its fortifications were too strong to breach, and he did not have the resources nor time for a siege.

At Narbonne, most of the milites were loyal to Matfred, the co-viscount with Maiol. There was not open rebellion, but

Matfred had placed excessive tolls on goods entering the port and those conveyed over land to Toulouse. He was opposed by the resident Arab merchants who shipped goods by sea to Narbonne. The Jewish traders, who transported those goods across land via Toulouse to the Atlantic and northward, were also against the tolls. Odulf had entered Narbonne with the help of Maiol and support from the merchants. After a few brief skirmishes, Matfred had surrendered and renewed his pledge of fealty to Ramon.

Hugh had marched his company of knights and milites northeast to Rodez. By the time he had reached the city, his father Ermengol had prevailed in several skirmishes with the rebels and secured the city, as well as the County of Rouergue.

The knights and troops returned to Toulouse. At the chateau, Ramon held council with his leading knights: Odulf and Pere, and the recently promoted Guilelm. Ramon raised his glass of wine and toasted:

"Sante pendant cent ans! Health for one hundred years!"

The knights answered, "Sante!"

"We had a successful campaign, gentlemen, but we could be called out to service again at any moment. That is the manner of our position and the way of the times."

"Now that Hugh has departed for Limousin, I need a replacement for my second in command. Odulf, I had proposed you become marshal, but you respectfully declined the position. Pere, you showed exceptional leadership in routing the Carcassonne rebels. I am designating you as Marshal of Toulouse. Guilelm, you show great leadership and I want you to command the second troop of knights and thus gain more experience."

The knights toasted Pere and Guilelm for their promotions. "I have been fortunate to be educated by the monks, who are fluent in Latin," said Ramon. "Pere and I had a brief conversation on the Via Aquitania, the old Roman road to Narbonne, about an inscription on a milestone. The education of a knight includes the ability to read Latin. I want to make sure all our knights can read well. We are not speaking Latin, as many think. Our spoken language is a, um, a . . . a cousin of Latin. Why am I talking about this? Because we may need to write important communications to each other. We do not write in the language we speak, Occitan. We write in the Latin. I am only reminding you to continue in earnest your Latin studies.

"Pere had asked a question about a milestone near the village of Brom. The Latin on the milestone read: 'Via Aquitaine. Eboromagnus. Unum mille passuum.' In our spoken language, it sounds like 'Aquitaine Road. Great Eboro. One thousand paces.' But over the years, the Roman name for the village evolved into 'Brom' and one thousand paces is a mile to us.

"So, to know Latin is only part of the solution. For example, on Pere's promotion we just signed and in his family's church records, Pere's name is listed as Petrus and Guilelm is listed as Guilelmus."

Pere said, "It sounds like we are ancient Romans!"

Ramon laughed. "We definitely have Gallo-Roman blood in us, Pere!"

Ramon continued, "After interrogating the rebels we captured, I now understand they are not only raiding our manors and villages. They have also delivered letters to King Rudolph alleging we are oppressing them and causing them to revolt."

The knights grumbled.

"Yes, I am sure one of the letters was from Acfred of Carcassonne. They are spreading false rumors.

"And that is very far from the truth," Pere added. "We are loyal to the king and we have rescued and aided our vassals, which you proved by defeating the Hungarians thus saving Carcassonne and Narbonne. The rebels are the insurgents."

"Agreed Pere, but Frankish knights arrived yesterday with a directive from King Rudolph. He ordered my Uncle Ermengol and me to journey to Paris and to explain the situation. I have asked the Duke of Gascony and my future father-in-law, Maiol, Viscount of Narbonne, to travel with us to show their support for the king and to verify my reputation. So I have informed you of the reason why I must travel to Paris. I am confident you will keep Toulouse safe while I am gone."

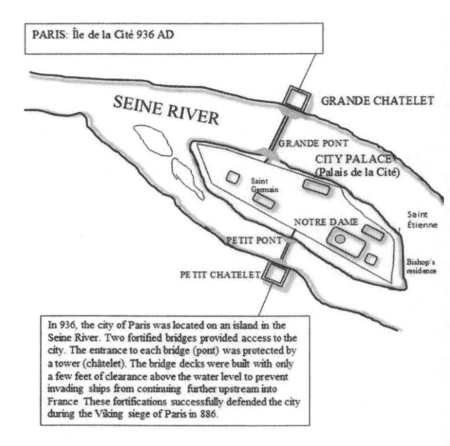

PARIS: Île de la Cité 936 AD

SEINE RIVER

GRANDE CHATELET

GRANDE PONT

CITY PALACE
(Palais de la Cité)

Saint
Germain

Saint
Étienne

NOTRE DAME

PETIT PONT

Bishop's
residence

PETIT CHATELET

In 936, the city of Paris was located on an island in the Seine River. Two fortified bridges provided access to the city. The entrance to each bridge (pont) was protected by a tower (châtelet). The bridge decks were built with only a few feet of clearance above the water level to prevent invading ships from continuing further upstream into France These fortifications successfully defended the city during the Viking siege of Paris in 886.

CHAPTER FIVE

It was in May of 932 when Count Ermengol of Rouergue arrived from Rodez, and Ramon heartily welcomed his uncle. They expected Sancho, the Duke of Gascony, to arrive any day from the capital of the duchy in Auch. They were also awaiting Maiol, Viscount of Narbonne, to join them in the expedition to Paris.

Ermengol and Ramon sat in his study in the tower of the Chateau Narbonne. "Ramon, the few knights we are taking with us will not severely compromise the defense of either Rodez or Toulouse. My oldest son is very capable."

"Uncle, I also am confident that the city will be in good hands while I am gone. I completely trust Pere's loyalty and abilities." Ramon paused. "What are the conditions of the roads heading north? You have been to Paris. Are the roads as good as the Via Aquitaine, the old Roman road to Narbonne?"

"No, the roads are like the route between Rodez and Toulouse. They are gravel and pocked every few miles by gouges. Although the Romans were accomplished engineers, these roads didn't last as long as the Via Aquitaine. But many of their bridges are still usable, and the aqueduct at Rodez continues to deliver water to this day."

"It is necessary for Toulouse to get water from the Garonne," Ramon said. "Our aqueducts were destroyed long ago by Germanic tribes."

"The Visigoths?"

"No, Odulf told me that according to ancient lore, when the Visigoths invaded the Roman Empire, their leaders recognized the value of civilization, and they promoted the continuation of the Gallo-Roman institutions. Then years later, when Toulouse was the capital of the Visigoth Kingdom, the Vandals destroyed the aqueducts. Eventually the Visigoths and their Gallo-Roman subjects intermingled, and we became their descendants. But now the Vikings, pagans like the Vandals, seem to merely live to destroy. Many still inhabit the coast of Gascony. They are not satisfied with just killing or enslaving the populace but put to flame basilicas and chapels and they even go so far as defiling the graves of the saints and scattering their bones."

"Uncle, thank you again for agreeing to go with me to Paris. I need your support to convince the king that we are governing fairly and are keeping the Frankish domains secure."

"Of course, Ramon. You are my brother's son. But it will help my standing as well. And you were clever to convince Viscount Maiol to join our mission."

"Yes, who better to testify for me than one of my vassals? He will negate the claims and false accusations made against me."

"Ramon, let's talk of more pleasant things. You will wed next year, no? What about your bride to be, Garsinda? Surely she will be very beautiful! She has Catalan blood. Hmm. I can envision her now with long dark hair, olive skin, and dark eyes that will melt your heart!"

"Uncle! You are talking about my future wife!" Ermengol laughed as Ramon continued, "Yes, I have thought about her. When her father Maiol proposed we unite the houses of Toulouse and Narbonne, he said she was attractive. But of course, he would say that to be convincing. My mother and father married for political reasons. They had a good marriage, and I believe I will also. I have my concerns about Viscount Maiol. He came to Toulouse to pay respects at my father's funeral, but shrewdly and almost insultingly, used the visit for political goals."

Just before sunset the next day a messenger informed Ramon that Maiol had arrived from Narbonne. Ramon and his uncle entered the chateau courtyard as the viscount and a handful of his knights removed their saddle bags and were turning their mounts over to Ramon's stable handlers. With them was a young woman wearing traveling clothes fabricated of a durable flax material. She was covered from head to toe in layers consisting of a long tunic, vest, surcoat, and cloak. Her dark hair was covered with a dull red scarf which was also draped around the front of her neck, exposing only her face.

Ramon greeted Maiol, "Welcome, welcome! Thank you for coming, Viscount!"

Maiol embraced Ramon. "My future son-in-law! Count! Look at you! You have become a famous man. Tales of your accomplishments soar across Languedoc. 'The Double Swordsman! The Vanquisher of the Hungarians!' Thank you, thank you. We were fortunate the Hungarians bypassed Narbonne, and they would have been back if you had not destroyed their army."

Maiol pounded Ramon on the back. Ramon was caught up in the emotion and returned the enthusiasm. "Come, join us for supper in my hall," Ramon said.

Maiol saw Ramon's attention on the young, dark-eyed woman. "Oh, oh, forgive me! This is Agde, Garsinda's lady-in-waiting. Garsinda wanted her to come to Toulouse to meet your staff and organize your wedding. It would have been Garsinda's mother . . . my wife, but she passed away . . . it's been five years now." He looked down.

"I am sorry for your loss, sir," Ramon said. He turned to the young woman. "Pleased to meet you, my lady." Ramon waved a servant over to attend the young woman. Ramon estimated she was about sixteen or seventeen.

She held up a burlap bag and said, "Count Ramon, Garsinda wanted me to prepare one of her specialties for you tonight for supper. May I have your permission?"

As she talked, Ramon stole a moment to study her features. *Maiol told me Garsinda was attractive. I wonder if Garsinda shares any of Agde traits? This young woman has a unique charm. At first glance she did not strike me as beautiful, as happened with Alda, but something different excites me. It is not her long straight nose and strong chin that gives her a distinctive beauty. No, it's her eyes framed by lavish eyebrows. Her eyes are uniquely green, not the dark, but lovely pools of a Catalan. They sparkle with intelligence, and are enticing. But, what am I thinking! I must stop these thoughts and reserve these feelings for Garsinda.*

Ramon's servant stood by the count awaiting his instructions. "Yes, please show, uh, Agde to the kitchen and make sure she has any required help in her preparation for this evening's meal."

The dining hall had high ceilings made of rough timbers set into the stone walls. The only furniture in the large room was a long wooden table and accompanying seating. Chairs with arms and backs were costly and the wealthiest nobles possessed only a few. Stools and benches were much more common. As count, Ramon sat at the head of the table in an armchair with a high back. A second arm chair with a lower back, at the other end of the massive table, sat empty, reserved for the future countess. Maiol and Ermengol took seats on benches. A maiden servant brought a bowl of water and the men took turns washing their hands, then dried them on a towel draped on the young woman's arm. Another servant poured wine from a pitcher and stood ready for a second round. Ramon felt awkward, as the small group occupied only one end of the huge table in an immense room. Garsinda's lady-in-waiting, Agde, guided the servants. She and the maiden servants each wore cloth headbands, their hair coiled atop their heads in braids. Their long tunics were overlaid by vests that matched the color of their headbands.

Ramon raised his cup and toasted, "Sante!"

The others joined his toast and their voices echoed in the great space.

"I hope you will enjoy the simple fare, a Basque specialty," Maiol said. He looked to Agde. "Please enlighten our guests on the recipe."

"The dry beans are added to cold water in a pot and then brought to a boil. A bit of olive oil is added, and the pot is simmered for about three hours with bay leaves. Some cooks add vegetables or lamb, but those ingredients are not in this original recipe. In this way, you will enjoy the true flavor of the tolosa beans."

"Tolosa beans?" Ramon said.

Maiol said, "Yes, the recipe was a Basque specialty brought by my wife from Tolosa. God rest her soul."

"Tolosa is the Latin name for Toulouse," said Ramon. "Is there a connection?"

"Who knows? Do any of us know the origin of the names of most of the rivers, towns, and places where we live? Perhaps scholars in a monastery might have time to think about such details. My wife was from the Basque town of Tolosa, far from your Toulouse. Is the similarity just a coincidence?"

A servant brought a plate of hard bread for each guest. Agde placed a pitcher of water on the table, then went to the kitchen. She returned with an iron pot, holding the hot container with a cloth wrapped around its bail. The contents were steaming. When the count requested she serve the guests first, she ladled dark red beans into Maiol's bowl, then Ermengol's bowl. She then dipped her ladle into the pot to serve Ramon. As she leaned over to pour the soup, Ramon's vision moved from her brown eyes to her ears. *Her earlobes are long, delicate, and lovely.* His gaze drifted to the gentle swells in her vest. Suddenly he felt a hot sensation in his lap. Ramon jumped up as he brushed the soup off his tunic. "That's hot!"

She straightened to her full but diminutive height, squared her shoulders, and locked eyes with Ramon. He said, "Um, excuse me. Mistakes happen. Do not worry. And, pardon my. . . pardon me, madam!"

She answered with steely eyes, "Pardon me, Count Ramon Pons!"

She left the pot on the table and retreated to the kitchen. Maiol followed her.

"Ramon, I could swear she spilled the beans on purpose!" said Ermengol. He laughed. "Nephew, I guess Garsinda's lady-in-waiting was upset with your stare."

Maiol returned to the table and said, "Agde is very sorry. She is rather new at this duty, Count Ramon."

"It is well enough." He spooned the beans into his bowl and said, "I just want to taste the tolosa beans! The aroma makes me hungry."

After the men finished their food, a servant served spiced wine, sweetened for a soothing after dinner drink. Ramon noted that the awkward lady-in-waiting was no longer serving.

Ermengol commented, "This sweetened wine is a nice change. Is this cinnamon that I taste?'

"Yes, thanks to the Jewish merchants who pass through from time to time," said Ramon. "For several years now, they have traveled through Toulouse on their way to Bordeaux. Some of them trade with the Muslim sailors who put in at Narbonne. A few others trade in the Levante and return on Arab ships, bringing their wares to Europe."

Maiol added, "One such merchant told me he saw Pisan ships at sea near Nice."

"Amazing!" said Ermengol. "Perhaps someday Narbonne and Marseilles will recover and resume trade across the sea. Now with the coasts of Provence and Gothia controlled by the Arabs, we are fortunate there are even a few Jewish merchants in Narbonne.

"Viscount Maiol, tomorrow Duke Sancho will arrive. We hope to let him rest and then leave the following day for Paris. It will be a long journey. I estimate longer than a fortnight."

Maiol replied, "I propose we leave in three days. Ramon, you will need a couple days of rest."

"Why do you say this?"

"Tomorrow will be your wedding with my daughter Garsinda! The young woman who spilled the beans. She has approved of you." He chuckled. "If you value Narbonne's loyalty, the marriage must take place before we leave for Paris. That is my prerequisite to accompany you and to represent you before the king."

"You have not mentioned a dowry, Viscount," said Ramon.

"You dare ask such a question? That is highly unusual!"

"Viscount Maiol, I want to marry Garsinda and will soon call you father. What husband do you want her to marry? A weak-minded man, or . . . someone who can negotiate like . . . you?"

Maiol calmed. "Tomorrow, yes, tomorrow, you will see her wear her mother's jewel necklace. It is a family keepsake and very treasured. That will be her dowry."

Ramon changed the subject. "Viscount, the king may ask us about the reasons for the disloyalty in Rodez, Carcassonne, and Narbonne. Are you ready to tell him the truth? That you backed down and let your co-viscount Matfred support the rebels?"

"We rule the city together. Each can veto the other's decision. I was against the rebels, but he did not agree. Besides, after the rebellion was put down, he pledged loyalty to you again."

"Yes, and I appreciate your influence," added Ramon. "I have a villa on land north of Narbonne where the Jaur flows into the Salesse River. You have holdings that are contiguous with the property. That would be a generous dowry for Garsinda."

Maiol laughed and slapped Ramon on the back. "Ramon, Son, you are remarkable! Garsinda is the lucky one!"

"She will have the land."

The next morning, the bishop performed a swiftly planned yet sanctified marriage ceremony at the La Daurade, and the wedding party led the guests to the Chateau Narbonne for the celebration party. The distance to the chateau was just over a mile, and the procession of nobles gave the townspeople the opportunity to see their new countess. Citizens crowded along the street to watch and then headed toward the forum after the countess passed, eager to join the feast and festivities being held for them.

The wedding party arrived at the chateau and entered a great hall. Inside, scores of people took seats along an enormous table. Flute music filled the air and stringed instruments added to the festive background. Ramon sat in his chair at the head of the table, with Maiol sitting at his right hand. His uncle and Duke Sancho of Gascony sat at his left. Garsinda seemed far away at the other end of the table. Ramon saw his new wife smile for the first time. He watched her from across the length of the table, as she talked with the ladies of Toulouse. *She is clever. Just like her father! But she is also very pretty! That was her, acting as a servant last night, testing me! What will our marriage be like? I am certain it will not be dull. She seems engaged and continually absorbed. Could she be hiding a little fear? Is she nervous at all? I imagine my mother must have been fearful when she married Father, never having seen him before the wedding, never having had a conversation, and never getting to know him. I must be considerate and have only a few cups of wine tonight.*

Garsinda was now dressed in the layers of a noble woman. Her linen smock was covered by a sky-blue dress, the blue representing purity, and the dress was covered by a dark blue surcoat. A gray silk drapery covered her head and concealed her neck. Garsinda caught Ramon looking at her, smiled, and held up her wine as a toast.

Ramon said to Maiol, "Your daughter is very smart, and gracious as well. Viscount, uh . . . Father, did you teach her that skill, or is it she cannot help being her father's child?"

Maiol laughed. "Watch and learn, my son. When we get to Paris, you will be gobbled up and spit out with your naivete and sincerity. The politics and entanglements that we must deal with there will spin your head!"

Hmm. He thinks I am naive? No matter. He is my ally, not my enemy, but I believe if I am projecting that image, just slightly, it may make my adversaries less cautious with me. "Then I am fortunate to have my new father attending me!"

Maiol said with an enthusiastic smile, "Our trip will take at least three weeks. I will teach you much. Sante!"

Ramon and Garsinda stood on each side of the table that was stacked with the small cakes the guests had brought, according to custom. When they both leaned over the top of the cakes to kiss, Garsinda was too short to reach her husband's lips. The guests' laughter turned into a roar when Garsinda jumped just high enough to plant a kiss, falling among the cakes. The guests then escorted the couple to Ramon's quarters and left them to each other, returning to the celebration in the great hall.

Garsinda sat on the edge of the bed, unraveled her scarf and began unbraiding her dark hair. Ramon sat on the bench near the end of the bed. She said, "My mother died three years ago when I was thirteen, but she told me how to be comfortable on my wedding night."

"Garsinda, you are my wife. If I do anything that makes you uncomfortable, tell me."

She began to brush her hair out. *She is enticing, and very beautiful. Only sixteen and I am thirty-two, twice her age! But perhaps it is better this way. Ten years ago I would not have had the maturity to hold myself back right now. Besides, she seems to have a plan.*

Garsinda stood then unbuttoned and removed her surcoat. She draped it across the end of the bed, sat down, and smiled at Ramon. "It's your turn!"

"What?"

"I removed a garment, now you remove one."

He hesitated.

She smiled, but appeared nervous.

Ramon looked puzzled.

"Ramon, you are making me feel uncomfortable!"

He had already taken off his long outer tunic when he had entered the bed chamber. All he wore now was his inner tunic over his leggings. When Ramon stood and pulled his tunic over his head, Garsinda gasped. "You are all muscles and scars! It is scary, but intriguing!"

She walked to him and held up her right hand, pointing to a large scar across his arm. "May I touch your scar?"

Ramon nodded. She examined several more and traced muscles on his chest. Ramon embraced her and kissed her deeply. Garsinda drew back and said, "Wait, Mother said I am supposed to have a warm inner feeling first." She stepped back and untied the front of her dress and exposed her breasts. "You are probably thinking, 'That was not what I imagined' when you tried to stare through my vest last night!"

"Garsinda, no it isn't what I imagined. You are more beautiful than I ever dreamed."

She looked Ramon up and down with amorous scrutiny. Ramon reached and tipped her chin upward and kissed her gently.

Hours later they awoke. The noise from the festivities had ended.

"That was perfect, Ramon! You are strong but you are a gentleman!"

"And you are a very beautiful girl, uh, a beautiful young woman, Garsinda."

"You are just being kind. I am not a tall, regal woman, but Mother ensured that I became highly educated. She said that would be my attraction."

"Garsinda, you are a beautiful woman. The most beautiful countess!"

She went on as if she did not hear his compliment. "So, my education could help you manage your county and manors. I have read many books. Of course, I have read the Bible many times. What I tell you next, you will not tell anyone, will you?" Ramon shook his head and she continued, "Jesus's words are beautiful and full of love, but King Solomon and David were adulterers! And Lot was incestuous with his daughters! Do you think that is why the priests don't want the people to read?"

Before Ramon could answer, she said, "I have talked too much. I barely know you. I have never told anyone these thoughts!"

Ramon squeezed her shoulders as he said, "'The heart of her husband trusteth in her, and he shall have no need of spoils.'"

She was tearing with joy. "Ramon, you are a dream come true for me. You know the Bible! We can discuss the verses, which I find much more interesting than the boring Mass at the basilica!"

"I also wonder about the meanings of many of the Bible verses," Ramon said.

"But what will it be like for me in Toulouse? Will you always be away, like my father, to govern on horseback and fight battles? Will we have time to talk?"

"I will make time, Garsinda."

"Ramon, you must have visited many places, but have you been to Santiago de Compostela?"

"No."

She jumped out of bed and went to the door and yelled down the hallway.

"Esti! Esti, wine and cakes, please!"

"You make friends fast, Garsinda! Did you arrange for the maiden to be on call?"

She ran back to the bed and slipped under the covers with Ramon.

"My mother and I went on pilgrimage to see Saint James's relics at Compostela when I was about ten. Of course we had an escort, a troop of knights, and a carriage was brought, but for penance we walked almost the whole way. It took us over two weeks to get there."

"All my life, I have seen many pilgrims on their way to Compostela," said Ramon. "They take rest here at Saint Sernin Abbey. Many go barefooted, they said it was for atonement. I know most of them could afford shoes, because they made contributions, some quite generous, to Saint Sernin Church," said Ramon. "The abbot says he offers aid to the pilgrims for free, but he mentioned the church coffers are overflowing from the accumulated donations. The church leaders are beginning to think they will someday replace the church with a large cathedral in honor of Saint Sernin. The pilgrims come from all over Europe."

"Yes, when we were there, we met people from Provence, Burgundy, West Francia, England, and Italy. In the mountains, we stopped at a pass where Charlemagne had fought a great battle many years ago. A troubadour had camped there too and sang poems to the pilgrims. He sang about Charlemagne's bravest knight, Roland—and he chanted the 'Song of Roland.' It moved me and I memorized parts. When we traveled on, I recited the song during our journey, but I had to sing it in a whisper, as my mother said it irritated her."

"You said the song was beautiful. Why did it bother your mother?"

"The song described a battle between the Muslims and Charlemagne's Frankish army in the Pyrenees mountains.

Charlemagne and his men would have been massacred, had not Roland and his band of knights fought to the death to allow the Franks to escape. When my mother heard me singing the song, she told me the battle was really between the Basques and Franks. Charlemagne was retreating from the Muslims in Spain, after he had destroyed Basque cities, claiming they had allied with the Muslims. In revenge, the Basques ambushed his army in the mountains. My mother's grandfather lived during that time and told her the true story. So she was upset because the Franks had been so unkind to her Basque ancestors and the song was twisting the truth.

"I understand why she was mad, Garsinda."

There was a knock on the door and the maiden Esti carried in cakes and wine on a wooden slab.

"Garsinda, I saved cakes for you, like you asked! "Bon apetis!" said Esti as she closed the door behind her.

They enjoyed their sweet fare as Garsinda continued, "At Compostela, I learned that Saint James had preached the gospel in Spain long ago, but he returned to Judea when he saw a vision of the Virgin Mary. After his death, his disciples sent his body to Spain to be buried at Santiago de Compostela. The ship crashed during a storm, and his body was lost at sea. But miraculously, it washed ashore, covered in scallops."

"Scallops?"

She pointed to her rumpled gown on the floor. "Yes, see, there sown on my dress is a scallop shell, a souvenir from my pilgrimage."

"Hmm. An interesting story. Several years ago I asked pilgrims returning from Compostela wearing the shells about their meaning. One told me the lines on the shell represent the web of roads and routes converging from all over Europe at Compostela. The second pilgrim insisted that because Compostela was near the westernmost coast of the world, the lines represent the rays of the setting sun.

"So my wife, Garsinda, do you remember any of the verses from the Song of Roland? I'd like to hear them."

"Ramon, my husband, my Roland! This verse also fits you well. You defeated the Hungarians, and after all your trials have the vigor to make love to your young wife!"

We shall make a stand in this place.
The first blow and the first cut will be ours.
That's the sort of valor any knight must have
Who bears arms and sits astride a good horse!
He must be strong and fierce in battle,
Otherwise he is not worth four pennies,
Instead he should be in one of those monasteries
Praying all the time for our sins.

"Garsinda, that is beautiful, especially when you sing it. *I have married an inquisitive and intelligent woman! It makes her even more beautiful to me.* They put down the food and drinks and returned to each other.

Two days later, Ramon led the nobles northward in their journey to pay homage to King Rudolph. With Sancho, Maiol, and the knights, the group had increased to twenty. They traveled along the route traced by old Roman roads. A few segments of pavement remained along sections of the old roads, but most parts had deteriorated and become beaten gravel and dirt tracks

Ramon was exhausted. *But our time together was delightful. I am more tired from our long nights lying in bed and talking well into the morning than our love making! She asks so many questions! I already want to return to her.*

Maiol spurred ahead to ride next to Ramon and woke the count from his reverie. "Son, here is your first lesson."

His self-assurance is irritating, but I must endure it.

His father-in-law continued, "Why do you think I wanted the marriage to happen early?"

"Loyalty. Secure our relationship?"

"Yes, and the timing?"

"Your timing was perfect. I could not reject the proposal."

"But son, what advantage did I achieve?"

"You reinforced your alliance with Toulouse."

The conversation was starting to grate Ramon. *I think this is all obvious!*

"Yes, and why is Duke Sancho going with you?" added Maiol.

"He is an ally. His father before him was an ally with Toulouse."

"Yes, but the Vikings?"

"They are still a problem? The Vikings have not invaded the upper Garonne valley for a generation, thanks to my father and uncle."

"But they still hold Gascony's major seaport, Bayonne. That is why the Duke's capital remains at Auch, to stay out of the reach of the Viking longboats. Also, Ebalus, the Duke of Aquitaine, hides the fact from the king that he does not control Bordeaux. It is still under the rule of the Vikings. Fifty years ago, those pagans tore down part of the city walls and told the inhabitants if they repaired the wall, they would return and kill everyone in the city. Meanwhile the Vikings live in enclaves along the coast, collect tribute from Bordeaux, and raid coastal cities as they wish.

"Sancho will ask King Rudolph to send military help to rid the coasts of the Vikings."

Ramon said, "So he is exploiting our relationship?"

"Of course, Son! That is what life is all about!"

"So, my advantage is marrying your beautiful daughter."

Maiol said, "You are smart to say that first."

Ramon laughed and continued, "My other benefit is that the king will believe you when you report that I am not abusing my vassals."

"And Son, your people will realize another long-lasting benefit. Sancho will recover Bayonne to renew trade with the British Isles. For now, the small amount of cargo smuggled past the Vikings results in only a few trade boats a year that make it upstream to Toulouse. If Bordeaux is freed, you will see fleets of boats at your docks and when they offload, there will not be enough mules in your city to transport all the goods to Narbonne! Narbonne and Toulouse will prosper."

Ramon rode on and chastised himself. *I was wrong in thinking the Viking threat had been reduced. I did learn something. I must tell myself more often to clear my mind and listen.*

###

The scouts preceded Ramon and his men by a day's travel to inform the local lords of the group's arrival. They announced the coming of the nobles and their expedition to see King Rudolph. So far, they had secured comfortable lodgings at the castles and manors of allies. On the third day of travel, Ramon sent a messenger ahead to notify the Lord of Aurillac du Perigord, Pons of Aurillac, that he would arrive the next afternoon.

Lord Pons met the entourage at his castle gate. Pons welcomed the nobles, embracing Ramon last. "Count Ramon, I am honored by your visit! I know you have been in the saddle all day and are tired, but I have procured more comfortable lodgings at the nearby abbey. It is also large enough to accommodate your knights. Forgive me, but my small manor is not worthy to host your assemblage. The Saint-Sour monastery is only three or four miles away."

Ramon's cousin mounted his horse and directed a pair of his knights to lead the procession toward the abbey. Lord Pons and Count Ramon rode beside one another.

"Count, we have never met. Your Uncle Ermengol's daughter married my father. So, we are cousins."

"And we have the same name."

"Yes. But why are you Ramon Pons and not just Pons or Ramon?"

"My father told me Pontius was an ancient Roman family name."

"But I have only one name, Pons; Pons of Aurillac."

"What is your written name, your Latin name?"

"Pontius, of course. Is that your written name?"

"Yes, Raimundus Pontius. My parents said they wanted to use the old family name to distinguish me from my father and grandfather, who were both named Ramon."

"I do not know of that, but we are cousins, and we both are Pons or Pontius. In any event, I am glad we have met. And I am looking forward to a delicious dinner at the abbey, already being prepared for us."

The road began to parallel a river, and a watermill came into view on the opposite bank. Lord Pons said, "It is only about a mile to the abbey past the mill."

"Is it your mill?"

"No, the monks of Saint Sour Abbey own and operate the mill. We pay them for grinding our grain."

Ramon added, "There are a handful of flour mills south of Toulouse, also owned by the monasteries in the city."

The dinner that evening was like a banquet. Ramon was curious how his cousin had convinced the abbot to serve them such a sumptuous fare, because the monks were devoted to a stoic life based on their Benedictine Rules. During the dinner he told his cousin Lord Pons of his plan to establish a monastery in honor of Saint Pons. By the end of the night, Ramon had a good feeling about the cousin he had just met. *We are in Limousin, where the lords are independent of allegiance to the king or a count. Lord Pons, however, pledged to help me in any way, I believe based on family loyalty and not merely fealty as a vassal.*

On the sixth day of travel the group approached the manor of Hugh and Alda, east of the town of Limoges near the Vienne River. The estate was lush and green, encompassing the fertile river bottoms. The gentle south facing slopes were covered with vineyards.

Ramon jumped off his horse when he saw Hugh and Alda waiting in front of their castle to welcome them. He embraced Hugh and pounded his back. He then kissed Alda's hand. "I am so glad to see you both, Cousin and . . . Lady."

Ramon had thought of Alda often, but he did not detect anything out of the ordinary in her eyes. *Good, it will be easier to forget her, since she has already forgotten me.*

The senior nobles collected in the hall to relax and share wine. Hugh and Alda gave Ramon a tour of the manor as they strolled about the buildings and fields. Hugh updated Ramon on the prosperity Alda and he had achieved in County Limousin. The two men reminisced about the times in Toulouse. "Remember jumping off the old bridge into the river years ago when we were boys?" said Hugh as he chuckled.

"Yes, that was when we were thirteen or fourteen. The most fun was when we stole out of the chateau and jumped into the river in the dark. You never knew when you were going to hit the water!"

"No! The best time was when you jumped in shallow water and got stuck in the mud! It would have been funnier if you had dived!" They both were caught up in laughter.

They had fun telling the stories to Alda, who was amused, but not being part of the adventure, her mirth was subdued compared to their outbursts of laughter. "So you were wild young men always exploring the city at night?" said Alda.

"But, Alda, what about the night you insisted we steal a horse from the stable and ride through the city?" answered Ramon.

Hugh said, "What? I don't remember that."

Alda had an uneasy expression as she looked at Ramon. Hugh looked back and forth at them, his smile fading.

Ramon said, "Hugh, it was one of the times we went out late then asked men leaving the tavern if they would bring us a cup of ale. For some reason, Aylmer, the chateau's mouser, followed us all the way to the forum. We thought it very funny, but we later lost track of the cat. When we got back . . ." He looked at Alda and she nodded slightly. "When we got back you went to sleep and, I um, . . . talked to Alda and told her about the cat. She was distressed that Aylmer had not returned."

"Aylmer slept in my bed most of the time," added Alda.

Ramon continued, "She talked me into going back to find the cat and insisted we get a horse to search the streets for Aylmer.

Alda convinced the stable boy, who had a keenness for her, to let us have a horse—"

Hugh interrupted, "We all had a fondness for Alda."

"Um . . . you are right, Hugh," said Ramon. "We found the cat and, believe it or not, I took the reins and Alda held the cat behind me as we rode back to the chateau. I am sure Aylmer knew the city better than us and would have come back anyway."

Hugh laughed and while still in a state of mirth said, "Are there any other secrets you two have for me?"

Ramon was shaken. *Does Hugh suspect Alda and I were once together?*

Alda put her arms around both men and squeezed them into a huddle. She whispered, "Both of you know all and all are happy."

The nobles of Ramon's troupe chatted over a pleasant breakfast with Alda and Hugh the next morning, then after a short ride, arrived at Limoges. The town's monastery contained one of the largest libraries in West Francia. After attending Mass at the monastery, Ramon inquired about commissioning a copy of a book from their library. Ramon wanted to return with a special wedding present for Garsinda. He asked if there were any copies of "Roland's Song." The monks had heard of the song, but they did not know of any written record of the poem. It took weeks or sometimes months to copy a book, so they agreed to let Ramon choose from one of the volumes which they were in the process of copying. Ramon chose the book "On Free Choice of Will" by Augustine, the former Bishop of Hippo Regius in North Africa. The monks were already halfway through making a new copy of the manuscript. They would be able to finish it by the time he returned on his way back to Toulouse.

After a good night's rest at the monastery, Maiol, Ermengol, Ramon, and Sancho continued their journey north. The terrain was level and the horses followed the road with little guidance.

"It has worked well so far," said Ramon. "The lords have been friendly, the accommodations comfortable."

"When the scouts issue silver before our arrival, it helps," Sancho said.

Ramon added, "It makes sense. We would want our hosts to remember us in a positive way, not as a burden."

"We are now leaving County la Marche and entering the Royal Domains," said Sancho. "You may see the attitudes change. Be aware. Our next stop is the city of Orleans."

In Orleans, they used commercial stables and stayed at an inn. The city was as large as Toulouse and had accommodations for their troops. Sancho agreed with Ramon to let the men have freedom after the long journey. The knights had an evening on the town, gamboling from tavern to tavern, and a few visited some less reputable locations.

Ramon sought out the cathedral instead and then retired to his room. He had just dozed off when he heard a knock at the door. He held his dagger and looked through the space between the door and the jamb. In the hallway was a woman holding an oil lamp.

"What do you want?"

"I have a present for Count Ramon Pons."

"What do you mean?"

"I am here for you, Count Ramon, to satisfy your needs!"

She opened her cloak, exposing a voluptuous figure.

"You are a very beautiful lady, but I say, find a good man." He laughed as he said, "Like Jesus would say, 'Sin no more.' I am married and happy."

The following day they approached Paris. It was smaller than Orleans, and the king considered it his capital, although he often resided temporarily in strongholds in other cities. As they neared Paris, Ermengol said, "This is my second time to Paris. The first time was with your father. The city is located on Île de la Cité, the City Island, in the Seine River. Up ahead you can see a fortified bridge also protected by a castle. It is the Petit Ponte, the shorter of two bridges. The longer bridge, the Grande Ponte, is on the other side of the island. The bridges were built very low, close to the river surface, so boats cannot pass under them. They have protected Paris from the Viking long boats many times. We will cross over to the island and meet King Rudolph at his residence, the City Palace."

They stabled their horses and found accommodations for their knights at the nearby Saint Denis monastery. The king invited the nobles to stay at his palace, and within two days they were afforded a meeting with King Rudolph. They were advised that before he would hear their appeals for help against the Vikings or the rebels, the king would first play the courtly games for which he had a keenness.

Shortly before they entered the king's chamber, Ramon whispered, "Maiol, Father, what is this? This is rather unusual."

"Ramon, I told you. It is give and get. The king has his way and we must play along."

Ramon played chess with Rudolph. They relaxed, sipped wine, discussed many topics other than the game, and played at a leisurely pace. A few hours into their matches, Rudolph examined the chessboard as he decided his next move, then said, "Count Ramon, we have much in common. Two years ago when I was Count of Burgundy, the Hungarians tried to invade by crossing the Alps. I blocked the pass with my knights, and the King of Italy was coming from the south, chasing them after they burned Pavia. But they were swift and stealthy, and we only killed a few hundred before they escaped. Unfortunately, I could not kill enough of them, but only stopped them, and as you painfully experienced, they descended on Nimes and Toulouse. You have my respect! How did you defeat them?"

Ramon, remembering the report about Rudolph fighting the Hungarians years earlier, described the loss of half the Hungarian army to disease, and the details of the tactics he used in the battle. Rudolph said, "You are speaking humbly, Ramon. I know the Hungarian horse archers. On the open plains where you fought them, they are almost invincible. They are wily! Just last year they crossed the Alps and attacked Rheims, only eighty miles from Paris. By the time I organized my army, they had fled back east.

"Ramon, back to our game. Did you know we adopted chess from the Arabs, our greatest enemies?"

"No, sire. This is my first exposure to the game." He did not admit Maiol had given him some instructions.

"Ah, check and checkmate. You owe me another silver coin! This is very entertaining! Let's play again."

Ramon said, "You are rather crafty, sire!"

During the next chess game the king asked, "So, Ramon, you married Maiol's daughter the day before you journeyed to Paris?"

"Yes, sire."

"I am grateful for your loyalty, as well as leaving so soon after you were married. Was your wedding night amorous?"

"Um . . . uh . . . why, yes, it was, sire."

"I want to give you a gift to take back to her, to . . ."

"Garsinda, her name is Garsinda."

"To Garsinda. We may have a few swaths of rare silk for her. Does she like precious stones?"

"She is very curious and enjoys reading. I am having a book copied for her in Limoges, which I will pick up on the way back to Toulouse."

"Does Garsinda like poetry?"

"Yes, in fact, she wanted me to find the 'Song of Roland,' but the monks in Limoges said they did not know of any copies."

The king called over a servant and whispered something to him. "Ramon, I will have my library searched for an appropriate book."

"Thank you, sire. That is very generous of you."

After several more chess games, which Ramon lost, Rudolph said, "I understand that the Duke of Aquitaine has been causing some trouble in County Rouergue, but your uncle took care of it. I suggest, to increase your . . . our influence, you could establish support by founding an abbey in the adjoining county of Auvergne. I own land near Chanteuges. I will donate the land if you fund construction of a new monastery. The people will remember you for your donation.

"Come, let's watch Count Ermengol and Duke Sancho play the board game tafl."

They crossed the large study to watch the men seated at a table, upon which a checkered pattern had been carved, much like the chess board. On the squares were what appeared to be carved figures representing three armies.

77

"The objective is for the king, with his men in the center of the board, to escape the two overwhelming forces. The Northman Rollo taught the game to me, although we did not get along very well."

"I have heard of the Viking sieges of Paris decades ago. How were you able to put a stop to their raids?"

"I invited Rollo, one of the Viking chieftains, to settle with his people along the coast at the mouth of the Seine River. In exchange, he agreed to end his raiding and give us his protection against further incursion by other Vikings. Rollo died, but his son William Longsword and I get along just fine, although many of his nobles think he is becoming more Frankish than Viking. Perhaps they are right, it has been just one generation after their settlement and most of them now speak French."

Ramon's uncle and Sancho continued to play tafl. As he and Rudolph sat at another tafl board nearby, his father-in-law stood drinking wine and watched the interactions. He winked at Ramon. Ramon lost every game of tafl. *Does the King really enjoy these games or is he simply trying to empty my pockets?*

After a mid-day meal, the king insisted they play more games. He said, "Please try our ale. I know wine is the more popular beverage in Toulouse and the south, but many in the north want ale over wine. Next, we will play dice. All four of us can take part in the match."

Sancho and his uncle sat with them as the king explained the rules of the dice and the betting. Ramon paid close attention. *If I keep losing my money, I will not have enough to pay for Garsinda's book!*

Rudolph downed a swallow of ale, then said, "Gentlemen, did you know the word dice comes from the Latin 'dadus,' which means given? Before they became Christians, the pagan Romans believed that the throw of the dice was not a random happening but was given from the gods. You may find it interesting that when I first met Rollo, he said control of dice was by Oden, the Viking god of wisdom and prophecy! But later Rollo was baptized. Many Northmen have also converted to Christianity."

He likes to show off his knowledge, but how interesting! Garsinda would enjoy this. I am missing her already! After examining the dice, Ramon decided he could estimate the odds. *The sevens were the most likely, followed by the sixes and eights. I need to win enough back to pay the balance for the book being copied at the Limoges library.*

Finally Rudolph took a break from the games. As they had dinner together, the king announced, "Gentlemen, men of Narbonne, Gascony, Toulouse, and Rouergue, I have played with you and consider you worthy." He laughed.

Ramon joined his fellow travelers and forced out a hearty laugh. *That was difficult, I am getting a little irritated with this. Either my uncle and father-in-law are good actors at feigning interest or they are enjoying these diversions.*

The king continued, "Ebalus, the current Duke of Aquitaine, continues to allow the Vikings to do as they want in the duchy. I will gather my Frankish knights and lead them to Bordeaux to rid the Northmen from Francia. Elabus will go with me." The men clapped and cheered.

A servant brought a rolled manuscript and a codex of several pages and handed them to the king. He unrolled the manuscript, glanced at it, nodded, and handed it to Ramon. The king announced, "For your defense of Toulouse, the south of Francia, and your loyalty to the crown, I appoint Ramon Pons, the Count of Toulouse and Marquis of Gothia, to also hold the title of Duke of Aquitaine. You will replace Elabus. This document is my official declaration."

Ramon glanced at his uncle and father-in-law, who both seemed very pleased. He answered, "For generations, since the time Charlemagne designated our family to hold the title of Count of Toulouse, we have been faithful to you, King of the Franks, and we will continue to remain loyal vassals."

Rudolph handed Ramon a booklet. "I do not have a copy of the 'Song of Roland.' However, here is a gift for your new wife. I think a very proper book. It is a poem by Decimus Magnus Ausonius, a poet, educator, and general who was born in Bordeaux, but his early education was in Toulouse. He eventually retired in his hometown and wrote many more poems. That was hundreds of years ago, during the Roman Empire. We are fortunate that the monks have copied and preserved this volume." Rudolph then held his mug of ale high and toasted, "Sante!"

Ramon's entourage rode south the next day. Ramon was now used to his father-in-law's questions and testing. He decided it was his turn. "Father, why do you think the king did not mention the letter of complaint the rebels had sent to him?"

"Hmm? What did you say, Son? Oh, yes. He probably got so involved with his games he forgot. He is such a fop!"

"I think he trusts us and believes the accusations were unwarranted," said Ramon. "And he is honoring us even more by not even mentioning the letter. Yes, he is odd, but I have an intuition our visit was very successful."

Maiol hesitated, then said, "Rather perceptive! Yes, I am very pleased you married my Garsinda."

After several more days journey, the group separated north of Toulouse. Sancho and Ermengol returned to their domains. Ramon passed through the massive gateway into Toulouse, glad again to be home. Garsinda was very pleased with the two books and delighted to have Ramon back.

Ramon and Garsinda were having dinner with her father before he left the next day for Narbonne. They all sat at one end of the large table. After they savored tolosa bean soup and baked fowl, they relaxed and sipped blackberry spiced wine. A servant placed a pie in front of Maiol, who said, "What a wonderful surprise! Garsinda did you bake this pie? Blackberry is my favorite! I feel like I am at home."

"You may always consider this your home, sir," Ramon answered.

The viscount announced, "Would anyone like a piece of my blackberry pie?"

Garsinda was silent, but peered at Ramon, anticipating an answer. Ramon looked for a hint. *No clues. Strange. Yes! This is another one of Maiol's tests! The prostitute in the inn. Testing my patience with the king's queer habits. He did say "my" pie, although he stared straight at me when he said it.* "No sir, I am full," answered Ramon.

Garsinda smiled.

Expedition to Tomieres-
founding of St. Pons Monastery 936 A.D.

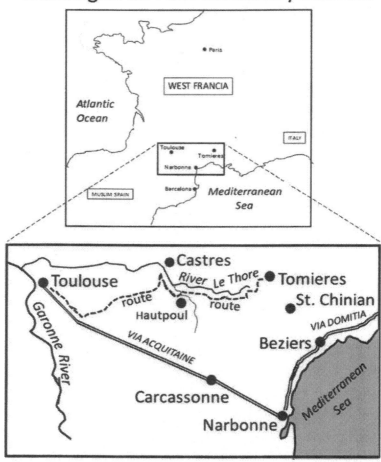

CHAPTER SIX

Garsinda wrapped the remainder of the blackberry pie in waxed cloth and hid it with the rest of his food in her father's travel pouch. The parting with her father was tearful though she assured him she was indeed happy and content.

That afternoon, she asked Ramon what she could do to help with the duties of the county. They sat in his study at the chateau, as Ramon showed Garsinda how to manage and figure the accounts for his manors and the county's expenses. *I have fond memories of Alda when she was showing me the same procedures. But Garsinda's heart belongs to me and mine to her. I never felt that way with Alda.*

Ramon paused and looked up. "My love, you learn everything so fast. Your enthusiasm is contagious. I feel ten years younger being with you."

Garsinda laughed. "You would still be older than me, husband!"

Ramon frowned. "So, you think me old?"

Garsinda looked over her shoulder, laughed, and whispered, "You have the strength and passion of a young man. You are my Ramon, my husband, my Roland!"

###

The next several months Ramon tutored her in ways to support him in ruling the county. Garsinda and Ramon were inseparable during their work and long hours of personal and intimate time. As he had assured Garsinda, Ramon had limited his travels. He sent his marshal, Pere, the second in command, to make calls at the counties and towns under his authority. Pere filled in expertly and thus Ramon kept his promise to Garsinda to spend time with her.

With the hours at home, Ramon had also arranged the building of a monastery in County Auvergne, as King Rudolph had suggested. He had secured the manpower and materials and had appropriated funds to start an abbey in Chanteuges, in the county adjacent to his Uncle Ermengol's residence. Ermengol's oldest son had agreed to oversee the construction of the abbey. The monastery was almost complete and Ramon was planning a trip to attend the dedication. However, he was surprised when a troop of King Rudolph's knights arrived in Toulouse with a summons. They reported the king had occupied Perigueux, the capital of Aquitaine, and was preparing to launch a campaign against the Vikings on the coast. Rudolph demanded that Elabus, the former Duke of Aquitaine, go with him and fight for his new title, Viscount of Perigueux. Ramon's role was to hold the king's base at Perigueux while he campaigned to the west. Ramon would thus assume his role as Duke of Aquitaine, as he had been appointed in Paris. Within two days Ramon had assembled a troop of knights. As the chevaliers gathered in the courtyard and prepared to depart for Perigueux, their families joined them to say their farewells. Garsinda held him close, not concerned about her display of affection in public.

"Husband, please return very soon. I will miss you."

"Duke Sancho is sending a force of milites to reinforce the king, so perhaps the king's campaign will not be long. Garsinda, you are my love. I will return.

"Pere has learned much in the last year, and I am confident he will provide support for you as you govern in my absence. I know you are very faithful to the Church but be well aware of Bishop Armandus. He will try to take control. Do not agree to any of his proposals while I am gone. In any event, you must maintain your sovereignty to govern the city yet still support the Church."

While Ramon was occupied in Aquitaine, Bishop Armandus made frequent visits to Garsinda at the chateau. During one of his calls, they sat comfortably overlooking the city from the upper level of the chateau, sipping Cahors wine and enjoying the hard-crusted fresh bread that the chateau ovens baked so well. Garsinda relished drinking Cahors, as it was Ramon's favorite and the aroma made her think fondly of him. After pleasantries, the bishop said, "Countess Garsinda, during my last visit you politely declined my offer of assistance to help you manage the royal accounts during Ramon's absence. May I ask then if you would consider donations to the Church? Ramon's father asked him to found a new monastery dedicated to Saint Pons and your husband told me he would honor his father's request."

"Your Excellency, I have been very busy learning about my husband's domains. He has not mentioned founding another monastery. There are already two monasteries in Toulouse. I understand La Daurade is devoted to leading the people in faith, maintaining the library, and to education. Saint Sernin helps the pilgrims on their way to Compostela."

"You are very learned, young Countess. I suggest we consider a location outside the city, but within Count Ramon's realm. There is a need to . . . keep it under our control. As you said, the Saint Sernin Abbey of Toulouse provides one of the stops for the pilgrims. The Bishop of Marseilles has informed me that the pilgrims must travel almost fifty miles between the monasteries of Saint Chinian and Saint Benoît de Castres until they can find a safe place and shelter. Now they must camp outdoors subject to the weather and bandits. A new monastery in Gothia between Saint Chinian and Saint Benoit would be ideal for the pilgrims. Travelers must now camp outside the castle and village of Hautpoul, populated by those who call themselves 'good Christians.' However, the Bishop of Marseilles communicated to me that the church of Hautpoul is unconsecrated. They are probably Arians as were their Visigoth ancestors, who believed Jesus was distinct from the Father, and thus they do not believe in the Trinity. Even if they did aid the pilgrims if they were in need, they would be subject to Arian contamination. We should find another place of rest for the faithful Christian travelers. Although I do pray that the people of Hautpol will repent and follow the true Church's way before the End."

"The end? The end of what?" Garsinda exclaimed.

"Why the end of the world, of course! The second coming of Jesus. It will be at the Millennium. The year 1000 anno Domini. We will not live to see it, but your children will be alive to welcome the Lord. That is another reason to build this monastery and many more, to make our world ready for Christ's return."

Garsinda looked dumbfounded.

"Countess, we can develop the design of the abbey while the count is in Aquitaine. When he returns, we can submit the plans for his approval."

Now I understand my husband's warning. The bishop is pressing. I should avoid continuing this discussion. Or . . . I can try to gain an advantage. And the end of the world? Did I miss something in my reading of the Bible?"

"Bishop Armandus, I will send expeditions to search for a location, on this condition. I would like to see the new abbey include a nunnery as well as the monastery for men."

The bishop squirmed slightly but kept his composure. "Countess, your wisdom is beyond your years. I agree. You and I work well together. I await with optimism your communication."

That evening Garsinda found several passages in her Bible about Christ's second coming. Bibles were expensive and rare, and she had brought her personal Bible from Narbonne. There were only a handful of Bibles in Toulouse, two at the chateau, and the rest at la Daurade and Saint Sernin. Garsinda found a quotation of Jesus in Luke: "Truly I say to you, this generation will not pass away until all things take place. Heaven and earth will pass away, but My words will not pass away." *Jesus' followers expected His return within their lifetimes, but that did not happen.*

She discovered another passage in the Gospel of Matthew: "And this gospel of the kingdom shall be preached in the whole world for a witness to all the nations, and then the end shall come." *"All nations"? The Muslims still control Spain and the Holy Land. Will they be converted in sixty-three years? Before the year 1000?*

The third passage Garsinda found was in Mark: "No one knows about that day or hour, not even the angels in heaven, nor the Son, but only the Father. Be on guard! Be alert! You do not know when that time will come." *These differences in the Bible trouble me. How can the bishop say it will be the year 1000, if this is true? Oh my, it would be much easier to be a common person, and not be able to read the Bible. I could simply reflect on Christ's sacrifice. Then I would never have such perplexing questions.*

The bishop and Garsinda met several more times during the following week and negotiated the means to pay for construction of the new monastery. They also discussed how to recruit monks for the abbey. King Rudolph expelled the Vikings from their permanent settlements in Aquitaine and subsequently recovered Bordeaux. Viscount Elabus fared strongly in the battles against the Vikings, so King Rudolph endorsed Ramon's appeal to have Elabus rule the duchy in Ramon's name. The king departed for Paris, and Ramon, confident that his holdings in the Aquitaine were secure, returned to Toulouse. He arrived at the chateau late in the afternoon and retired to his quarters with Garsinda. There was no talk of his ventures in Aquitaine, and there was no talk of her dealings with the bishop. The night was theirs only. They ate alone, followed by spiced wine and the sweet cakes that Garsinda relished so much.

Ramon and Garsinda slept late into the morning. As soon as Ramon exited their bed chambers, a servant handed him a message from the bishop, who desired an audience that afternoon. Over their breakfast of warm porridge and milk, Ramon asked Garsinda, "How were your dealings with Armandus? I hope you were able to hold firm against his ambitions."

Garsinda smiled.

"I can tell by the look on your face you are proud of something! My sweet, what did you do?"

"I committed to build the monastery that you promised your father."

"What? Without my approval? I have not even inspected the new monastery at Chanteuges. And I never told you about the plan for Saint Pons. For all you know, the bishop could have invented the story!"

"You mean it is not true?" Garsinda looked upset and began sobbing. "But I gained the bishop's approval that the Church will provide half of the money and manpower to construct the buildings, and to include a nunnery in the abbey. He will recruit monks from other locations to begin the monastery. The bishop also agreed to build on the land in Gothia that my father gave me, still within your jurisdiction."

She is crying. I overreacted. Indeed, she is an excellent negotiator! I need to hear the whole story.

Ramon moved around the table and kneeled next to Garsinda, putting his arm around her shoulders and kissing her on the cheek. "I am sorry, sweet. Give me the details before the bishop arrives."

Garsinda recovered her composure and continued, "One more item, husband. The land that I donated for the monastery was the dowry from my father. The bishop wanted the monastery to fill a gap in the pilgrims' route between Saint Chinian and Castres. Commander Guilelm has just returned from Gothia and approved a site on the River Jaur."

She retrieved a scroll from the shelf and unrolled a map of the proposed area. "Guilelm sketched the best location to build the monastery. It is less than two miles from an ancient Roman quarry. Marble will be easily accessible."

"Garsinda, I am sorry that I overreacted. I see the site is only a few miles from a villa I own at Courniou, although I have never been there. You have planned this well, but I still think it will be difficult to hire workers and support them so far from Toulouse."

She traced a line with her finger from Toulouse to the site. "It is about eighty miles from Toulouse, but we might recruit help from the monks at Saint Chinian, thirteen miles southeast. Hautpoul is eighteen miles to the west, but the bishop does not approve of the people. He says they are likely Arians, a term I have never heard. He said they are Christians that do not believe in the Trinity."

"Arians? No, I also have not heard of them. If they are Christians, I do not see a problem with trying to obtain workers from Hautpoul."

"Ramon, I have another idea that might help if we cannot find enough workers. Remember the codex by the poet Ausonius that King Rudolph sent me as a gift?"

Ramon looked puzzled. "Yes."

In the poem, Ausonius wrote about a place in ancient Gaul, during Roman times, that had a water mill powering saws that cut marble!"

"What?"

She recited a few lines from the poem, "'Renowned is Celbis for glorious fish, and that other, as he turns his mill-stones in furious revolutions and drives the shrieking saws through smooth blocks of marble, hears from either bank a ceaseless din.'

"There were notes written in the margin of the manuscript, that the River Celbis is in northern Francia."

"I do not know of that river. Even if we could determine where it had been, the mill would be long gone. There are flour mills in County Toulouse and I saw several watermills on my journey to Paris. They were operated by the monasteries. At the Saint Sulpice Abbey, where we stayed overnight, they also operated windmills. And I saw a pair of waterwheels on the Seine in Paris. But these mills were to grind wheat. I have never heard of a watermill that could cut stone. Perhaps the Romans operated them as the poem describes. But we cannot try to build machines like theirs, at least not without a model, or a book. I cannot solve it now, but we can study how the millstones are turned by the waterwheels and perhaps modify them to turn a saw."

Just after sunrise on a chilly spring day, an assemblage of travelers exited Toulouse through the Narbonne gate. A handful of Count Ramon's knights rode in the vanguard, followed by Ramon, Garsinda, Bishop Armandus, and Castellamonte,

Toulouse's master builder and an officer of the milites. Behind them was the baggage train with soldiers leading mules loaded with food, tents, and supplies. Skilled smiths and sawyers drove several two-wheeled carts which carried those tools too large for the mules. Ten more knights made up the rear guard. The first few miles were on the paved Roman road to Narbonne, but they then turned east onto a road that followed an eroded Roman road to Castres. They maintained a steady pace across a terrain of gentle rolling hills, covered with stretches of forest. Occasionally they encountered a hamlet surrounded by farmland. An hour before sunset the group reached the village of Puylaurens, where they camped near the church. Since they were not within a fortified area, Ramon had the knights take shifts and provide watch throughout the night.

The second day they reached the town of Castres. As they approached the fortified city, Garsinda asked, "Ramon, I have not heard you or Pere mention visiting Castres. Is it not one of your vassals?"

"We do not make routine visits to Castres, although they are vassals to us, indirectly. The Lord of Castres owes fealty to Ato, the Viscount of Albi, who in turn owes fealty to my Uncle Ermengol. As you learn more about the politics of Languedoc, you will find that there exists a patchwork of loyalties and alliances, and those agreements change as nobles marry or die, or per the whims of aristocrats."

"I need a scribe to follow me around and update the records of all the relationships," laughed Garsinda.

"That is a bright idea, love."

They were welcomed by the Abbot of the Benedictine monastery of Saint Benoît, and the Lord of Castres. That evening at dinner the abbot told them of Castres.

"The ancient Celts settled here, followed by the Romans, who built roads, baths, and public buildings. In fact, the name Castres evolved from the Latin word castrum, a Roman military camp. The first Christian missionaries arrived during the Roman Empire and the people were mostly Christianized when the Visigoths replaced the Romans as rulers. When the Abbey of Saint Benoît was built, it generated growth and prosperity for our city. We are fortunate to have this knowledge of our history, which we owe to Gregory, the Bishop of Tours. He wrote the history of the Romans, Visigoths, and Franks."

Garsinda glanced at Bishop Armandus, then asked, "Abbot, I have been told that the Visigoths practiced a different version of Christianity, called Arianism. Does this still exist?"

"Not that I know. To celebrate the conversion of the Visigothic King Reccared to Trinitarian Christianity, our monastery was built by the Catholic bishops of Catalonia and Iberia in collaboration with the Frankish King Sigibert, hundreds of years ago. They interred the arm of Saint Vincent, the martyr of Saragossa at the new abbey. Before that time, the nobles, mostly Visigoths, were Arian Christians and the Gallo-Roman people were Catholic Christians. After King Reccared's conversion, my understanding is that Arianism disappeared from Languedoc."

"What about the unconsecrated church in Hautpoul?" Bishop Armandus asked.

The abbot chuckled and said, "They do keep to themselves and are a curious lot, but I do not think their faith is much different than ours. I have never been in Hautpoul. Why do you ask?"

"I heard that they refuse to pledge oaths as a vassal to any count or duke," said Armandus.

The abbot's face seemed nonjudgmental. "That is a secular issue and not of my concern, Bishop."

Ramon changed the subject, hoping to diffuse any tension. "Abbot, when my men passed through your city last year, they notified you of our plan to build a new monastery between Castres and Saint Chinian to aid pilgrims. We need men to help build the monastery, which will be a few miles east of my manor at Courniou, about thirty miles east of Castres. Can you recruit any skilled or unskilled laborers that might go with us? After the monastery is complete, the workers would be rewarded with land in the Jaur Valley."

"Yes, Count, I will ask, and inform you tomorrow."

In the morning, the abbot held a private Mass for the travelers and prayed for their safe journey and success. The group headed southeast and the well-worn roads disappeared as they followed the pilgrims' path along the River Le Thore to Hautpoul. The abbot had been true to his word. With the addition of a score of men from Castres, the assemblage of travelers now stretched further along the riverside trail. Ramon rode beside Garsinda. "I had an amusing conversation with the abbot," said Ramon. He asked what saint we would honor with the new monastery. When I answered Saint Pontius, he responded, 'Pontius, yes, Pons, I have read of the martyr of Cimiez. A good choice. Saint Pons is revered in Languedoc and Provence.' Then he asked if I was related to the saint. I said yes because Pons is my family name, and I feel a special affinity to the saint. I do feel we have a kinship, across the hundreds of years."

"Ramon, what is so amusing about that?"

"Oh, oh, yes, then the abbot said his family also has a surname. It is Trencavel. His name is Frothaire Trencavel. The abbot laughed when he said his family chose Trencavel because it was the nickname of his older brother: Nutcracker. He laughed, and said, 'We are a bunch of nutcrackers!' He then explained that Trencavel was derived from the Latin 'breaks hazelnuts' because his brother consumes them in great quantities."

Garsinda laughed, then said, "So, what does Pontius mean? In Occitan pont means bridge. Is there a relation?"

"Yes, dear, they are similar, but Pontius is a very old name from Latin. Over one thousand years older than the Occitan word for bridge. As you know, Pontius Pilatus was mentioned in the Bible.

"But Garsinda, I find another odd coincidence. The word for bridge in Latin is pons. But we know the Pons name of Languedoc is derived from Pontius, not pons, because that is how the name is written in all the legal and historical documents."

Garsinda sighed. "It is mystifying. We may never know the origin of the family name."

In the afternoon, the river curved due east as a tributary joined the Le Thore. A scout returned and reported to Ramon.

"Sire, Hautpoul is a mile upstream along the tributary we just forded, so we must make a diversion south to make our overnight camp."

Ramon tilted his head for the scout to lead, and the guide waved the knights in the vanguard to follow. Soon they reached the edge of a steep trail leading to the village. The count looked over his shoulder at the bishop. "Bishop I assume you will join Garsinda and me to meet the citizens of Hautpoul?" Armandus responded with a feeble smile. Ramon sent the scout up the narrow trail to the castle to request accommodations for three.

The count gazed up at Hautpoul. The castle and village were constructed on a peak at the extreme edge of a mass of rocks overlooking the valley. Like Castres, Hautpoul was a vassal of the Trencavels of Albi. As Ramon's men set up their camp, he surveyed the site, approved of the encampment, and turned the command over to Castellamonte. The scout returned with two knights from Hautpoul in escort. One of the knights addressed Ramon, "Count Ramon, the consuls welcome you, the Countess, and your companions to Hautpoul, and are pleased you will stay the night." He glanced at Garsinda. "The trail is steep. We must dismount and lead our horses for a few stretches."

Garsinda said, "Please show us the way."

"Count Ramon, you can be sure the camp is secure," Castellamonte said. "What time should we expect your return tomorrow morning, sire?"

"Before the third hour."

The knights from Hautpoul turned their mounts and started up the slope. Garsinda and Ramon followed. Bishop Armandus shouted to Ramon, "It is too steep for me, Count! And I am afraid the walking is too much for my old body. I will stay here for the night."

Ramon called to his master builder, "Castellamonte, please make sure the bishop is comfortable!"

Partway to Hautpoul, they dismounted and led their horses up the precipitous trail. Ramon watched his young wife negotiate the rocky path. *She is very curious and I soon discovered her desire to learn and to have new experiences. That is why I agreed she could join me on this expedition. But it is good she is also very sturdy. This is not an easy trail, even for me, and she has not complained once.*

The light in the sky began to fade as the group arrived at the fortified village and passed through the gates into a square. A group of three men and two women waited as they dismounted. One of their escorts said, "Count Ramon and Countess, these are our village consuls."

Ramon and Garsinda were first shown their rooms. Awaiting them was a bowl of hot water and towels. They refreshed themselves and joined the consuls in the dining hall of the castle. As they described the background of Hautpoul, Ramon learned that the Lord of Hautpoul and the local priest had made frequent journeys to Narbonne. During one of their trips several years earlier, they had been killed by Saracens. The Viscount of Albi, to whom Hautpoul owed fealty, had not taken measures to replace them, so the local people had organized themselves and elected five consuls as leaders of the village.

The table was set with vegetables and roasted chicken. One of the consuls, a middle-aged woman, stood and held up her cup: "Sante! To our guests, Count Ramon and his beautiful wife, Countess Garsinda!"

All those at the table replied, "Sante!"

Ramon savored the wine, which was dark red and hearty. "Consul, your wine is an excellent vintage."

"Yes, our priest brought it from the Laroque vineyards, owned by the Bishop of Carcassonne. We have saved it for special guests. I am sorry our priest is not here to enjoy it, God rest his soul."

Another consul exclaimed, "Ah, wine! The habit of drinking wine daily is so universal. Wine is the democratic elixir. Everyone drinks wine: peasants, merchants, clergy, counts, and kings!"

There was mixed laughter and sighs from the group.

The man took a huge bite from a chicken breast and talked through his food.

"It is so appropriate we are enjoying chicken today."

Ramon smiled and asked, "Why is that?"

"Because we live in High Chicken," he laughed. Another consul and Garsinda chuckled. "I read the charter written by our founder, Pierre of Albi. It states our village is Alto Pullo, or high chicken."

"Hautpoul means High Perch, not High Chicken. You need to be drinking less wine!" responded an older consul.

They quieted as they ate. Garsinda savored the aroma in the room as she enjoyed a leg of chicken. She dipped her fingers in water, then said, "I am sorry for your priest's death. I see you do have a church. Bishop Armandus travels with us, but I regret he was not strong enough to climb the mountain. How do you conduct Mass?"

The senior woman said, "I lead prayers and administer the Eucharist, Lady Garsinda."

"I thought a priest must lead the Mass and the Eucharist."

"Yes, true, Lady, for the Mass, but nothing in Scripture says only ordained clergy can administer communion. We are all priests in the kingdom of God."

Garsinda hesitated, then said, "Madame, you are fulfilling a wonderful duty taking care of your people, and you are very learned in the Bible as well."

"I learned Latin from the priest and was assisting him before he passed away. I have taught a few others who are interested and we read the Bible aloud to each other every day."

"So, you are a deacon?"

"Yes. I am not an ordained priest, but I do care for the people, and we believe in Christ. We are good Christians."

There was a pause in the conversation and Ramon glanced around the table and then asked, "We are on our way east to start a monastery a few miles from Courniou, two days from here. We need more workers. Will you ask your citizens if any are interested? They will be paid and rewarded with land."

Garsinda added, "And I will talk to Bishop Armandus about helping your church."

When she awoke, the first thing Garsinda told her husband was that the female consul had confided in her not to tell the bishop about her activities. She feared what he might think if he knew a woman was performing the communion and leading prayer meetings. Ramon agreed there was no reason to mention it to the bishop.

Ramon and Garsinda left Hautpoul at daybreak. Two new recruits, a smith and an unskilled laborer, accompanied them on foot to join the expedition. When they arrived in the valley, the camp had been struck and Ramon's caravan was ready to travel. They returned to the trail along the Le Thore and continued east. The valley became wider and they forded often to shortcut the bends in the shallow river. In the early afternoon, they stopped at a large stone set into the earth, a pace wide and as tall as a one-story house, covered with undecipherable symbols. The scout had notified Ramon to stop the troops and rest at the landmark while he rode ahead. As they paused, Ramon and Garsinda ate hard bread, quenched their thirst, and studied the stone monument.

"Ramon, that stone looks very old. It is not Roman."

"Yes. These engravings are not like the Latin letters or numerals on the milestones in Narbonne and Toulouse."

Bishop Armandus saw the stone and shouted, "Soldiers, get tools and ropes! We must tear down this pagan shrine!"

Ramon said, "Wait. Bishop, we don't know that it is religious. Perhaps it was a marker between two ancient tribes."

"It could be milestones, like the Romans left on the roads," Garsinda added.

The bishop remained angry. "No, the stone is evil. We shouldn't be staring at it."

They heard galloping as the scout returned from reconnoiter ahead. "Sire, this menhir marks the spot where we will travel due east."

"Menhir?"

"Yes, sir. On my first trip to the monastery site, an old man at the Jaur springs said menhir is an old Celtic word for the stones. A mile due east is a second menhir, near Courniou. There are several more menhirs between Courniou and the hamlet that align and point to the springs at the building site."

"Bishop, these are useful to us and for others who are traveling to Courniou and eventually to the monastery," said Ramon. "Later if you want, we can remove the carvings, but I would like your agreement to leave them as they are now."

"Very well, Count Ramon."

Ramon addressed the scout, "Did you tell the steward at the villa that we will be there soon?"

"Yes, sire. They are looking forward to your arrival."

They forded the Le Thore once more and headed east. Soon the track became wider and followed the Salesse River. Within an hour, Ramon saw the terra cotta roof of the Courniou villa. A colorful banner hanging from a window flapped in the breeze.

"The villa is not much more than a farm, considering the few outbuildings and the small acreage that is tilled. But they have a banner?" Garsinda asked Ramon.

"I assume they planned to grow into a manor."

The stone villa was a sturdy structure, surrounded by a stacked stone wall which encompassed a large area including a barn and raised vegetable beds. Behind the villa were smaller grassy enclosures demarcated by stone walls, holding goats, mules, and a few milk cows. A middle-aged woman and man waited at the bottom of the villa's steps. Next to them were three young women, each dressed in brown wool tunics, dark brown aprons, and orange and brown plaid scarves.

Ramon called to the man, assuming he was the steward.

"Sir, my men will camp within the walls to keep their horses fenced."

He nodded and Ramon directed Castellamonte to organize the camp. Ramon, Garsinda, and Bishop Armandus dismounted. He turned to greet the villa residents and saw they were genuflecting. Ramon said, "His Excellency Bishop Armandus has endured a tiring journey and we are fortunate to have him with us."

The bishop offered his right hand. Each kissed his ring. The bishop said, "Rise, children of God." He then added, "These are your lords, Count Ramon Pons and Countess Garsinda."

The steward said, "My family and I are here to serve you, Your Excellency, Lord, and Lady."

Garsinda began helping the bishop up the steps to the villa. The steward nodded to his wife and she said, "Please, Lady, may I have the privilege?"

"Of course, thank you."

As the steward and his wife assisted the bishop up the staircase, Garsinda perused the young women's clothes. "You have such pretty dresses. Your scarves are unusual. I have never seen that pattern."

The youngest of the girls said, "We made them ourselves."

A second girl elbowed her.

"I'm sorry. We made them ourselves, *Lady*."

The second girl added, "These are not our daily clothes. We only wear them once a year in the autumn when we have the Chestnut Festival on Saint Martin's Day. Today we wore them in your honor."

Garsinda smiled and asked, "I am pleased. Where is the festival?"

"In the village."

"The village of Tomieres?"

"Yes, Lady Garsinda."

Ramon and Garsinda slept in the master chambers in rather austere surroundings as compared to their home. Chateau Narbonne in Toulouse was a multi-storied castle of stone filled with a labyrinth of rooms and chambers topped by a tower overlooking the city. Although most rooms were simply furnished, the royal chambers had a soft bed with felt mattresses and high bed posts from which fabrics were draped during cold weather. Their Toulouse chambers also had comfortable padded chairs and richly carved furnishings. In contrast, the villa was a two-story wooden structure built on a stone foundation. There were only stools at the kitchen table, and the beds were simple wood and rope frames, each with a woolen mattress stuffed with straw.

The house guests and men in the camp awoke just after daybreak. The smell of cooking fires drifted into the villa's dining room as Ramon, Garsinda, the bishop, and the host family ate breakfast. They had goat's cheese and chestnut bread sprinkled with the honey that Garsinda had brought as a gift for the household. Garsinda had insisted the three young women eat with them. She enjoyed their company as she and the girls were similar in age. Garsinda said to the steward's wife, "This bread has a pleasant and distinct flavor. Where do you get the chestnut flour?"

"Why, we make it ourselves, Lady. The forests are full of the trees. And thank you, Lady, for bringing the honey. It is very generous."

"I have a fancy for sweets. This is Narbonne honey, from my hometown."

Ramon said, "Our journey was primarily along the river bottoms where beech trees were widespread, so we didn't see any chestnut trees until we reached these hills. Yes! The chestnuts are on the Courniou banner. I was also proud to see the Cross of Toulouse on the flag."

Garsinda added, "But please explain the bats on the banner."

"Bats are very common here because of the many caves and caverns," one of girls answered. "We have explored a beautiful cave less than a mile away. We can show you."

"Thank you. There may be more time later. Today we will go to Tomieres and explore the location for the monastery."

The workers, soldiers, and knights assembled for the short trip to Tomieres, less than three miles distant along a well-beaten track. Leaving the villa, they climbed a gentle hill. At the top they arrived at another menhir and looked down into the Jaur Valley. Green hills covered by chestnut forests filled the landscape. As they sat on their mounts, the scout described the countryside. "There is plenty of water. You can just see River Aguze through the trees on the left and the houses of the hamlet to the right, climbing the slopes of Artenac Hill. In the center of the hamlet are springs that are the source of the Jaur River. The mountain across the river is called Lauzet. To the far right the valley widens. That is where the River Jaur flows into the Salesse. From the river junction, we will be able to see the old quarry which was worked by the ancient Romans.

They continued and within a half hour the expedition arrived at the springs, where clear water gushed from a cave. The sun rising above the hills created a misty glow inside the grotto. The troops dismounted in a cobblestone plaza bordered by the springs, a small church, and a cluster of stone houses. Standing in front of the church was a figure in monk garb, his wool habit the color of the dull brown stucco walls. A few women and curious children were in front of the houses, watching as soldiers led the horses to drink.

Ramon, Garsinda, and the bishop went to greet the monk. His head was shaven in a monk's tonsure and the strip of gray hair remaining hinted at the man's age. The monk spread his arms wide. "Welcome to Tomieres!" He knelt at the bishop's feet and kissed his ring. Your Excellency, I am Friar Taenerus.

"Count Ramon Pons and Countess Garsinda, we are honored with your presence."

Ramon gently helped the man to his feet and embraced him. "Friar, we are pleased to meet you. I will do my best not to upset the peace here."

Garsinda kissed the man on his right then left cheek. "Tomieres, your village, the valley, the springs, everything is so fertile and lush!"

Taenerus led them to a sturdy wooden table under a large plane tree beside the springs. They sat on benches and the friar passed around plates of bread and cheese. He poured them wine and water. "Count Ramon, your scouts told me weeks ago that a new abbey will be built here. A very good thing. Our poor community has not been able to give much help to the pilgrims that travel from Saint Chinian through Tomieres."

"Yes, it will be located on the other side of the Jaur." He nodded toward the forested land across the river. "My men will camp over there to help maintain the tranquility of your hamlet."

"Thank you. So, do you feel something? The wonder of this place? This site is a very fitting location for a monastery."

"Yes, the sound of the water. The beauty of the valley," the bishop said. "Your church is in a location that encourages prayer and meditation. And so it will be for the monks and nuns of the abbey. A good choice!" The bishop glanced at Garsinda and she beamed with delight. "Friar, tell us about your church. No priest has been assigned here?"

"I was born and grew up here, and became a priest, ordained by Fructuarius, the Bishop of Beterris. It seems like a lifetime ago. My wife left me and years later I met a wonderful lady, but the Church would not allow me to marry a second time and remain a priest. I chose marriage and was demoted to deacon, but I do not regret it. We had a gratifying life together, but she passed away several years ago.

"I became a monk at Saint Chinian Abbey less than twenty miles distant. My life there consisted simply of work, prayer, and contemplation. The bishop decided I would be the best to lead the small flock here in Tomieres. I am humbly grateful."

"We are sorry for your loss, Friar," Ramon said.

"Thank you, Count." He lingered, as in thought, then said, "What can we do to help? The men of Tomieres have strong backs and need work. I do ask they receive at least nominal pay. They are poor and can barely feed their children properly. As for me, I volunteer to work. Gardening is not enough work for me; I need something more robust and I still enjoy hard work."

Ramon chuckled and said, "A true monk! Worship, reading, and labor. You are welcome to help, Friar.

"My troops will cross the river shortly and begin clearing the trees. I am going downstream to determine what is necessary to reopen the old quarry. I see your church has columns imbedded in the walls. Are they made of marble from the quarry?"

"Yes, Count, they were part of an open-air pagan temple erected by the Romans. The Romans enclosed it after they became Christians hundreds of years ago; they filled in between the marble columns with bricks and cobbles, added a roof, and applied stucco to build the structure you now see."

"It is a durable sanctuary for worshipping, sir. I hope to quarry the marble to build the abbey and church to honor Saint Pontius of Cimiez."

"Very good! That is appropriate. Here in Gothia and even more so to the east, in Provence, Saint Pons of Cimiez is much venerated."

Garsinda and the bishop remained with Friar Taenarus as Ramon's men forded the Jaur River and began clearing the site for the monastery. Ramon and his master builder and engineer, Castellamonte, were escorted by knights to examine the quarry. Friar Taenerus led Garsinda and Bishop Armandus to the church.

"Welcome to the Church of Saint Martin de Jaur. As I said earlier, the Romans became Christians here in the fifth century and transformed the pagan temple into a Christian church.

However, the history of the site is much older. I am fortunate to lead the Christian church because, like my predecessors, I serve as a vessel to pass on the ancient history of the site."

As they entered the interior, even in the subdued light, they could see that the church was simply furnished. There were a few wooden benches along one side, and a kneeling rail at the far end in front of a large wooden cross. The air was damp and cool. In the center of the floor was an elongated stone protruding from the ground and like the menhirs they had encountered, it was covered with engravings.

The bishop pounded his cane on the stone floor, the sound echoing in the large enclosure. "What is this? You have brought one of the pagan idols into a house of God?"

"No, no, your Excellency, I mean . . . the menhir has been here for many hundreds of years. The Romans built the columned portico around the stone. Then the first Christians here found it in this exact place and built the church around the columns. You can see the columns embedded in the walls made of pink marble from the nearby quarry."

As he waved his cane at the pillar, the bishop became unsteady. "But I see again, here are those strange symbols like at Courniou! They are evil. We must remove this stone at once!"

Garsinda steadied the bishop and said softly, "Please Bishop Armandus, sit. Let the Friar explain."

She pulled over a bench. Taenerus seemed thankful. "Your Excellency, no one worships this stone. The menhir is just a record of the naming of this place, of our hamlet."

The bishop calmed and said, "But what are those . . . uh, letters? Hmm . . . I do not know Greek, but I recognize a few Greek letters."

"Precisely, Your Excellency!

"Yes, you see these Greek letters?" He pointed to the engravings. "I made a copy of the engraving on parchment, and pilgrims carried it to the Bishop of Bezier, who passed it on to the clergy at Marseilles. I thought it was lost, but almost a year later pilgrims returning from Compostela delivered the translation. There are still monks in Marseilles who copy Greek manuscripts.

"The name of our hamlet, in Occitan, is Tomieres, derived from the Greek word spelled 'Tau-om-mu-iota-eps-rho-eps-sigma, or T-o-m-i-e-r-e-s.' Tomi means to cut out or carve out a section of ground, or to delineate a section of ground. Ieres means sacred. So Tomieres means sacred ground. The Roman columns enclosed the original sacred area designated by ancient Gauls, then the Christians built the church around the space. It is not surprising the sacred site is next to the springs."

"Who wrote the inscription in Greek?" Garsinda asked.

Taenerus shrugged. "I am guessing that it was the early Roman Christians. I know from my training at Saint Chinian Abbey that the first writings of Saint Paul and the disciples were in Greek."

Bishop Armandus nodded and commented, "Now I see the Greek letters as you have described. There are also two more words, just before Tomieres."

"That was difficult to decipher. They are Greek letters, but the words are Celtic. The legend passed down reveals that the words mean abundant source."

Garsinda said, "Yes, yes. Perhaps they referred to the springs, the source of the Jaur, always providing bountiful water."

"Those are also my thoughts, Countess," said Taenerus. "Your Excellency, would you hold Mass during your visit here? I lead the people in prayer and communion every Sunday, but we have not had a Mass since a priest visited from Saint Chinian, months ago. We would be very honored!"

Bishop Armandus smiled and surveyed the church, "How many of your people will attend?"

"All of the hamlet, about fifty."

"Yes, Friar Taenerus, we will have Mass tomorrow. Saint Martin's Church will have room for all the expedition's soldiers in addition to the townspeople."

Ramon, Garsinda, and Armandus returned to Courniou for the night. The next morning, the three daughters from the villa accompanied them for Mass along with the townspeople and the members of the expedition. Afterwards, the people of Tomieres, although meager in goods, invited everyone to an outdoor feast by the springs. Chestnut bread, venison, and wild boar were the main fare. Castellamonte contributed food from the expedition's supplies to share with the townspeople.

Ramon sat with Garsinda, and both were enjoying the food as well as socializing. "Garsinda, we will be able to pay men from Tomieres. This will help them as they have modest resources. The men here shepherd goats and harvest an occasional red deer or boar. The women gather mushrooms and chestnuts from the forest and grow vegetable gardens.

"A local man guided us to the nearby marble quarry. Remember when you quoted that ancient poem about water-powered saws cutting stone? The Romans may have had a sawmill next to the quarry. We found the ruins of a millrace cut into the rock. Likely it fed a mill, but we found no equipment to examine or discover how it worked. I am sure Castellamonte will determine how to build such a sawmill."

"Your excitement shows, Ramon. You will inspire the workers!"

Ramon placed his hand on hers. "I am so glad you accompanied me here."

"And I am happy we are here experiencing this place together, my knight. Ramon, do you know much about Saint Martin, the patron of the church here?"

Ramon called to the bishop. "Your Excellency, can you enlighten us about Saint Martin?"

Bishop Armandus put down his cup. "This wine made by the monks of Saint Chinian is very good. Ah, yes, Saint Martin. He was a Christian who lived during the Roman times. When he was young, he was a Roman legionnaire. Once while he was traveling, Saint Martin saw a homeless man on the side of the road, freezing in the November cold. He used his sword to cut his own cloak in two and gave half the cloak to the poor man. Later, he gave the other half to a second man in need. He rode on through the sleet, almost freezing to death, but then the sun broke through the clouds and melted the ice and snow. The change in weather was credited to God's intervention and when this happens now, people called the occurrence Saint Martin's Summer.

"Later, he decided he could not continue to kill men in battle, due to his Christian faith, and was discharged from the army. That is when his religious calling began. He became the Bishop of Tours, opposed Arianism, and established a monastery near Tours."

"The girls at Courniou Villa said they have a celebration in Tomieres in the fall," said Garsinda. "Perhaps the festival honors Saint Martin?"

Friar Taenerus who sat nearby overheard her. "Yes, Lady Garsinda, Saint Martin's Day is November 11, when we have a feast much as we are doing today."

"And we are very thankful for everyone sharing their food, Friar," Garsinda replied. She returned to their earlier discussion as she asked Ramon, "So, what are your next tasks?"

"I sent messengers to Abbot Ahan of Saint Chinian this morning, asking him to come to Tomieres in the next few days. I know Saint Chinian is a small monastery and they will not likely be able to provide manpower, but the abbot might have some recommendations. I am also expecting the arrival of Marquis Bello from Lodeve."

"You told me about him. Is he the man you had to fight in single combat?"

"Yes, but that was years ago. We have had good relations since then and I am going to trust him to help protect this place while the construction is underway. I told him I will pay the men good salaries to join the workforce and build the monastery. The most welcome volunteers would be workers who would remain after the abbey is complete. They would be awarded land to till. He also said he would leave a garrison of milites to reinforce Castellamonte's men. Of course, we are paying them for their services."

A pair of riders entered the square, escorted by several of Ramon's milites, who had intercepted and questioned them outside of town. They led the riders to Ramon's table. An unfamiliar soldier bowed to Ramon and Garsinda. "A message from your father, Countess." The messenger handed Garsinda a scroll. She read:

Daughter, I send my love and apologies. I will not be coming to Tomieres as planned to join in the survey of the building site. Please inform me of the date you will complete the monastery and conduct the sanctification, which I look forward to attending. I have several matters I must take care of in Narbonne.

The letter was not signed, but the Viscount's seal was pressed into wax at the bottom of the note. Garsinda said, "Ramon, Father is not coming to Tomieres, but he writes that he hopes to be present at the opening of the monastery. Our plans are to finish the monks' dormitory before next fall. How long will the chapel take?"

"We must finish the monks' dormitory before next fall because a group of monks from the monastery at Aurillac have volunteered to come and start Saint Pons. The completion of the chapel depends on how many men we can muster. Perhaps another year. Did your father write why he could not come?"

"No." She handed him the note and as he read it, she said, "He just said he has to work on a few issues."

The messengers waited.

"Soldier did Viscount Maiol hand you this message?"

"No, Count Ramon. His second did."

"How are conditions in Narbonne? It is peaceful?"

"Yes, Count."

"Very good. Join us, men, the food is delicious."

CHAPTER SEVEN

After a demanding week, Ramon, Garsinda, and Bishop Armandus departed Courniou. Ramon chose to return home by a southern route through Saint Chinian, Beterris, and Narbonne. He wanted to mollify the abbot of Saint Chinian monastery who was concerned his abbey might be abandoned when Saint Pons monastery was completed. Ramon also wanted to obtain support for the new monastery from the nobles and religious leaders of Beterris. In addition, Garsinda wanted to see her father, Maiol, after he was unable to attend the dedication in Saint Pons.

During their stopover in Saint Chinian, Bishop Armandus assured Abbot Ahan that his monastery would remain open and continue to be important to the Church and to the pilgrims. Having relieved the abbot's worries, they were on their way early the next morning.

Ramon's returning party was small compared to the original expedition, consisting of only the knights, Garsinda, and the bishop. The mules, carts, and their handlers had remained in Tomieres as part of the workforce to build the monastery. Castellamonte had stayed to design and supervise the construction. He also had a detachment of foot soldiers at the work site for security and to supply game. They hired men from Tomieres as guides for hunting in the surrounding forests, where they harvested wild boar and red deer.

The troupe started at a nominal pace as they departed Saint Chinian. Ramon saw that the road was good and suggested they quicken their pace, so the horses were spurred into a steady trot south. They stopped to rest their mounts along the River Le Lirou. As Ramon and Garsinda dismounted, a knight gathered the reins and watered the horses. Garsinda said, "Ramon, how far is it to Beterris?"

"I think we are halfway there. The road has been level since leaving Saint Chinian, so we are making good time. I am impressed the bishop has not complained about the pace."

Bishop Armandus walked up behind Ramon. "I heard that, Count!" The bishop laughed and patted Ramon on the shoulder. "These old legs are weakening, but I can ride just fine."

Ramon smiled. "This road is adequate, but through Beterris, Narbonne, and to Toulouse where the roads are smoother, we may be able to make even faster time and ride our mounts at a canter."

Garsinda pointed to a broken column that had fallen down the river bank. Inscribed on the column was JULIA BAETARRAE, $\overline{\text{VIII}}$ PASSUM. "Look! There is writing on it. What I read is '*Julia Baetarrae, eight paces.*' Eight paces?"

Ramon answered, "That is a Roman milestone. There are hundreds of them along the old roads. I was confused the first time I read a milestone, but I solved it from experience. The line above a numeral means the number is in the thousands. That is, eight thousand paces, or to us, eight miles. And Baetarrae is the city that we know as Beterris, so the next town is eight miles."

"I am learning more and more every day," said Garsinda. "Ramon, I overheard your conversation with Marquis Bello when he arrived in Tomieres. Do you think the men will be safe?"

"We left a company of milites, and Marquis Bello added a troop for protection. Because the Saracens' base of operation at La Gardi Fraxinet is over a hundred miles away, I had thought the danger unlikely. But Bello was told the Arabs range afar and have recently occupied the passes through the Alps, robbing pilgrims and taking hostages. When I mentioned I had an agreement with Captain Samad from Fraxinet that his men would not invade Toulouse or Gothia, Bello said that Samad had been killed. Now the agreement is worthless. Also, Bello stated that the Count of Provence, Boson of Arles, does not forcefully defend his realm, but remains behind his walls if Saracens are raiding nearby."

"Yet travel through those areas," said the bishop, "will be required to retrieve Saint Pontius's relics from Cimiez."

Garsinda seemed worried. Ramon answered, "Yes, Bishop, that is a problem, but right now I am going to concentrate on making Saint Pons secure throughout its construction. That is one reason to go through Beterris on the way back to Toulouse. The lords in Gothia tend to be defiant and undependable, but you and I together may convince the secular and the religious orders in Beterris that it will be in their best interest to support and reinforce the people in Tomieres."

They continued south toward the city and passed by manors with vineyards spread over the plains. When they arrived, they were welcomed at the monastery by the Bishop of Beterris. In short time, the Viscount of Beterris and his wife joined them for dinner.

Garsinda gracefully used her knife to taste another flake of fish. "This is very delicious, both with and without the pomegranate juice. And the texture is so delicate. What kind of fish is this?"

The viscount's wife answered, "I'm glad you like it, dear. It is called barbel, and it's a freshwater fish."

Garsinda selected a vegetable from her plate and dipped it in a bowl of white sauce. "Mmm. And your aioli makes these vegetables especially tasty."

"Thank you, Countess. How does it compare to the Toulousean aioli?" said the hostess.

Garsinda took another taste. "It is very good, but, there is something . . . different."

The viscount's wife smiled and was about to answer, but Garsinda answered first. "My initial guess was that your olive oil was a different taste, but now I know. There are no walnuts used to make this aioli!"

"That's right."

"But very flavorful," said Garsinda. "And I must compliment you on the pomegranate fruit on the plates. The fruits are so decorative!"

Ramon cleaned his fingers in a bowl of water and added, "Yes, yes, a very delicious dinner. Viscount, the manors we passed had extensive vineyards that appeared healthy and well-established. Is this wine from local grapes? It is robust, but just sweet enough."

The viscount answered, "Thank you, it is local wine. We are proud of our vines. They are now maturing after they were replanted following the Saracen incursion."

"They destroyed the vineyards?" asked Ramon.

"Many years ago," said the viscount. "It must have been several generations ago. The Arabs occupied Beziers and cut down the vines. They do not approve of drinking wine."

Garsinda asked, "Did you say *Beziers*? I saw the Latin name for your city, Baeterrae, on a Roman milestone and I thought the city's name was now Beterris."

The viscount answered, "Yes, of course, over time language, words change. Many of the inhabitants call the city Beziers in their Occitan vernacular. Both Beterris and Beziers are used. Sometimes it can be confusing, Countess. And the milestones. Yes, many ruins and vestiges of the ancient Romans scatter the countryside. Several of the manors you saw among the vineyards were Roman villas at one time."

Ramon said, "As we discussed earlier, the Saint Pons monastery is being established to aid the pilgrims and to develop the land to be productive. This monastery will be in your diocese. We have the commitment of the abbot of Saint Geraud in Aurillac to transfer five monks to begin the Saint Pons monastery this fall. Will you be able to send a representative to welcome them and start their work for the Lord?"

The Bishop of Beterris said, "I would be honored! I will personally visit Tomieres and give them my support, Count Ramon."

Ramon turned to his host and said, "Viscount, we have almost one hundred milites at the building site for protection. Will you be able to commit soldiers for the next year to bolster their defenses?"

When there was no response, Ramon sensed rejection of his appeal coming and placed a small bag of gold coins on the table. "Here is compensation for assigning your men to the site."

The viscount gently bowed his head and slowly but briefly closed his eyes, accepting the proposal.

The ride to Narbonne from Beziers was along the Via Domitia, the road that had linked Italy with Spain during the Roman Empire. As they left Beziers, they crossed the Orb River on an old Roman bridge. Its nine arches had stood the test of time. Garsinda spoke to Ramon as their horses trotted along the paved road. "This bridge is hundreds of paces long, perhaps longer than the bridge in Toulouse! Both were built by the Romans. How many years ago, Ramon?"

"The Romans were living here when Christ was born, so I will guess the bridges were built at least 936 years ago, the current year of our Lord."

"Ramon, everything seems to be going according to plans. You have started the construction. Marquis Bello has contributed soldiers to the garrison at Saint Pons and the Viscount of Beziers promised to send more. How did you convince the Abbot of Aurillac to send monks to begin the monastery?"

"It was not from my initiative. On our way north to Paris several years ago, I talked of the new monastery with my cousin, Lord Pons of Aurillac. He arranged it.

"Are you looking forward to seeing your father? We should be in Narbonne well before sunset."

"Yes, yes, I am. Have the scouts gone ahead to tell him? He doesn't know we are coming. I have been looking for milestones along the way, but they are damaged or broken beyond reading. Oh, there is one." They slowed as she read the engraving, "'*Via Domitia, Narbo three thousand paces*'; that is three miles. But now I am puzzled! My steps are small, but even a tall man, like you, will need more than a thousand paces to cover a mile."

I am not surprised by her observation. She is always inquisitive! Ramon answered, "When I was a young man, I asked the same question once when traveling with my father. He told me the 'passuum' in Latin means pace, but one pace is two steps. A Roman legionnaire's steps, that is."

There was a short pause as Garsinda appeared to be in deep thought. "Yes, now it makes sense. That would figure right." She laughed. "Husband, one of these days, I will ask you a question you cannot answer."

Within several minutes, a pair of Ramon's knights galloped from the direction of Narbonne. One of the knights reported to Ramon, "Count, the gates of Narbonne are closed, and the guards said, 'The Count of Toulouse is not welcome.'"

Garsinda gasped. "It is Matfred again! My father could be in danger!"

"Are there any towns before Narbonne?" asked Ramon.

"Yes sire, there is a hamlet surrounded by farms and vineyards about two miles away."

Within a short time, they neared a cluster of houses. Set back among the vineyards were several villas, hundreds of paces from the road. The bishop said, "That is strange. Even the smallest hamlets have a church. But here, I see no bell tower or crosses on any buildings."

A knight heard the bishop and said, "Your Excellency, we rode through the hamlet earlier and I saw some men wearing the hats . . . um, the hats that are unique to the Jews."

They entered the village and a group of men in pointed caps stepped into the road, about a hundred paces ahead. The scouts drew their swords. Ramon shouted, "Wait! They are unarmed. Ride ahead and tell them who I am."

The villagers appeared excited as a scout rode back and reported to Ramon. "Sire, when I told them you were the Count of Toulouse, the men were relieved you have arrived. Samuel, their leader, said the people of Narbonne need your help once more, to temper the Viscount Matfred."

Garsinda moaned, "I knew it!"

Ramon proceeded to the knot of men gathered in the road and introduced himself to Samuel, who reported that Garsinda's father was unhurt, but a hostage in Narbonne. Samuel invited Ramon's troupe to his villa, a short ride through his vineyards. The knights dismounted, watered the horses, and rested outside near the stables, as the bishop, Garsinda, and Ramon were led to the villa. As they crossed the courtyard to the entrance, the surrounding landscape was filled with a panorama of vineyards, grazing livestock, workshops, and activity that lent an air of prosperity and well-being. Inside the villa, Samuel's wife served them from a pitcher of wine.

Garsinda said, "Sir, please, I thank you for your hospitality, but my father . . . and the people of Narbonne need our help. Can we bypass the pleasantries?"

Ramon was silent, letting the conversation continue. Samuel answered her, "I am sorry, Countess, I should have told you. Preparations are already underway. Remember, Countess? Before you were married and lived in Narbonne there was another time when Matfred caused problems. At that time, the people of Narbonne waited to act until Odulf arrived with soldiers from Toulouse. It was Odulf who was the captain you sent, is that right, Count Ramon?"

Ramon nodded.

"So now Count Ramon is here and again we will fight. Narbonne is a haven for my people and we make up a quarter of the city's inhabitants, but we are merchants, educators, and philosophers, not soldiers. When Odulf arrived the last time during our troubles, we opened the gates through part stealth, part bribes, part . . . but very little part aggression. When you arrived, I sent out word to the other manors to organize and be ready to infiltrate the city again. It may seem to you that I am wasting time, but I am waiting for them to arrive, so we can open Narbonne once again. Meanwhile, drink." He raised his cup: "Success!"

Ramon raised his cup. "Well planned. Timing is everything." Garsinda hesitated, then reluctantly joined their toast. Ramon paused, then said, "Samuel, the bountiful fields, these manors, they all belong to the Jewish community? I have been in Narbonne and I am familiar with the Jews as talented and shrewd merchants, but not as landowners."

"Many years ago, King of the Franks, Pepin the Short, rewarded the Jewish community a third of city and surroundings, for their help recovering Narbonne from the Saracens. We earned these lands. But we have never forgotten the Frankish king's help nor the munificence of the Count of Toulouse. Before your family ruled Toulouse, Guilhem d'Orange, a Frankish count, was the Count of Toulouse."

Ramon seemed puzzled. Then suddenly he remembered. "Yes, now I recall the stories about Guilhem! After the Saracen rulers were expelled from Narbonne, they regrouped with Muslim reinforcements from Spain. Guilhem is still celebrated for defeating the Saracens when they attacked Toulouse."

Samuel added, "And we as well are indebted to your predecessor, Guilhem. He supported our Rabbi Makhir to establish the Judaic Academy, still flourishing in Narbonne. At the school the Talmud is studied, and poetry is composed. It has attracted great scholars from across the sea.

"But over the last few generations, our people's rights and freedoms have been restricted. And there have been farms taken away under suspicious reasons. We are encouraged that you have arrived, Count Ramon!"

Garsinda said, "Yes, I have heard of your Talmudic school, but I was not aware that a count of Toulouse had helped establish it. With this knowledge, as countess, I will provide support to your institution."

A man entered the courtyard and bowed to Samuel, addressing him by his title, "Nasi, we are all ready."

"Let us meet in the courtyard," said Samuel. "We will describe the plan to our followers."

When they exited the villa, they saw that hundreds of men had joined Ramon's knights. The Jewish men bowed their heads and random whispers were heard. "Nasi. Nasi. Nasi."

Samuel announced to the crowd, "It will be as before. Enter Narbonne through the secret way. Each of you will gather your Jewish, Christian, and Arab comrades. This time the signal will not be the church bells. We used those last time and I am afraid Matfred will be wary of them. This time the signal will be given by blowing the holy shofar, the ram's horns. Then gather in the streets and use carts to block the roads to the front gates. With this distraction, our men will use their daggers on the guards and open the gates. The Count . . ." He looked at Ramon, who nodded, "Ramon Pons, the Count of Toulouse . . ." The crowd shouted praises. "When the horns are sounded, the count will charge into the city. Yahweh deliver us!"

Garsinda, Bishop Armandus, and Samuel remained at his villa during the assault. The elderly nasi was not a military leader, and his followers would not let him be subject to harm in the city. The plan to open the gates succeeded and the united forces entered the city with only a few casualties. When the townspeople saw that Ramon was the leader of the rescue forces, they lost their fear of Matfred. Many of Matfred's milites changed sides and Matfred retreated to the citadel with Garsinda's father Maiol as hostage. Ramon negotiated with Matfred and as compensation, agreed that Narbonne's annual tribute, historically paid to Toulouse, would now be retained in equal shares by Matfred and Maiol. This sum would appease Matfred and replace his unauthorized tariffs of the merchants' imports. The negotiations were public, shouted across the moat to the castle, and the townspeople could hear the conditions of the agreement. The drawbridge was lowered and Maiol was freed. To seal the armistice, Ramon and Matfred embraced. The townspeople cheered, but Ramon whispered into Matfred's ear as they clinched, "If you do this a third time, I will personally hunt you down and kill you."

Ramon chose to remain a few days longer to be certain the peace held and there were no repercussions. At Maiol's chateau in Narbonne, Ramon and his father-in-law deliberated on strategies to stave off future problems from Matfred. In addition, Ramon learned from Maiol that Jewish merchants traveling from the north had reported of King Rudolph's illness and subsequent death.

"Father, do you think King Rudolph's death prompted Matfred's aggression?" asked Ramon.

"It is likely," answered Maiol. He may have viewed the selection of Louis IV to king as a weakness. Louis had been living in England and Matfred may have thought Frankish support would diminish toward Narbonne and the southern counties."

"We should still have the king's support," said Ramon. "From what you told me, it was Rudolph's brother-in-law, Hugh, Count of the Franks, who put Louis on the throne."

"Yes, but Matfred rebelled despite that."

115

"Then perhaps I must send knights to garrison in Narbonne?" asked Ramon.

"No, the people would see them as outsiders," said Maiol. "I have another plan, Son."

After the city was secure, Garsinda and Armandus arrived from Samuel's manor to stay at her father's chateau. She decided to visit Samuel who had returned to his residence in the city. Her escorts waited in the anteroom as Garsinda sat with Samuel. "Nasi Samuel. Is that correct? I heard your men call you nasi, perhaps it is a sign of respect, or a title?"

"Yes, Countess, nasi means prince. I am a descendent of Rabbi Makhir. He was our leader and founded the academy with funds from the former Count of Toulouse, many years ago."

Samuel was discovering how many questions Garsinda could ask as she continued. "And this palace, or chateau you live in when you are in Narbonne. It is called Cortada Regis Iudaeorum. In Latin that translates to indicate the cut, the property of the royalty of the Jews. So, are you a count or a king, or prince?"

Samuel heaved a sigh. "My people have been wandering throughout the world since the Romans destroyed the temple and dispersed us. The Talmudic term used for our exile is galut. But the Jewish community who speak Greek use the term diaspora. As for the title of nasi and the name of the property where the chateau is located, they both represent the hope that someday my people will have a kingdom again. As of now, our properties in Narbonne are greatly cherished and I hope you will be our patrons, as King Pepin, Emperor Charlemagne, and the former Count of Toulouse were."

"I will support your academy," said Garsinda. "Study and knowledge are my dreams. May I visit the Judaic Academy?"

Even with her great magnanimity, years of tradition hindered Samuel. He tried to hide his discomfort. "Countess, women are not routinely allowed . . . but you are the countess. I will escort you to the academy."

Peace finally restored, the count led his small party back to Toulouse. Along the Roman road they traveled quickly. Carcassonne would have been a convenient stop, but Ramon knew they would not be welcome. They detoured and stayed the night at the Saint-Hilaire Abbey in Limoux, a sister abbey to their Saint Sernin Abbey in Toulouse. The following evening, they camped near the ruins of an old Roman post station where a hamlet had grown up around a small unfinished castle. The next afternoon they were back home in Toulouse. Pere and Odulf welcomed them at the city gate.

Weary from their travels, Ramon and Garsinda slept late into the morning. Ramon invited Pere and Odulf to a midday meal. Over a repast of fresh bread and ewe cheese with black cherry jam, Pere updated Ramon on the status of Toulouse.

Then Ramon described the conflict in Narbonne. Odulf said, "You did that with a small troop of knights? Bravo, Count Ramon! During their first revolt, I had crossbowmen and foot soldiers to support me. Maiol can't seem to balance Matfred's hunger for power. Um, pardon me, Countess. I did not mean to be disrespectful of your father."

Ramon said, "I left Matfred with an ultimatum regarding his dissent, but simply eliminating him would have caused unrest, since half the people in the city still support him. Odulf, I want you to go to Narbonne and train a company of milites to act as the special guard for Viscount Maiol. Recruit the men from the citizens of Narbonne, based on Maiol's recommendations. I want to protect him with a balanced unit consisting of crossbowmen, shieldmen, and pikemen that can coordinate with his knights. Take enough funds and give the money to Maiol so he can pay the milites. I want their loyalty owed to him."

"Excellent idea, Count! I will organize and leave within a few days."

Ramon gave them an account of the work at Tomieres. Garsinda added, "We plan to return to the site next spring to dedicate the monastery."

"Castellamonte must complete the monks' dormitory before cold weather," Ramon said. "At least before the brothers from Aurillac need accommodations."

"It is good you returned," said Odulf, "the Aurillac monks just arrived here yesterday and are eager to continue on to Tomieres. I asked them to wait until we provide them an escort. They are a spirited group, especially their leader! Not like the monks I see in Toulouse."

Ramon looked interested. "Spirited? And I did not expect them until the end of the summer. Toulouse is not the most direct route from Aurillac to Tomieres. Why did they come here?"

"They wanted to obtain your approval. As you would expect of Benedictine monks, they are traveling very lightly. They wear only their habits and sandals, and each has merely a shoulder bag. Instead of long walking staves as you would expect, they have garden hoes. I was jesting with them and said, 'True Benedictines! You are frugal and efficient. I see you are bringing your garden tools with you.'

"Their leader answered, 'The hoes are good walking sticks. We also dig up roots to eat on our journey and will use the tools to plant our gardens in Tomieres.'"

Ramon and Garsinda laughed.

Odulf continued, "The monks walked unescorted for a week to get to Toulouse and said they only requested directions to Tomieres, that God protects them, and they were not in need of escorts. When I reminded him that brigands and Saracens could attack them, he said, 'Our hoes are also very effective tools of defense.' Once he saw the doubtful look on my face, he demonstrated his skills. I was impressed."

Ramon asked, "What did he do?"

"He walked to the center of the courtyard. Holding his hoe with one hand, he started circling it overhead in large arcs and said, 'Throw your dagger at me.' I said, 'Good monk, I do not want to hurt you!' And I refused.

"Instead, the other monks surrounded him in a circle, several paces away. He shouted, 'Throw!' The monks threw the hoes all at once. A couple flew straight at him like an arrow, the others spinning end over end. His comrades did not hold back, but threw with all their might. The hoes all surely would have struck him, but his circling hoe intercepted and redirected all but one."

Ramon said, "So one got through. That isn't too bad. Did it strike him?"

"No, sire, he caught the fourth hoe with his free hand, and stood holding both in his possession."

Ramon laughed and said, "He is confident he can defend himself, but we must be sensible and provide them with an escort. They are the future of Saint Pons Abbey. What is their leader's name?"

"Varadolanus,"

Garsinda said, "I would like to meet them before they leave."

Ramon added, "They should not go without an escort. Once a month, Castellamonte will be sending messengers here with reports on their progress. When these messengers leave for Tomieres, they can be the monks' escorts, but they are not expected in Toulouse for several weeks."

"Where are the monks now, Odulf?"

"At La Daurade with their monastic brothers."

Two evenings later, several soldiers arrived unexpectedly from Tomieres. They waited in the courtyard for Ramon and Garsinda. Anxious, Ramon did not wait in his study for the messengers but went to meet them in the chateau courtyard. *This is two weeks early for a report from Castellamonte. I hope they do not bring bad news.* Garsinda struggled to keep pace with Ramon as they crossed the bricked courtyard to receive them. Ramon calmed as the messengers appeared to be in high spirits. "Count Ramon, I have good news from Castellamonte. The engineer built a water mill that can drive a saw that cuts through marble. We are ahead of schedule!" The messenger handed Ramon a leather case. "The details are in his letter."

Ramon, much relieved, said, "Thank you, soldier. I will call you when I compose my response to Castellamonte. You will have at least an extra day of rest before you return to Tomieres. There are five Benedictine monks that will travel with you upon your return to Tomieres."

Out of respect, Ramon chose to visit the monks at the abbey rather than call them to the chateau. He also wanted to see

Bishop Armandus, who had been exhausted after their long trip and whose health was of concern. Garsinda and Odulf accompanied him as they walked along the river to La Daurade. Citizens waved and bowed along the streets, pleased to see their count and their adored countess in the city once again.

Ramon and Garsinda met with the Aurillac monks at the abbey situated next to La Daurade Basilica. Ramon addressed the monks' leader, who wore his hair long and tied behind instead of the common tonsure of the Benedictine monks.

"Monk Varadolanus, we thank you for volunteering to be the first monks of Saint Pons."

"Count, we are ready to serve God in any way. Your captain insists we travel with soldiers."

"I heard about your impressive display of self-defense. Do all the brothers of Aurillac train with garden hoes as weapons?"

"A Benedictine monk has a hoe in his hand for many hours of each day and to pause between gardening, we entertain ourselves."

"Yes, I understand, Varadolanus, a soldier is . . . um, also intimate with his sword, spear, and dagger. As for the escorts, that is not a problem now. Messengers just arrived and will be ready to guide you to Tomieres the morning after tomorrow."

"Excellent. Our wish is to help with the construction. We pray, we study, and we work. We work hard. It is good for the soul."

"I agree, Varadolanus. You have an interesting name. Is it Latin?"

"No, but it's Latinized. My late father was a Hungarian. He left his people and went to east Francia to learn about Christianity. There he married and only later became a monk.

"Count, may I ask you about your name?"

Ramon nodded.

"We were told that the monastery will be built in honor of the Roman martyr Pontius of Cimella, um . . . as you say in Occitan, Pons of Cimiez. Are you related to the saint?"

"I identify with Saint Pons by name and I do believe we are related. And I am compelled to recover Saint Pons's vestiges in Cimiez and deliver the saint's holy relics to sanctify the monastery at Tomieres. It is a mission I am called to pursue."

Garsinda swallowed hard but suppressed an audible gasp. Her manner betrayed no emotions.

They called on the bishop who was resting in bed but feeling stronger each day. He talked of their journey to Tomieres and the dream of completing the abbey. They prayed together and wished him better health. Garsinda looked tense and was silent during their walk back to the chateau. As soon as they were in private, Garsinda said, "Husband, why didn't you tell me you planned to go to Cimiez yourself to obtain Saint Pons's relics? Don't you think it best to send Pere, Odulf, or a loyal knight to lead the mission? We could have talked about it."

"I am sorry, love, that I announced it like that. It has been welling up inside me for months. I often think of the indebtedness we hold for Saint Pons and for all the martyrs. I feel obligated to honor his sacrifice and at least take the risk myself. But I have a way to lessen the danger.

"While you were with Samuel visiting the Judaic school in Narbonne, your father and I went to the waterfront where he introduced me to an Arab trader who was his close friend. The merchant owns a small ship which he uses to trade along the coast. His family lives in Narbonne, and Maiol trusts him. He agreed to take me to Nice by sea. From there, Cimiez is only a few miles inland. This way I would not have to pass overland through Provence where the Saracens are a threat."

Garsinda sobbed, "How many soldiers could you take? Would they have crossbows? How long will you be gone?"

"Garsinda, love, I will be prepared and I will take enough guards."

She smiled and wiped the tears away. "It is hard to be a countess!"

Ramon hugged her, laughed, and said, "I am surprised you didn't ask to go with me!"

"You know me. Yes, I would have, but I also have a revelation for you. I am carrying our child."

MICHAEL A. PONZIO

Mission to recover Saint Pontius's relics

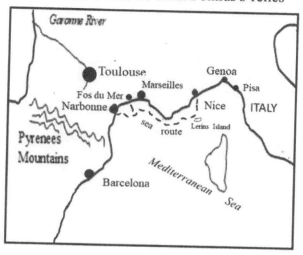

MICHAEL A. PONZIO

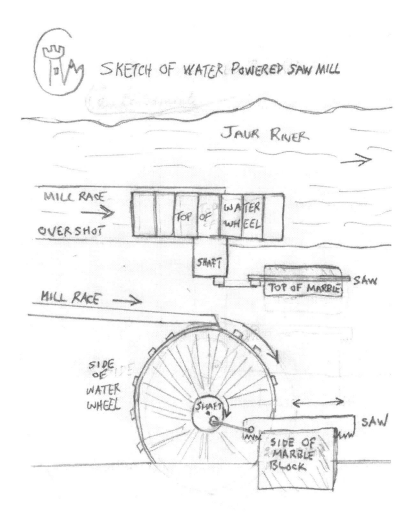

SKETCH OF WATER POWERED SAW MILL

JAUR RIVER

MILL RACE

OVERSHOT

TOP OF WATER WHEEL

SHAFT

TOP OF MARBLE

SAW

MILL RACE

SIDE OF WATER WHEEL

SHAFT

SAW

SIDE OF MARBLE BLOCK

MICHAEL A. PONZIO

CHAPTER EIGHT

It was now October of 936 and four months after the start of construction of Saint Pons monastery. Ramon had just received a message from Castellamonte. The count had written to the master builder requesting a detailed description of the mill he had built for sawing the stone and marble blocks. He examined the sketch the engineer had sent, which illustrated how the watermill could use the same saw as a two-man crew. Ramon paused. *How creative! I need to share this with Garsinda right away.*

His wife eagerly studied the engineer's drawing as Ramon read the letter to her. "'The Roman mill race that had been cut into the rock had been eroded and there were no remnants of any of the original mechanisms, so it was impossible to determine the original design. With only a few repairs, however, we easily installed an undershot waterwheel, which channels the water to flow along the bottom of the wheel. This initial mechanism did not have much power and barely outpaced two sawyers. It required a few more weeks to build an elevated millrace. The water was then channeled over the top of the wheel, and with the fall, provides additional drive to the blades. This is the overshot design and the configuration now saws blocks of stone and marble ten times faster than a team of sawyers.'" Ramon looked up from the letter and considered their shared expressions of wonder.

Ramon was increasingly pleased with the news as he continued the letter from Tomieres. The Aurillac monks had arrived at the site and had joined the workforce. By the end of the first summer the foundation of the church had been completed and the erection of the walls had begun. The monks' dormitory had been completed, as well as stone houses for those workers who would stay permanently. They had also finished a bridge across the Jaur River to connect the Saint Pons site to Tomieres. The sawmill had allowed increased production of the building stone and marble, and Castellamonte predicted completion of the project by fall of 937. As he looked over the sketch again with his wife he said, "I assume Taenarus or one of the monks wrote this letter and added captions to the drawing. Sir Castellamonte is brilliant but is not literate nor can he write. His sketches are superb and he is creative—see his sign: C-M and a castle symbol."

Throughout the fall Ramon received encouraging updates of the construction at Saint Pons monastery. Progress slowed during the winter, but the quarters for the monks, workers, and soldiers, had been completed before cold weather. With his expedition ready to recover the relics of Saint Pontius, Ramon was eager to leave for Cimiez. Garsinda had organized a feast to be held the day before Ramon departed. That April afternoon was pleasant as they gathered outside in the chateau courtyard. Garsinda arranged to serve Cahors wine, Ramon's favorite. She asked for the attention of the ladies and knights.

"I was fortunate to visit the Judaic Academy in Narbonne. They study their holy scriptures of course, but also compose 'wine poems.' As a toast, I will recite part of a poem by Samuel na Hagid." She raised her goblet.

> *To fill the cup with coral drink,*
> *Put up in kegs in Adam's time,*
> *Or else just after Noah's flood,*

A pungent wine, like frankincense,
A glittering wine, like gold and gems,
Such wine as concubines and queens
Would bring King David long ago.

"To my husband, the Count of Toulouse Ramon Pons, who would risk all to honor Saint Pons of Cimiez."

A chorus followed: "Sante!"

Music from several flutes and a pair of vocalists filled the courtyard. Guests returned to their food and conversations as Ramon and Garsinda sat close together.

"Garsinda, my love, as you wanted, I have planned this journey with safety in mind. I will take two knights and four bowmen."

"That is not very many soldiers."

"The ship I have bought passage on is small, but swift. It can only hold a crew of two sailors, their captain, and the six of us."

"Again, Ramon, tell me how long it will take to sail to Nice?"

"The captain said if winds are favorable, it will take two to three days. We will only sail during the day and we will always be within sight of land. Does that make you feel better?"

"Ramon, I am sorry I argued again last night about your journey. But I have accepted your obligation and now I am more assured you will not take unnecessary risks. You promised your father you would rebuild Saint Pons, and you have promised me you will return, for our son Ramon."

"Nothing will stop me from returning to you." He looked over at their son's nurse, holding Ramon Pons, three months old. "Now I have two reasons to return." Garsinda nodded at her nurse who handed the infant to her. Ramon chuckled. "I want to see young Ramon grow, so I can teach him to fight with two swords. Are you and Ramon going to spar with wooden spoons?" Garsinda laughed.

"We will stop at the island of Saint Honorat, near Nice," said Ramon. The bishop's records show a monastery on the island. Saracens have sacked Nice many times over the years, and the captain will not know the conditions at the city until he enters the harbor. We plan to wait on the island while the captain continues to Nice and decides if it will be safe there for us to land."

Garsinda sat and rocked their son. She said, "You told me you will stop at Fos sur Mer after the first day's sailing?"

"Yes, Pons de Fos has a castle on the bay, west of Marseilles. I sent him a message by way of traveling merchants. Hopefully he received it and will accommodate us for the night. Hmm, another possible cousin, and one I have never met."

Within a week, Ramon and his men were at the docks in Narbonne. They carried their food, blankets, and a small cask of wine onto the deck and stored them below in the cargo hold. They kept their weapons close. The sailboat was twenty paces long fitted with a single triangular sail. The only part of the deck that was covered was a low cabin in the aft section, with enough space for the captain to sleep.

The men settled in and Ramon reviewed the course with the captain, Hamid al-Tulaytuli. As they studied the chart, Ramon's second-in-command joined them. "Hamid, anytime I am absent, Jordan as my second will make decisions for my men."

Hamid and Jordan both nodded. Hamid pointed to the map. "We will be able to sail to Fos sur Mer before sunset, as planned. The castle of Fos is located on a bay that provides good shelter. Have you arranged consent to anchor there?"

"Yes, I have sent Lord Pons of Fos a message. They should expect us and I will have you hoist the flag of Toulouse when we draw near the castle."

"Good. The following day we should arrive at the island of Saint Honorat. I have never landed there, but I know of several good places to anchor where we will be hidden. You said earlier that a monastery is on the island?"

"Yes, as we discussed we will wait there, while you reconnoiter at Nice."

"Count Ramon, remind your men that when we are at sea, if we see an Arab trading ship you must all go below into the cargo hold."

"Agreed. What if we see any other ships that are not Arab?"

"That is not likely, except in Nice, which is a port of call for Pisan merchant ships. I have heard their armed galleys have been there, but that is as far west as they sail from their home port. Nice is considered a neutral port although I am cautious and I will not enter the harbor if a Pisan warship is docked."

Ramon said, "Are the Pisans the only Europeans that have ships?"

"I only sail as far as Nice. But I have talked to sailors who have seen the Roman galleys in southern Italy. It is said when they spray the Greek fire on your ship, water cannot put out the flames."

"Romans, you mean Romans from Constantinople?"

"Yes, you too have heard of the greatest city in the world? There are stories that the Christians built a church there that is as big as a mountain."

Hamid guided the ship down the river channel and out to sea. His men set the sail, and the captain tacked against the wind. Ramon, like his men, tried to hide the initial uneasiness of being on the sea. A few vomited over the side and recovered. After several hours, they all seemed to adapt to the rolling motion. Ramon, interested in the operation of the ship, went to the stern where the captain manned the tiller. "Hamid, I am impressed! The wind is blowing from the south and you are still headed southeast—that is almost into the wind. How do you do that?"

"The method of sailing this way is called tacking. It is done by the angle we turn the sail. With our alshirae, we can sail on a slant against the wind. A square sail cannot be used that way."

"Captain, you said, an alshirae?"

"Yes, the alshirae, the three-cornered sail."

"I do not know anything about three-cornered sails or square sails, Hamid, but you have quite a skill!" *I have respect for these sailors' knowledge. Garsinda will be interested.* "It is invigorating being at sea, Hamid!"

"Yes, I have the best work. I ferry goods between Nice and Barcelona and make a living from that. It is a good life. Soon we will turn east to parallel the coast."

"I sense your fulfillment," said Ramon. This is the first time I have been on the sea, but I feel as if I am revitalized! Curiously, almost as if I belong here. It is a strange feeling.

"You said the sail is called alshirae?"

"The sail is called alshirae and the three-cornered sail is called a mizan alshirae. And this ship is called a kharraq."

"Your ship has a name?"

"Yes it does, but what I meant is this type of trade ship with one sail is called a kharraq. But, yes, ships are named. This ship is named Arbouna."

"It sounds almost like Narbonne."

"Yes, Arbouna is the Arabic name for Narbonne. Count Ramon, perhaps your ancestors were sailors and that is why your spirit rises on the sea. It runs in the blood . . . Count, I see the top of a sail up ahead, take your men below."

After a tense half an hour, the captain called to Ramon.

"Come above deck. The ship is passed. It was an Arab merchant vessel."

Several hours before sunset their ship turned northeast and approached the coast. Hamid guided the ship into a large bay. As they sailed nearer to the shore, the towers of a castle came into view. The captain called out to Ramon, "Count, that castle is Fos. Give me your banner and I will hoist it for them to see."

They raised the flag of Toulouse, its gold Occitan cross in contrast with a bold red field. Ramon was proud. *It is stirring to see our flag flying strong in the ocean winds!*

A horn trumpeted from the castle. A watchman at the castle waved a red flag adorned with the design of a castle tower. The motif reminded Ramon of a rook piece and he had a flashback of playing chess with the king. "Head toward the shore. They have acknowledged us."

Within minutes a soldier from the castle rowed a small boat to their ship and came alongside. The Arab crew, Jordan, and half of Ramon's men stayed on the ship, anchored near the castle. Ramon and the rest of his men were rowed ashore. The castellan, the governor of the castle, Pons of Fos, greeted them at the dock. "Welcome, cousin!" He laughed. "Well you greeted me as cousin in your message. We do have the same name!"

Ramon embraced him. "Lord Pons, thank you for your generosity. I am honored to meet you."

"And to meet you, Count Ramon Pons, Vanquisher of the Hungarians! I read your message. You are on a special mission, to recover the relics of Saint Pons. Here in Provence, the people much revere Saint Pons of Cimiez."

As they entered the castle, Ramon was impressed with the triple layer of fortifications. Through the crenellations atop the walls, he could see soldiers monitoring them. "How have you survived here in Provence? Marseille was burned. The Hungarians ravaged Nimes. I was told that Count Boson is not supporting his vassals."

"True, the count has not aided us. And security has not improved here on the coast even after Provence became part of the Kingdom of Arles several years ago. The king of Arles has never helped us and after his recent death, his son Conrad is no better. We have seen the Saracen horse archers assessing our stronghold, but there have not been any assaults. Perhaps the Saracens thought our small castle wasn't worth attacking. I tried to convince my father to retreat to this citadel, but he stayed in Marseilles and perished."

"I am sorry for your father, Lord Pons."

"Thank you, Ramon. We should be addressing each with our familiar names. Am I right, Ramon?"

"Yes. What is your given name?"

"I was named after my father, Ison. Ison Pons.

"How is the work on the new monastery progressing? I shall want to donate to the monastery, and I will send a message to my half-brother, Pons l'Ancien, Viscount of Arles, to make a donation as well."

Over a jug of wine, the cousins talked late into the night of their lives, their families, and possible common ancestors.

The weather was pleasant the next morning, and the wind continued from a southerly direction. Hamid guided the ship past Marseilles toward the Lerins Islands, twenty miles west of Nice.

By late afternoon, the islands of the archipelago were within sight. Hamid signaled Ramon to come to his post at the tiller.

"Count, the pirates, who can be either Arabs or Pisans, frequent these islands to collect water. We must avoid them. Since you said the monks will take you in for the night, I will leave you at the monastery. But I have been told the Arabs raid in this area so be very careful. There will be enough light for me to reach Nice. If Nice looks safe, I will stay there overnight and return to retrieve you tomorrow morning. Otherwise, I will anchor along the coast, then come back to the island."

As the ship approached the shoreline, the bell tower of the monastery was visible above the trees. The shore was rocky, but a dock had been built by the monks and afforded a place for them to disembark. From the dock, Ramon watched the captain guide his ship away from the rocky shore and set sail. The men from Toulouse entered a walled courtyard through a portal in the stone wall. The wooden gate had broken off its hinges and lay on the ground. The courtyard was empty, other than the raised garden beds lacking any cultured plants. On one end of the courtyard the building's roof was blackened from fire and had collapsed.

Ramon shouted, "Hello! Brothers of Saint Honorat, are you here?"

There was no response. They searched each building, finding only evidence of fire and destruction. There were no signs of any monks.

"Let's collect firewood before dark; we'll eat, then get a good night's sleep before Hamid returns tomorrow."

They camped in the corner of the courtyard. The sun set during their meal, and the men prepared to bed down. The first man to keep watch picked up his crossbow and blanket and sat with his back to a wall. A voice was heard in the darkness. "Men of Christ, will you share communion?"

Ramon heard an archer set his bowstring. "Soldier, hold your fire!"

A man entered the circle of light provided by the fire. His clothes were shreds of cloth hanging from his body, his hair fell to his shoulders, and his beard was a long white mat. The man held a stout walking staff. He said, "Welcome to Saint Honorat Abbey!"

Ramon drew near to the man, not knowing how to respond. The man embraced Ramon and held him tight. "I am not the best hermit."

Ramon returned the embrace, and then gently extracted himself from the man's friendly, but slow to yield clinch. "Please join us. We have bread and wine. Let us all join in communion!"

After their ritual, Ramon asked, "What has happened to the monastery?"

Wizened yet eyes sharp with intelligence, the man said, "It was years ago, I can't remember how many. I was a young man and had just arrived here on the island. Saracens attacked and killed almost all of us. Since then we have lived off the land, as best we can, and we pray."

"We? Who else survived?"

"Just one other monk. He lives on one end of the island. My home is a cave on the other end of the isle. We rarely see or talk to each other. The most time we spent together was in burying the ten brothers who died in the attack. I should be going now."

Ramon stood. "Please wait. Do you want to leave with us? There will be a ship arriving tomorrow." Ramon told the monk of the construction of Saint Pons Abbey and his mission to recover the saint's relics. He finished by inviting the monk to join the new abbey.

"You are undertaking a very holy mission, Count Ramon. No thank you, sir, but thank you for the bread and wine. I choose to continue to live the life of a hermit in accordance with Saint Anthony's example."

"Brother, you mean Saint Anthony of Lerins? I have heard of a monk from this abbey named Anthony, who lived here hundreds of years ago. Bishop Armandus mentioned him when he told me the history of your monastery."

"Saint Anthony of Lerins was one of our revered monks, yes, but I am referring to Saint Anthony the Great, Anthony of Egypt. He was a Christian who lived long ago in Alexandria during Roman times. He left the city and subsisted in the desert alone. He cultivated a garden, wove rush mats, and meditated. Others seeking enlightenment sought him out and lived nearby, emulating his simple life of work and prayer. Anthony, however, moved again, wanting isolation. The devout continued to follow him deeper into the desert. He did not establish a monastery, but a commune grew around him based on his example in living an austere and isolated life."

Ramon said, "It seems Saint Anthony set the example for the Benedictines, who continue to follow his stoic practice. After all these years of meditation and prayer, can you give advice to us?"

"Work, study, and pray."

After Ramon's men finished a meager breakfast, they lightly sparred, feeling the need to exercise after several days at sea. Practicing together at a tempered speed, Jordan parried another sword strike from Ramon. The soldier on watch shouted, "Count Ramon, I see a sail on the horizon!"

Jordan stepped back and ended their match. "Count, it has been several hours since sunrise. It must be Hamid."

Ramon glanced through the portal in the stone wall. "Men, halt your practice, and stay behind the walls out of sight. There is a ship approaching, but it is too far away to determine yet if it is Hamid's."

Hamid docked his ship and reported his findings as Ramon and his men boarded. The captain had discovered there were only local fishing boats and a few trading vessels in the harbor. It would take them two hours to sail to Nice. After an hour under sail, Ramon and Jordan searched for land across the swells in the sea. "We must first find a church," said Ramon. "The priests are our best hope for locating the relics of Saint Pons. Hamid said the town has not fully recovered from the Arab raids, but one church is still in use. I remember Armandus telling me there has not been a bishop in Nice for over a hundred years! And, more surprising, Hamid said the Arabs that attacked Nice were from North Africa, not Spain or Fraxinet. That is the reason the Saracen stronghold in Provence is not on the coast, or the Africans would attack them as well."

Jordan looked disgusted. "It is sad, but in that way, we are much like the Arabs. We fight and kill our own kind."

The sun was overhead in a cloudless sky, the wind steady from the south. Their ship moved briskly, sailing parallel to the coast, then turned toward the land. The southerly wind enhanced their speed and within minutes Hamid shouted as he pointed to a cluster of buildings on the shoreline. "That is the city of Nice! We will dock soon."

They sailed into the harbor. The seagulls had already found them and were pestering the boat. The docks were lined with small trading ships. A flag emblazoned with a white cross waved from a mast, the ship partially hidden by merchant vessels.

Jordan pointed to the flag and said, "Look! A red flag with a white cross. It is much like our flag, except ours has a gold cross."

Their ship swerved sharply, and Hamid yelled, "That is a Pisan warship! It was not here this morning. We are leaving!"

The ship came about and Ramon lost balance, quickly grabbing a rope. "You told me Nice was an open port, that a truce is honored in the harbor!"

Hamid's eyes were wide. "Yes, but I do not enter when warships are present, only traders. I do not trust the Pisans. If we dock, they can simply wait for us to leave and follow us. I cannot outrun their ship. It has both sails and oars. Right now, we can get away. The crew is likely on shore and scattered throughout the town."

Ramon opened a leather sack and held up two gold coins. "I will give one of these if you dock, and the second one to not leave without us."

Two of Ramon's soldiers remained on the boat with Hamid and his crew. Ramon's men left their shields and their supplies on the ship and took blankets for the shore venture. The bowmen kept their weapons in waterproof cases, yet they still drew stares as they walked toward the main square from the waterfront. Ramon noted the Pisan ship at dock was a galley almost twice the length of Hamid's ship. He saw scores of Pisan sailors on the streets. A few of them said something to him that he could not understand. He smiled and answered in Occitan, "Bonjorn!" One sailor answered, "Buongiorno." It was close enough to Occitan, so he asked, "Where is the church, the gleisa?"

The sailor shrugged his shoulders.

Ramon repeated and put his hands together and looked to heaven, as if he were praying. "The church, the gleisa."

"Oh, oh, the church, the chiesa!"

The sailor pulled one of his comrades over, who said something to him. He spoke slowly, and Ramon understood the directions to the church. The first sailor talking in Genoese, said his friend only knew Pisan. Smiling, he pointed to the Occitan cross on Ramon's tunic and then to the flag flying on the Pisan ship.

Ramon nodded and thanked him in Occitan, "Merces."

The sailor acknowledged in Genoese. "Prego."

Ramon and his men worked their way down narrow streets. A few buildings were burned and damaged. Jordan said, "Those sailors didn't seem like a bad lot."

"I agree," answered Ramon, "but at sea, if we were traveling with Arabs on an Arab-owned ship, I am afraid they would not be so friendly."

They came to a small plaza and found the church. Rubble and burnt wood was piled just outside the door. Above the entrance was engraved the chapel's name, *Santa Reparata*. Ramon left his men on watch in the plaza and entered the church. After his eyes adjusted to the dim light, he saw a few people kneeling at the rail in front of the altar. Ramon did not see anyone in a habit or priest's garb, so he explored the side aisles. After he knocked on a few doors without success, he returned to his men waiting outside. There Ramon saw a Pisan sailor exit the church, and he decided to try to communicate with the young man. "Where is the priest?"

The sailor looked confused and scratched his head of dark hair. "Who is the priest? The priest is Padre Guy."

"Is he here?"

"No! We are here."

"Where is the priest?"

"Oh, where, yes. The priest eats now. He will come back. You men are from Provence? I hear you speaking Occitan. I am learning Occitan here in Nice. If you speak slower, I will be able to converse with you, sir."

"Here? Occitan is spoken here?"

"Yes. Occitan, Genoese, Pisan."

Ramon said to Jordan, "I guess we should have asked a citizen of Nice for directions instead of that sailor back at the waterfront."

The stranger pointed to the gold cross on Ramon's tunic. "Who are from . . . I mean, where are you from? What city is your symbol?"

"We are from Toulouse."

"Does Toulouse have ships?"

"No."

"Pisa has many ships, grand ships. I have visited Nice many times."

"Yes. We saw your ship at the port. Do you know how to get to Cimiez?"

"Cimiez? Hmm. Is that Cimella?"

"Yes."

"There is nothing there, just ruins. Monastery ruins and Roman ruins."

"Have you been there?"

"Yes, but why would you want to go?"

He must be quite a devout Christian. He was praying in the church. Possibly he can tell us how to get to Cimiez. What a strange coincidence . . . no, the bishop would say it is God's plan. "Have you heard of Saint Pons?"

The sailor's eyes widened. "Yes! Of course! That is why! You venerate Santo Ponzio, er, um . . . Sanctus Pontius . . . um, in Occitan, yes, Saint Pons? I am from Genoa. We remember his sacrifice. The people who live here also remember."

Ramon continued more slowly and pronounced his words with care. "I feel a close relation to Saint Pons or as you said Santo Ponzio. I am Ramon Pons, the Count of Toulouse. We have founded a new monastery and are here to find the relics of Saint Pons to sanctify the new abbey."

"Count! You are related to the saint and you will honor him? But I have never seen a shrine nor tomb there, and I have never heard of any relics. Pilgrims who come to venerate him pray in the amphitheater where he was beheaded.

"I have a deep reverence for him that is beyond his martyrdom because I also believe I am related to him. I am Ponzio Gambaretto. My family name is Ponzio. But Pons and Ponzio, they are not the same."

Ramon said, "I will show you. Can you write your name, your surname?" Gambaretto nodded. Ramon picked up a charred fragment of the wood and handed it the sailor. "Write your surname, Ponzio, on the pavement."

Gambaretto wrote Pontius.

Ramon asked, "How do you write Pontius, as for Sanctus Pontius?"

Gambaretto paused and looked puzzled. "But it is . . . the same. Pontius."

"That is how I also write my name, Pontius. It is Latin. Our cities have been separated for centuries since Roman times and now we just pronounce the same name differently."

Gambaretto said, "I am not an educated man like you. And although you are tall with reddish hair and I am short with dark hair, I somehow believe we could be distant cousins. I must go back to my ship, but I can show you which road to take to Cimella."

The sailor scrutinized Ramon's men as if he had just seen them for the first time. "Count Ramon, how far is Toulouse?"

"You have heard of Marseilles?"

Gambaretto nodded.

"Toulouse is farther west than Marseilles."

"I see you and your men carry your blankets and supplies. Did you walk all that way?"

"No, um . . . our horses are stabled."

"Still, you have made a long pilgrimage to find Saint Pons's relics."

They walked several blocks parallel to the waterfront. Gambaretto said, "Your men are crossbowmen. I am also an archer. I was born in Genoa, but my ship was destroyed when the Arabs pillaged our city two years ago, so I have joined the Pisan fleet. I have killed many Arabs in battle, but not enough to gain revenge."

They came to a road that ran north and south. The Genoese pointed north. "Go on this road. After about five miles, you will see the ruins on a hill to your left. It will be easy to see. I am sorry we could not spend time together over wine, but I am pleased we have met. The faithful will be grateful you are doing a holy act for Santo Ponzio." Gambaretto embraced Ramon and departed south along the road.

They retraced their path to the church and Ramon entered. Seeing a stranger, the priest met him near the door to greet him. Ramon briefly kneeled and crossed himself. "Paire, um . . . Padre Guy, I am the Count of Toulouse on a mission to honor Saint Pons of Cimiez."

"Count. I speak Occitan. Are you on pilgrimage to Cimiez?"

"Yes, Padre. My wife Garsinda and I have founded a monastery near Beziers to honor Saint Pons. The construction will be completed later this summer and we hope to dedicate the abbey with the interment of the relics of Saint Pons."

"I see. Come, we should discuss this in my chambers. Are those your men outside the door? Tell them to come in and my aide will offer them bread and wine."

As his men were refreshed, Ramon and Guy talked in an office at the back of the church. "Count, why would you rebuild Saint Pons Abbey in such a remote place, far from the saint's martyrdom?"

"The most important reason is to protect the relics, Padre," answered Ramon. "Every monastery along the seacoast has been attacked by the Saracens. Also, the location of the new monastery will provide aid for the Christian pilgrims on their way to Compostela. Bishop Armandus of Toulouse told me the Saint Pons monastery nearby in Cimiez was destroyed many years ago and was never rebuilt. And I can see by the condition of your city that Nice does not have enough resources to revive the abbey."

The priest's face turned red. "Sir, you just walk in here and demand his relics? Do you think the counties of West Francia are so rich, they can dictate what the Church will do with its holy remains? For over a hundred years the Arabs have pillaged, destroyed, and killed along the coast! Even the Count of Provence will not help! God has forsaken us!"

"Padre, please do not be offended. I have a special devotion to the saint. My name is Pons and I feel close to him by relation. At my father's dying bed, I promised I would rebuild the monastery for Saint Pons. Will you help us?"

"You cannot have the saint's relics because no relics exist. They disappeared long ago when the monastery was desecrated!"

Padre Guy exhaled loudly. "Count Ramon, forgive me. I am sorry. Perhaps you can make a pilgrimage to Cimiez and return with a fragment of the amphitheater where he was beheaded, to commemorate the new monastery."

"Thank you, Padre, and thank you for the kindness to my men. We will be going now to Cimiez."

"You know the way?"

"Yes, a young man, a sailor gave us directions. I met him here at the church earlier today."

"Was it Gambaretto? Ponzio Gambaretto?"

Ramon nodded.

"He visits Cimiez every time his ship calls here."

The sun was three hours from setting when Ramon and his men arrived at the location of the former Roman city of Cemenelum. The local inhabitants of Nice called the place Cimiez, its Occitan name, and it was referred to as Cimella by the nearby Genoese. The rays from the late afternoon sun cast a brilliant glow on the marble stone of the ancient ruins. Only a few columns of the old Roman buildings were still standing, although the former baths were discernable and the amphitheater was mostly intact. The more recent buildings of the former monastery were scarred and scorched, and the roofs had collapsed into piles of rubble. The site was deserted except for Ramon and his men. He set up their small camp in the center of the amphitheater and sent the men to examine the ruins. After a light meal of bread and hard cheese, they bedded down for the night and took turns on watch. As he slept, Ramon dreamed that he witnessed the martyrdom of Saint Pons in the amphitheater.

The next morning, the campfire was rekindled to chase away the morning chill. Jordan said, "Count, we traveled all this way, thinking we could recover the relics."

Ramon stared into the fire. "We had to try. There was no way to send a message this far to determine the status of the relics. There is no bishop. Nice is in shambles. The local church barely functions, and the priest told me the relics were lost. But there is something strange about his behavior. First, he was kind and welcomed us into his church; then he had an angry tirade. Then that outburst was suddenly followed by an apology."

One of Ramon's men shouted, "Count, a band of men is approaching!"

Padre Guy was leading a throng of men. *Now what does he want? He brought an armed crowd? His troop bristles with spears!*

The knights took their place beside their count, their swords out. Ramon directed the archers to spread out behind the fallen blocks of stone and wait with ready bows. He shouted to the bowmen, "No one is to loose an arrow until I command! And do not hit the padre if we shoot!"

The crowd of men drew closer and Ramon realized what he thought were spears he could now see were shovels and picks. "Sheath your arrows!"

The padre marched unswervingly to Ramon and embraced him. He raised his voice and turned so his message could be heard in all directions: "You are right, Count! I thought deeply about what you told me yesterday, and I ask your forgiveness."

"Forgiveness?" Ramon answered with a puzzled look.

Guy cast a few tears. "I lied. The relics are here. They were buried when the attacks from the Arabs began and were never moved to Nice for fear that the holy remains would have been subject to harm. Nice may never recover. You will be the best caretaker of the saint's vestiges! The safest place will be at the new monastery. I am certain they will be honored."

The padre walked to the center of the oval grounds of the amphitheater, pointed to the ground and said to his men, "Dig here."

The men dug without results for over an hour. Then the sound of metal on stone rang from the bottom of the pit. The workers removed the soil to expose a stone box a pace long, half as wide, and two hands high. The excavation was narrow and deep; the head of the man working in the pit was below ground level. A rope was needed to bring the stone container to the surface. The padre slid the cover open just enough to peer at the contents. He allowed Ramon to take a brief look and he saw a few bones and the saint's skull. "This is the only time I have gazed at our martyr's relics, but I believed they were here. The secret burial place has been passed along through the generations by my predecessors. The saint's remains should only be openly viewed in a holy place—for example, at the church of your new Saint Pons Abbey."

The padre spoke to all present and explained that the relics would be transferred to the new monastery devoted to Saint Pons, and that they would be much safer there away from the predation of unbelievers. He then told the story of Saint Pons, known as Saint Pontius when he was martyred, how he grew up in Rome as a senator's son and then became a senator himself. He was baptized by Pope Pontianus, donated all his possessions to the poor, converted Emperor Phillipus to the Faith, and used his senatorial influence to help the Church. After Phillipus's death, Pontius fled Emperor Decius's renewed persecution of Christians and because of his faith in Christ was martyred in Cimiez. Ramon listened closely, knowing Garsinda would want him to repeat all the new details he had learned.

Ramon and his men returned to the church with Padre Guy, whose men conveyed the ossuary with care and reverence. The padre prayed with them for a safe voyage home. Ramon found a private moment to donate several gold coins to the modest church. There was no time to remain longer in Nice. Two of his men carried the stone ossuary to the waterfront. Ramon noticed the Pisan galley had sailed and Hamid seemed nervous.

Ramon asked, "Everything is good, Hamid?"

"Yes, but when we leave, I am afraid we could be intercepted by the Pisan ship. I could not determine if they were going east or west."

He handed Hamid the gold coin he had promised and said, "You told me the Pisans don't sail beyond Nice, so we should sail for Saint Honorat Island."

"As you wish, Count, we can make it before dark."

Their night on the island was uneventful, and the hermit did not seek them out again. The ship anchored the next night at Fos sur Mer. Pons de Fos was pleased they had recovered the relics and were safely on their way home. They set sail at sunrise. About two hours from Narbonne an Arab sailor shouted, "Sail on the horizon!"

Ramon's men crowded below deck. An Arab kharraq sailed by and the crew acknowledged Hamid and his men. An hour later there was another ship sighted. Just as Ramon moved below deck, Hamid held the hatch open and said, "I can see the ship has two sails. Traders with ships that large are rare. It could be a warship, but I cannot tell what flag the vessel flies."

From below deck, Ramon could hear Hamid and his crew speaking excitedly in Arabic. Hamid opened the hatch and said, "The ship is turning toward us. I am going to sail downwind toward the shore. But with the help of their oars, they can catch us. Our best hope is that they may give up the chase. I will warn you now, if the ship is an armed Arab galley and they find you hidden in the hold, they will kill me and my men. So be ready, I may tell you to come on deck; then when they discover that you are royalty, they will take you hostage. So, Count, you are in a lucky place. We are near Narbonne and your father-in-law is the viscount of the city. If you are taken hostage, they will soon have their ransom."

The captain returned to the tiller.

Jordan said, "We will show them how the count's men can fight!"

Ramon placed his hand on Jordan's shoulder. "Yes, I know you are loyal, but the relics are more important than any of us, and that galley could have a hundred sailors on board. We somehow must save the relics for the monastery, even if it means a humiliating capture. We must heed Hamid's advice and go on deck, whether the galley is Arab or Pisan. If Pisan, they will slaughter Hamid and his crew if we do not stop them."

There were minutes of tense silence, then the hatch opened. "It's a Pisan war galley!" Hamid screamed. "They will soon catch us. Come above now."

With full sails aloft and all 25 sets of oars churning the sea, the galley was rapidly gaining on them. Ramon ordered his men to mount their shields at the stern.

Hamid yelled, "They are trying to fool us! No face is showing on their bow or rigging."

As the ship barreled toward them, sailors abruptly emerged on the deck and some climbed up the rigging. A mass of crossbow bolts flew toward the Arab ship. Hamid's crewman on the tiller was impaled by several bolts and fell to the deck. Jordan stepped in front of Ramon and a bolt penetrated his armor, piercing his own chest. The other knight was also hit. The galley's oars were pulled in as the Pisan ship closed alongside the *Arbouna's* starboard side. Grappling hooks flew uncoiling ropes between the ships and stuck fast into the kharraq's wooden deck. As ropes stretched between the ships, one of Ramon's men became entangled and was pulled overboard. Crossbow bolts continued thudding into the kharraq and skittering across the deck.

Hamid lay on the deck and cried out, "We will all be dead before they even board us!"

Ramon's soldiers crouched under their shields at the stern. In the mayhem, the count had lost his shield. One of his men despite being hit by a bolt during his attempt, managed to drag a replacement to Ramon. The count covered himself as the clatter of crossbow bolts pelted his shield. *My timing must be perfect!* He waited. The noise from the projectiles stopped and a high-pitched whistle sounded. Ramon remained under the shield. When he heard the thuds of the sailors landing on the ship, he climbed on a crate, and spread his arms out to show that he was unarmed and to display the Occitan cross on his tunic. Ramon saw Gambaretto on the galley, pulling crossbows away from sailors, waving his arms at other Pisan archers, and screaming something unintelligible. Gambaretto pointed his own crossbow at Ramon. *But why, why . . . Cousin?*

A bolt hit Ramon in the thigh and dropped him to the deck an instant before a hail of bolts swept through the space he had just occupied. They streaked harmlessly into the sea.

Pisan sailors continued to clamber aboard. One ran his sword through the remaining sailor in Hamid's crew. Another sailor raised his sword to hack Hamid. Ramon struggled to stand and took off his helmet to show his auburn hair and beard. He screamed first in Occitan, then in French, for the Pisans to stop their assault, "Arresta! Arretez!"

The Pisan officer of the boarding party saw Ramon and shouted in Tuscan, "Arresto! Arresto! Arresto!

The killing stopped. Ramon surveyed the deck. Jordan, another knight, and two of his bowmen were dead, one missing overboard. Hamid was spared, but both of the Arab crew were among the fatalities. Only one of Ramon's men was unscathed. Another had taken an arrow in the leg. A third lay on the deck bleeding from a bolt to the abdomen. Ramon gesticulated with his hand as he asked the Pisan officer, "Sir, please allow me to treat my men's wounds."

The man nodded. Ramon said to Hamid, "Bring wine and cloth for bandages."

While Hamid was below, the Pisan sailors threw the bodies of his crew overboard. The sailors left the bodies of Ramon's men where they fell. Hamid returned shortly with a cask of wine, strips of cloth, and a handful of sea sponges. He removed the bolt from the soldier's abdomen and poured wine into the wound, then stuffed a piece of sponge into the hole and wrapped strips of cloth around the man's midsection. A bolt had passed completely through Ramon's leg, but had missed the bone. Hamid treated Ramon's wound and the soldier's leg wound and applied sponges. Ramon also had a lesion on the side of his head where he had been grazed by an arrow. Hamid cleaned the abrasion with wine, placed a small piece of sponge on the lesion, and held it in place, tying a strip of cloth tied around Ramon's head. He said, "Sponges make the wounds heal faster. An old sailor remedy."

Gambaretto arrived. "Count Ramon, you are alive!"

"Thanks to your perfect timing, Cousin, but I sorely regret I could not better protect my men."

Ramon's men and Hamid were confined to the hold and Ramon was taken to the Pisan ship. Gambaretto pestered the Pisan officer escorting Ramon as he followed them to the captain's quarters. He kept insisting that he interpret. The officer threatened lashes if he did not desist. The Pisan captain,

Basciano Doriano, received Ramon. He had difficulty communicating in Tuscan with him, so he called for Gambaretto to act as interpreter. After introductions, the captain said, "Count Ramon Pons, please sit and share this wine with me. We thought your ship was Saraceni. What were you doing at sea on an Arab ship?"

"I have built a monastery to honor Saint Pons of Cimella. I hired the ship in Narbonne to sail to Nice, to recover the saint's relics, and to sanctify the abbey."

"Yes, my officers have inventoried the hold and reported the ossuary. As a Christian, I will not interfere with the saint's relics nor put a ransom on them, but I will tell you right away my plans, so you can get to shore sooner."

"Thank you, Captain Basciano."

"According to the law of the sea, I claim this ship and all the contents on board, as well as any coinage. I also lay claim to the Arab and your soldiers. Your men will become good sailors, with a little training. We will now sail to Narbonne and anchor nearby. I will send two of your soldiers to Narbonne to obtain a ransom for your life. My demands will be in keeping with your position, Count, but you will be treated here as a gentleman of nobility. However, I do not want to stay in these waters more than a day or two."

"Captain Basciano, I would like to pay additional ransom for the Arab and my men as well."

"So be it."

"And take the bodies of my dead with me."

"Accepted, Count." The captain stood and raised his wine and toasted on the agreement. "Salute!"

Ramon added, "Sante! . . . Salute!"

The captain poured more wine and included Gambaretto. Ramon and the Genoese sailor looked puzzled as Basciano raised his cup and said, "To Ponzio Gambaretto, first class bowman! I heard the story. Thanks to him, Count Pons returns home and from his ransom, I will gain a grand profit!" He looked at the guards and officer and added, "Of course, I will divide it with my crew.

"And Gambaretto, a skilled archer, you will also be rewarded with one of the Toulousean crossbows. I hope you consider it a fitting memento."

A day later Ramon and Hamid joined in rowing duties as they guided a flat-bottomed punt up the river to Narbonne. Maiol had delivered the ransom money, and the Pisan captain had honored Ramon's request. In the punt, they conveyed the bodies of his deceased men, wrapped in their blankets, and the ossuary containing the relics of Saint Pons. Hamid said, "Thank you again, Count Ramon, for paying the ransom for me. My family will be very grateful. I will find a way to pay you back, although with the ship gone, I will need to find work."

"Your family loves you, Hamid?"

"Well, of course!"

"Then I am paid back, already. You are a worthy citizen of Narbonne and live peacefully among Christian rulers and Jewish merchants. I was surprised when you told me Samuel was the owner of the *Arbouna*, and not you."

"Yes, a ship has a personality. I spoke as if the ship was mine, only because a captain tends to have an intimate relationship with his ship."

"I will certainly talk to Maiol about your needs, and in the future when I visit Narbonne, I will hope to hear news of your good health and well-being.

"Thank you, Count Ramon. We will have tea together."

CHAPTER NINE

In June of 937, Ramon departed Toulouse to deliver the relics of Saint Pons to the new monastery. Garsinda remained at home with their seven-month-old son. The excitement about the dedication was tempered by the passing of Bishop Armandus. Garsinda and Ramon were saddened knowing that the bishop, who had put much effort into establishing the abbey, would not be present for its dedication. Hugues, a senior monk who had grown up worshipping and studying at La Daurade, was elected by the brothers as Armandus's replacement.

Months before, Ramon and Hugues had sent messengers to religious and secular leaders across Gothia and Provence, requesting their attendance at the dedication of Saint Pons Abbey. Now, Ramon and his men escorted a long mule train carrying extra foodstuffs intended for the expected delegations from across southern France. They spent the first night at Castres. The next day, Frothaire, the Abbot of Saint Benoît, and Frotarius, Bishop of Albi, joined Ramon's company traveling to Saint Pons. As they followed the pilgrims' road along the River Thule, Ramon and Hugues discussed the upcoming dedication ceremony.

"Count Ramon, I was recalling the list of dignitaries we invited to Tomieres. I sent letters to the bishops of Gothia and Provence. There is Bonnaricus, the Bishop of Orange and there is Manasse, who has been the Archbishop of Arles for over twenty years. Also I sent invitations to Rainard, Bishop of Nimes and Odolric, the Bishop of Aix. And I hope Fulcherius, the Bishop of Avignon will come. He is one of our most distinguished and respected clergymen. He is known for his hard work leading the two churches of Avignon: Notre Dame and Saint Etienne. The letters of invitation also announced the recent passing of Bishop Armandus."

"Thank you, Excellency. My messengers carried invitations to the bishops Raoul of Beziers and Aimery of Narbonne. It was difficult to contact Bishop Pontius. The Saracens had occupied Maguelone and his bishopric was moved inland across County Melgueil. I also asked Abbot Ahan of Saint Chinian to attend."

"Perhaps Bishop Pontius is another one of your far-flung cousins?" Hughes said as he laughed. "What about Arnulf? Did you invite him or is he too busy with his abbacy at the new monastery at Chanteuges?"

"Oh, yes, I did ask him to come. I am sure he will have beneficial advice for Varadolanus in his new role as abbot of Saint Pons. And the viscounts of Bezier and Narbonne have been invited."

"That Varadolanus! He looks like such a rebellious fellow, with his long hair and sometimes martial attitude, but he is very pious.

"Ramon, the ride today along the Thule is quite pleasant. It seems more tranquil than yesterday. What makes it seem calmer?"

"Shh. Don't curse our peaceful ride." Ramon continued his whisper, "The cats have stopped their protestations in being confined in their cage. The first two days they yowled on every bump in the road."

Hugues laughed. "Was it your idea to bring them, Count?"

"No, it was actually Garsinda's plan. She provided a male cat from our chateau, and the monks of Saint Sernin monastery donated a female. It is a good and very useful gift for the abbey of Saint Pons. The pair will prowl the new monastery for mice and rats. Their offspring may also be future mousers at Saint Pons abbey.

"But Bishop Hugues, you brought a most prized gift for the new abbey, a stunning Bible. The monks of La Daurade did a spectacular job creating a masterpiece. The title pages shimmer with gold and brilliantly colored letters."

"Yes, they started when the project was first announced and just completed it in time for the dedication."

"Ramon, you have done so much to establish the new monastery. I would say the relics of Saint Pons, which you risked your life to recover, are most precious."

"I feel it was my duty as a Christian and as a descendant of Saint Pons. I promised my father. But I want to help the monks also, especially with their writing, so I had ten pen knives crafted for them. The handles are engraved with the name of the abbey's patron saint, Sanctus Pontius."

"Very good. The monks will need those knives to sharpen their quill pens, Count. I asked the Provence bishops to donate a pair of geese to provide quills. The towns of Nimes, Orange, and Avignon are so close to one another, I left it up to them to organize the task. Now we only need the ink and parchment."

"That has been arranged, Bishop. I have asked Abbot Arnulf, an expert in making ink, to collect the ingredients with help from the townspeople of Tomieres. Perhaps the local shepherds can supply goat hides for the parchment."

"Also, during my last visit to Saint Chinian, Abbot Ahan said he would bring starter vines from his vineyards. Mount Lauzet, which rises behind Saint Pons village, has a south-facing slope which will be good for cultivating the grapes. And, let's see . . . yes, I requested seeds for the monks' vegetable garden when I sent my invitations to Arnaud and Raoul."

"I hope we have planned well. But . . . there is one more bishop you did not mention. Did you invite Bishop Honoratus from Marseilles?"

"That is another dark shadow on the dedication. I sent a group of messengers, but they never came back to report whether the invitation was delivered. I know the Saracens from Fraxinet still control Marseilles, but I thought they were allowing Christians to go on pilgrimage.

"The other unfinished issue is the women's abbey. I never arranged for a nunnery to be included in the plans as Garsinda desired. And she has not had time to give her recommendations because she was with child and is now taking care of young Ramon."

"Count, I believe God will provide a way. Will you be staying at your villa in Courniou?"

"Yes, with my father-in-law, Maiol. Bishop, you are welcome to stay, as are any other clergy. There will be ten visiting bishops and at least one assistant will accompany each of them. Add them to the five monks of Saint Pons and the total is about twenty-five. We built the dormitory at Saint Pons to accommodate twenty monks, anticipating further growth. A few of the clergy will need to stay at the villa. Besides, Courniou will be more comfortable than the monks' dormitory."

"Thank you, Count, but I plan to follow the tradition of Saint Benedict and his rules of renunciation. I will stay at the dormitory, even if I must sleep on the floor."

Two days later Ramon led the dedication party into the valley of the Jaur River. They descended the west side of the valley which overlooked the monastery and villages. Ramon marveled at how much the location had changed since his first visit. On the near side of the Jaur was the hamlet of Tomieres, with its new bridge connecting it to Saint Pons. Across the river were the buildings of Saint Pons monastery, which included the monks' dormitory, work shed, storehouse, and the partially completed cathedral. The village which had sprung up around the abbey already had more houses than Tomieres. They headed for the bridge connecting the two villages.

Ramon pointed. "Hugues, you can see the dormitory for the monks. It is the two-story building made of the marble from the nearby quarry. I imagine the same marble will be used for the church, the altar, and the choir."

"Count, what is that buzzing sound? I think it is coming from the south."

"That must be the water-powered sawmill that cuts the marble and stone into blocks for construction of the monastery. Castellamonte sent me a drawing of its workings. During our visit, we'll go to see how it operates."

They crossed the bridge linking Tomieres to the village of Saint Pons. There were several monks stirring the contents of a large iron pot. With them were two of the young sisters from the Courniou Villa. Ramon directed one of his knights to lead the procession on to the monks' dormitory as he and Hugues stopped to investigate the monks' work.

Ramon dismounted. "Abbot Arnulf! Abbot Varadolanus! Good to see you both again!" He laughed as he said, "Are you cooking a stew to celebrate our dedication ceremony?"

The two monks, Arnulf crowned by a tonsure and Varadolanus with his long hair tied behind, said in unison, "We are making ink!" They laughed at the coincidence. Arnulf continued, as he smiled at his comrade, "We are almost done with this batch."

Ramon and Hugues embraced the monks and greeted the young women, who responded with curtsies. "How is this ink made?" asked Ramon.

Varadolanus extended his arm toward his fellow abbot, bowed, and chuckled. "Arnulf, you are the expert, please go ahead."

"The ingredients needed to make ink are oak bolls, glue, and copperas, all mixed together in water. First, we searched the forests along the ridges above the valley for oak bolls. It took a while, since chestnut trees dominate the forests, but we found enough oak trees with bolls. Then as a substitute for glue, we fashioned glair, a sticky binder made by over-whipping chicken eggs. The final ingredient was found in the nearby caves. The two girls have explored many of the caves and knew where to find the white crust we were seeking. We made the copperas by heating the crust along with flakes of iron. A week ago, we placed all these ingredients in this pot and with the low heat and occasional stirring, the ink is almost ready."

"Well done, brothers, and . . . ladies. The ink will be ready for us to write the charter for the Saint Pons monastery. And it is fitting we are using ink made from the nearby resources." With this, Ramon and Hugues bid farewell and rode the short distance to the monks' dormitory. Construction of the new cathedral was underway across the road. They dismounted and left the squires to the care of their horses. Ramon commented, "The elegant marble laced with pink strikes me as appropriate for a holy building." The pair crossed the road and surveyed the unfinished walls of the cathedral. "It's sad Garsinda could not come. She would have appreciated the beauty of these buildings!"

The villages were bustling with men working on the monastery and townspeople carting items about in preparation for the dedication ceremony. The escorts for the bishops were making camp on the fringes of the new Saint Pons village. Bishop Raoul of Beziers joined Ramon and Hugues as they studied the work on the church. In his entourage was a middle-aged woman in a nun's habit. Two of the sisters from Courniou and a third young woman unknown to Ramon accompanied the bishop. Raoul said, "Count Ramon, I am pleased to see you again, but regretful Garsinda is not here for the dedication. Congratulations on the birth of your son!" He embraced the count and continued, "Count, please meet Abbess Lena. She is the senior at the nunnery in Beziers."

After pleasant introductions and greetings, the abbess bowed her head and addressed the count. "Count Ramon, I have a proposal. As part of the dedication ceremony, will you please announce the inclusion of a nunnery at Saint Pons?" She nodded at the three young women behind her. "These young women have taken vows to become nuns to spread Christ's word. Because of their earnest commitment, I have volunteered to remain here to guide them until they can lead the nunnery themselves."

"But where will you?" . . . *As Hugues said, God would show his plan. Thank you, Lord. Now I can keep my promise to Garsinda.* "Um, I mean, you and your nuns will have a place to live, to work, to pray, and to study. I hereby donate Villa Courniou as a nunnery for those women dedicated to Christ. It will complement the Saint Pons Monastery."

As they discussed the idea, a second group of women approached from the east along the road. They wore long dresses and vests of spun wool in earth tones and of matching style. Shawls covered their heads and draped their shoulders. The durable clothes, satchels on their shoulders, and walking staffs gave the appearance they had trekked a good distance. Ramon said, "Welcome! You have arrived just in time. The dedication is tomorrow. Have you traveled far?"

One of the women stepped forward. "We are from Saint Mary Magdalene's commune." From her satchel she produced a small ceramic vessel, fitted with a cover. "We have brought the ashes of Maria to join with those of her husband, Pontius Marcellus, Saint Pontius of Cemenelum."

Abbess Lena gasped. "I thought the commune was just a legend."

Bishop Hugues said, "How do you know the saint's given name?"

"We preserve the true accounts of Saint Mary Magdalene and of Maria, Saint Pontius's wife."

After a short silence, Varadolanus asked, "You three women walked all the way from Provence by yourself, without escorts?" He looked incredulous.

At this, the leader of the women kicked the bottom of her walking stick and it snapped up from the ground. Although her long dress hid the kick, Varadolanus was quick and raised his knee to block the ascending staff. A pebble that the staff had struck from the ground flew at his face. He blinked. Using this distraction, the woman redirected the staff with a twist of her wrist and stopped the tip less than a finger's width from his temple.

"Excellent maneuver!" Varadolanus laughed nervously. "My apologies, madam, uh, . . . I am Varadolanus, very much humbled. What is your name?"

"I am Cateline."

"Well, Cateline, you are exceptionally capable!"

Hugues interjected, "Count Ramon, we must inform the bishops of these women's arrival."

Later in the afternoon, even with all the work of preparation for the ceremony, the young women from Courniou had found Ramon's tender side and asked him to talk to the friar about the cats who would live at the monastery. *Garsinda considers the young women her friends. She would also think this is important and besides, I would like to see the friar.* Thankful for the diversion, Ramon crossed the bridge with the sisters to visit Friar Taenarus in Tomieres. They soon arrived at the church of Saint Martin. "Friar, glad to see you!"

"Welcome back, Count. I have been busy! With all the workers here from the village of Saint Pons, my church is full every Sunday! How are you? And the countess?"

"She is staying in Toulouse with our new son."

"Oh, wonderful! I mean . . . wonderful for the birth of your son! I am sorry Countess Garsinda will miss the dedication."

"Thank you, Friar. I have an, uh . . ." he glanced at the young women, "an important question for you. We need your help to, um," Ramon laughed, "name the two cats that will protect the monastery. You told us that the name Tomieres was from ancient Greek. The young ladies thought it would be appropriate for the cats to have classical names."

The Friar laughed. "Hmm. Well, their primary duty is to catch mice. So, the female's name must be Artemis, a Greek goddess who was a huntress. That makes sense.

"And do they look similar?"

"Yes, they are both gray striped cats."

"I suggest we name them after twins in Greek mythology, Artemis and Apollo."

The young women ran off to find the cats, and Ramon crossed back to Saint Pons and welcomed the bishops and abbots of Provence. They all declined Ramon's invitation to stay at Courniou. Instead they chose to adhere to Saint Benedictine's rule of self-denial and would sleep in the monks' dormitory. Ramon asked Hugues to tell the clergy about the women from Mary Magdalene's commune, while he went to the dormitory to be certain his men had delivered Saint Pons's ossuary. The stone container was in the refectory, being guarded by several of his soldiers as he had ordered. Ramon heard a commotion outside and went to investigate. He saw a group of his knights embracing a handful of familiar men. *They are the scouts I sent to Marseilles!* He joined them. "I was worried the Saracens had killed you! What happened?"

A scout kneeled before the count. "Count Ramon, forgive me, under my leadership, I lost two of our men. We had almost reached Marseilles when the Arabs attacked us. In the fight, Bernard and William were killed, but the rest of us made it into the city. Still pursued in Marseilles, we only survived because Bishop Honoratus intervened."

"Stand, soldier! I am sure you did your best. Where is Honoratus? Did he come?"

"No, he decided he must remain in Marseilles to negotiate with the Saracens and protect the citizens. He bribed the Saracens to let us deliver the relics of Saint Pons. Honoratus's second, Etienne, will explain."

Ramon cried out, "What? You have the relics of Saint Pons?"

Etienne bowed. "Bishop Honoratus said the saint's relics should be brought here, Count Ramon."

"But the relics of Saint Pons are already here! I brought them from Nice myself!"

Ramon immediately collected the bishops to ask them for decisions on two pressing issues. They convened at Saint Martin's church in Tomieres, where he told the bishops of the first issue: the women from the commune and their claim that Saint Pontius had a wife. The women's request to inter Maria's relics with Saint Pontius's remains brought on a heated discussion among the clergy. The initial consensus was to send the women back to the commune with Maria's relics. Instead, Hugues proposed that the women keep her ashes at the nunnery of Courniou. The bishops voted and agreed to this plan.

The more significant matter was that two sets of relics were each claimed to be the true remains of the saint. Hugues suggested the bishops view the relics, and both containers were opened. The remains brought from Marseilles were stored in a wooden casket which was engraved with figures depicting the beheading of Saint Pons. Inside was a skeleton with a detached skull. The stone ossuary that Ramon had recovered in Nice contained a jumble of debris and bones, which included a skull.

"Because of the dim lighting inside the church, this superficial inspection has not revealed which are the true relics," said Hugues. "Friar Taenarus, please bring us a few oil lamps for a better view of the relics. Meanwhile, I ask that each party who claims their artifacts are the true relics of Saint Pons describe how they obtained them."

Ramon said, "Also, I recommend each tell the account of Saint Pons's martyrdom. This may shed light on how the relics were acquired."

The bishops agreed. Benches were moved from along the walls of the church, so the bishops could sit. Etienne stood confidently before the council. "I am humbled to recite the story of Saint Pontius as passed down for centuries in the city of Marseilles. Saint Pontius, our revered saint, was a senator who fled Rome during Decius's persecution and arrived in Cemenelum, the Roman name for Cimiez. Pontius refused to sacrifice to the pagan gods, so the Roman authorities tortured him on an easel, a machine used to tear apart victims. The device broke, however, and two bears were released in the amphitheater to attack Pontius, but instead the wild beasts mauled their trainer. The executioners then tried to burn Saint Pontius, but the pyre was ineffective. After all those measures did not work, they took him to a cliff overlooking the Paillon River and decapitated him. The saint's head fell from the heights and rebounded three times. Springs gushed forth out of the places where the head touched."

Ramon heard huffs from the group of bishops.

"Pontius's head landed in the river and it floated between a pair of torches, continued Etienne. "The river carried his head to the sea where it was found by fishermen from the Islands of Hyeres. They took the head to the Abbey of Saint Victor at Marseilles. Waiting there was his body which had been transported by two angels the night after his beheading. Since then, the monks of Saint Victor abbey have preserved the relics of Saint Pons there in Marseilles."

There were a few murmurs from the assembled bishops. Then Ramon stepped forward. He was a confident speaker from his experience encouraging men before battle and negotiating with his vassals. Although he thought Etienne's story was an exaggeration, he suspected there were bishops who believed it. He was optimistic the story Padre Guy had told him would speak for itself. Ramon cleared his throat and bowed his head. "Thank you, holy bishops, for the opportunity to recount the martyrdom of Saint Pontius as told to me by Father Guy of Nice. Yes, Pontius fled Rome. He hid in the foothills of the maritime Alps near Nice, but he became remorseful that he had left his Christian brothers and sisters, and he returned to the nearby cities to preach Christ's word. He went to the amphitheater of the town we now call Cimiez and declared the Good News. The Roman prefect told him he could go free if he stopped preaching, but he chose to continue. He inspired many Christians and non-Christians in the audience, but many of the pagans wanted a spectacle, and the bears were let out of their cages to kill him. Pontius, however, kneeled and prayed. The bears ignored him and attacked their trainer instead. The Roman military commander had Pontius beheaded. Pontius's lifelong friend Valerius was present and buried him nearby. Valerius returned to Rome, recording his comrade's martyrdom in the Acts of the Martyrs. They kept the relics at the Saint Pons monastery of Cimiez until the abbey was destroyed by the Saracens, which compelled the faithful to hide the saint's remains under the amphitheater."

The oils lamps were lighted, and the bishops had another look at the relics as they congregated near the two coffers. Lamps were held above the containers and a bishop commented, "Look, there are sparkles of gold and colors—red and green, from the stone ossuary." Several others acknowledged his discovery.

Hugues reached into the clutter of bones and cobwebs and retrieved a skeletal hand. The fingers held two gold rings. One ring was mounted with a pair of gems, one red and one green. The other ring had an insignia. Hugues removed the ring to examine it more closely. He gave the ring to the Bishop of Orange. As it was passed around to the clergymen to examine the ring, Hugh announced, "Who is familiar with this inscription: *SPQR*?"

There was a long silence. Then Ramon heard low voices among the bishops.

After Fulcherius, the Bishop of Avignon, inspected the ring, he said, "As recounted today, Saint Pontius and his father were both Roman senators. This ring belonged to a Roman senator!"

Several nodded, but there were still mumbles of doubt among the bishops.

"For those who are still puzzled, I will have our monks in Avignon make you a copy of Cicero's works, where you will find reference to the ancient symbol of the Roman Republic: *SPQR*, which stands for *Senatus Populus que Romanus*, The Senate and People of Rome."

The following morning, on June 10, 937, the Bishop of Beziers held Mass in the church of Saint Martin in Tomieres. The townspeople crowded into the church and overflowed into the courtyard alongside the springs of Jaur. After the Mass, the four monks of Saint Pons abbey exited the church and carried a wooden litter which bore the saint's limestone ossuary and remains. Abbot Varadolanus led the monks. The bishops, abbots, their retinues, and the townspeople followed as the procession crossed the bridge to the unfinished church. Workers had partially completed the walls. The monks entered the incomplete enclosure and set the ossuary on a large block of marble at the location where they would erect the altar. To provide benches for the clergy, monks had placed wooden planks on stone blocks. The rest of the assembly stood.

Raoul of Beziers had written the charter for the monastery and given the bishops and abbots prior opportunity to review the document. The deed confirmed Garsinda had donated the land, and the funds to build the monastery had been donated by Ramon Pons. It also stated the abbey's ecclesiastical inclusion into the diocese of Beziers. He placed the charter next to the ossuary to be signed by the bishops. A wide range of ages were present in the ranks of the senior clergy: the youngest striding, the middle-aged moving less assuredly, and the eldest tottering with the help of a cane or an aide at their side. Raoul gave the benediction and the throng moved to the celebration in the courtyard beside the springs of Jaur. Tables were set up outdoors and there was plenty of boar meat, venison, and chestnut bread provided by the residents of Tomieres. Also in abundance were vegetables grown by the monks of Saint Pons and wine that had been brought by the monks of the Saint Chinian monastery. During the festivities, Ramon visited table after table and toasted the workers, townspeople, monks, and leaders, and all those who had made the project a success.

The clergy returned to their respective towns the next day, after depositing generous endowments of candles, candleholders, sacred communion ware, monies, and other items for the church. The monks had built a vault beneath the dormitory to accommodate such artifacts until the monastery was completed.

Ramon finally had a chance to accompany Castellamonte downstream near the quarry to examine the water-powered saw. Shouting above the piercing racket of the machine, Ramon marveled at its operation. "From the sounds across the valley, the saw must run from sunup to sundown."

"Other than delays when a blade wears out or breaks, we keep the saw running all day. We have built a workshop and forge which fabricates new blades and sharpens worn out edges," the engineer answered.

"Why is the sawyer pouring sand in the crevice where the saw cuts? Wouldn't that dull the blades?"

"Sire, using the sand to deepen the cleft in the rock outweighs those negative effects. We have discovered the sand may do more cutting than the metal blade itself."

"Interesting," said the count. Then Ramon slapped his engineer on the shoulder in approval. "I am fortunate to have such an able engineer and comrade as you, Castellamonte."

"Thank you, sire. The water power will allow us to complete the church in half the time compared to using only manual sawyers."

"And when does my master engineer expect the church will be completed?"

"By the end of this fall. After that, we will convert the sawmill into a gristmill. That will return tranquility to the valley."

Maiol had already departed for Narbonne, and Ramon ate breakfast at the Courniou villa with the steward, Cateline from Mary's commune, and Lena the Abbess of Bezier. At a nearby table were the steward's daughters and Lena's companions. Ramon addressed the steward, "Your role here maintaining the villa does not change. You will still have your room. And your daughters will be here although two of them have decided to train as nuns. Your manor, now a nunnery, will thrive. I see a young woman from Tomieres has also joined the nunnery."

"Count, I will also be a helper. An abbess still follows the Benedictine decree of work, study, and prayer," Lena added.

"Of course, Abbess Lena. And again, you have our deepest gratitude for leading the young women."

The steward excused himself to attend to his chores. Ramon nodded and then addressed the two women, "After learning further of Mary Magdalene's commune, I have a proposal."

Ramon noticed Cateline stiffen. *She intended our conversation last night about her commune to be private and I will not divulge anything. That is for her to do if she wishes.* "Cateline, Lena, do you think it would be beneficial if the sisters of Courniou and of Mary's commune could meet?"

Lena glanced at the women sitting nearby and said, "I can see they get along well and I have not perceived any issues these last few days." She coughed. "I would prefer the ladies of Mary Magdalene to visit here. Under my supervision."

Cateline looked more relaxed. "I welcome the idea and I agree with the abbess, the women of the commune will visit Courniou. I would enjoy remaining here for a time."

CHAPTER TEN

The swords clashed, but neither opponent could break through. They continued to circle each other and slash with their weapons. Ramon fought with a sword in each hand against his larger foe, who dueled with a sword and shield. His enemy, now down on his knees, lunged once more as Ramon blocked his sword, then scissored the man's wrist with two swords. His adversary screamed, "My hand! You cut off my hand!" and shoved his shield into Ramon's shoulder, knocking him to the ground.

"Husband, you are being too rough with him!" Garsinda exclaimed.

The father dropped his wooden sword and helped his son to his feet.

"No, Mother, I am fine. My timing was not correct."

"Well, I am proud of you, young Ramon," said his mother.

Count Ramon studied his son's eyes, making sure his blow had not been too hard. "Your timing was perfect, Son. It was the angle of your right sword. You can lock my sword with the x-block and still stop my shield strike if you hold the pommel of the sword elevated like this and lean just so. It would have intercepted the shield. Then you would have your one-handed enemy at your mercy. You are doing very well. We will practice more tomorrow."

Young Ramon, now four years old, dropped his helmet and wooden swords on the floor and dashed out of the room.

Garsinda laughed. "He loves to spar with his father, but when it is over, he eagerly runs off to explore the chateau."

"I will teach him to put away his weapons when he is older," Ramon said. "He should now have the life of a child, and little by little, increase his discipline. He never complains when I tell him it is time to spar and he is always full of energy. But I have also found him in deep thought, sitting in the tower gazing out over the city with Chester asleep on his lap."

Garsinda nodded. "There is something between him and that cat. Other than your son, Chester only tolerates one or two strokes from anyone before he bites."

"And he never brings his kills to anyone but young Ramon." Ramon hugged Garsinda and looked down at the swell in her abdomen. "Will his sibling be another sword fighter or a beautiful woman like her mother?"

"Both!" said Garsinda. Ramon laughed. She added, "No, I don't care, as long as our child is healthy." She kissed Ramon. "Must you go to Aquitaine tomorrow? Haven't you been there already this year?"

"There is no pressing issue, but I want to meet Maurice Pons in Perigueux. He is the cousin of Lord Pons of Aurillac."

"Is Maurice from Aurillac?"

"No, he is from the nearby castle at Polignac and was recommended by Lord Pons to be my advisor at Perigueux. He is the third son in the family and unlikely to inherit, so he is free to find his fortune elsewhere."

"Ramon, you have always been able to keep the loyalty of the vassal counties with little bloodshed, but this method of implanting your own chosen advisors? Won't it offend the local rulers and interfere with their control?"

"It will work if I pick men with the right skills and those that I can trust. They are not to interfere with any of the vassals' decisions but only to observe."

"They are your spies?"

"They are to provide me with accurate and unbiased facts about the status of each county."

"So, Rouergue is secure, your uncle is in control, and his son is loyal to you. My father is in Narbonne and now with his special contingent of bodyguards, the security there is much better. Hugh rules the county of Limousin. The brothers Ison Pons of Fos and Pons de Arles have Gothia secure. Yes, I see, you need someone in the counties of Perigord, Quercy, and Poitou—in Aquitaine. I hope Maurice meets your expectations."

"Garsinda, I could die tomorrow and I am certain my vassals would transfer their loyalties to you."

"Ramon do not say that!"

"You have governed before when I have been away. I am confident you have kept up with the alliances and understand the politics. You would be regent for young Ramon, would you not?"

"Yes, yes, but I have not personally met any of your confidants except, of course, my father and your uncle. You think the others would be loyal to me?"

Ramon paused. "Yes, but you would need to go and reinforce the relationship, just as I do now, honor them with royal visits and of course take young Ramon."

"Those are your political associations. Who are your religious allies? Of course, I know Bishop Hugues respects us and we can trust him."

"Remember Arnulf, the Abbot of Chanteuges? I trust him."

Garsinda added, "And Varadolanus, the Abbot of Saint Pons, who stopped here in Toulouse?"

"Yes, he is our close ally. There are many others high and low that will rally around you. There are the politics of exchanging favors and the politics of family loyalty. I try to secure our domains primarily through the latter. I'd rather give unconditional loyalty to my family rather than trade favors with political allies. But the family members I trust most are those who do not keep count of favors. They will support you no matter what the situation, and I will do the same, not expecting a reward in return."

Within several days, Count Ramon left for Perigueux, the capital of Aquitaine, to meet with Maurice Pons. Garsinda took up the duty of daily walks about the city to be seen by the people. On this day, she was escorted by a few knights, their ladies, and young Ramon. When her son suggested they stop at a tavern, as the count had done when he accompanied his father around the city, she declined. The summer day was humid, and the air was still. As they traversed the forum, Garsinda was troubled by the odor of human waste coming from the streets and alleys. It was common for citizens to throw the contents of their pot de chamber into the street. The only feasible cleaning that could be done was in the streets next to the river by flushing the waste with buckets of water. The rest of the city depended on cleansing from the rain.

As the entourage crossed the forum, they came to a group of soldiers crowded around a cavity in the pavement. Stones were missing and a few adjacent cobbles were sagging into the hole. The chasm was a pace wide and deeper than a man's height.

"Why is there a hole there?" asked young Ramon.

The leader of the milites bowed to Garsinda and then answered the boy. "Young sire, we believe those who built the forum constructed it over a hole, or the ground underneath has washed away. Now . . ."

"My father said the Romans built the forum."

"Uh, yes, yes they did, young master, they did. We expect Sir Castellamonte to arrive soon."

The engineer arrived shortly and bowed. "Lady Garsinda and Master Ramon, I am pleased to see you today. I discovered that this hole lines up with the ruins of a concrete structure at the riverside. I believe this was the main sewer of the ancient Roman city. I know the Romans continuously flushed their sewers with water from the aqueducts, but the watercourses have not been in operation for centuries. We can fill in the hole and repair the forum pavement."

"Mother, I heard you talking about the smelly streets!" Ramon exclaimed. "They could dump the pots in this hole and the stinky stuff will go away!"

The adults were surprised. Garsinda smiled. Then Castellamonte said, "That's not a bad idea, young master! We do not, however, have a source of flowing water to flush the sewer as did the Romans. Countess, I can build a low stone wall, a curb, around the hole for people's safety with openings lower than the forum level. That way when it rains, the runoff will flush the sewer. Although we will be transferring the odor from the streets to here, it will be a major improvement. Citizens could empty their pot de chamber contents into the opening. I respectfully submit my . . . um, Master Ramon's advice, Countess. You could write up a decree, post the order, and enforce it."

"Begin work, sir. I will make it a law of Toulouse. I am certain the citizens will support the rule as they will have fresher air to breathe," said Garsinda.

Just over a week later, Ramon Pons's second in command, Pere, visited the chateau to report to Garsinda. "Countess, the citizens are slowly getting accustomed to carrying their pots to the forum sewer. It will take a few more weeks to supervise them and enforce the edict before it is routine."

"Thank you, Pere." She held his eyes in her gaze long enough to unnerve him and said, "You are not withholding anything from me, are you, sir? I want the solid truth, so I can make the right decisions."

"I am sorry, Countess. So far, it is not working as well as we hoped. Perhaps it will take time to convince the people it is healthier."

"Pere, I would like to create the position of . . . say, a disposer. Men who will take the chamber pots to the sewer for the citizens, and then return their containers. As part of managing the city, I will pay their salary. What do you think?"

"Yes, Countess, that is a good idea. I will institute this as soon as possible. And, um, there is another problem. The shopkeepers are complaining that there were not odors near their establishments before, but now it smells bad all the time."

"I will talk to Castellamonte about a solution, Pere. Thank you."

The marshal bowed and hesitated before he exited the room. "Countess, forgive me for relaying an incomplete report."

"I have already forgiven you, Marshal Pere. I understand it is hard for men to accept a woman's judgment."

"Thank you, Countess, it will not happen again."

After his return, Count Ramon spent the day with his family. He reported success in Perigueux. However, Viscount Elabus's rebelliousness was stirring again. Ramon realized he had made the best choice to select Maurice Pons as his advisor in Aquitaine. Maurice Pons would cooperate with Elabus but would set the Pons family interests first.

Ramon and his son toured Toulouse the following day. As they entered the forum, young Ramon was eager to show his father the recently discovered sewer. He ran up to a circular depression in the pavement, covered by a round wooden disc. "Father, this is new, there was no wooden top before, there was just a hole, and it smelled bad!"

Ramon leaned down and examined the wooden cover. "The odor is not so bad." He studied the metal rods protruding vertically through holes in the lid. As he inspected the apparatus and its workings, he heard the bump of wheels on the uneven pavement behind them, and he turned to see a man pushing a two-wheeled cart containing a wooden barrel.

"It's caca man! Hi, caca man!" said the boy.

"Hello, Petithomme, or should I say Petit Comte, Little Count." He bowed to the count. "My fellow, uh, . . . disposers and I are most gracious to have this job, Count Ramon."

"The city is thankful for your work, sir! The odor from the streets is gone," said Ramon.

"Count, your son has been named by the citizens as *le petit homme*, as serious and clever as a man, but, well, it is good to see him having a chance to be a child, too.

"Do you see how your master engineer has solved all the problems?" said the disposer. "The rainwater runs into the hole and the wooden top floats up along the metal rods to let the water in, but when the water stops, the lid drops and, voila, no stinky!" Petithomme laughed. The disposer added, "At first the lid itself didn't float that well, so the engineer made the lid into a round wooden box. He said the air inside would make it float better. He was right!"

Father and son walked to the Garonne River and followed it downstream to the discharge of the sewer. The count was learning that the Romans had been very clever. He was sure they had intentionally located the discharge point downstream of the city. The areas where people now drew water were upstream of the discharge point, safe from the discharge of the sewer system. As Ramon discussed the design of the floating manway and the sewer to his son, a recurring thought surfaced. *He truly understands this. He has inherited his mother's curiosity and intelligence.*

Father and son trained that afternoon with their wooden swords. Ramon, on his knees, tested his son repeatedly on the two-sword x-block. After the warm-up, Ramon told his son to prepare to spar with sword and shield. Young Ramon picked up his weapons and stood en garde with his sword in his left hand and shield in the other.

"Son, what are you doing?"

"I want to hold the sword in my left hand."

"But that is not how I taught you."

"I want to do it."

Ramon, wielding a sword in his right hand, tested his son, who did well defending himself. "Son, I just realized I have never fought against a left-handed man, or in the stress of combat I was not aware of it. If I hold a sword in my right hand and you hold your sword in your left hand, both of us have the same advantage and disadvantage. The most common sword strike, the downward strike, is usually delivered at an angle, like this. When opponents are opposite handed, the strike must be blocked using a sword instead of the shield, and thus the stronger man now will have more of an advantage. It requires more strength to defend with a sword than a shield." This gave Ramon an idea.

"Hold the shield in your left hand. Son, pretend I am a big Viking." He grasped the dull wooden blade of the sword with two hands. "And this is a heavy battle ax." Ramon swung the weapon as a right-handed man would, making his son block with his shield. He struck over and over, hitting a bit harder with each blow. "Good defense, Son."

"Now, hold the sword in your left hand." He repeated the same attack, but this time his son's efforts to block with a sword could not stop all the strikes. Although Ramon made sure the contact was controlled, he struck Petithomme a few times.

"Father, stop! Yes, yes! I will be right-handed!" Petithomme flung his weapons down and stormed off. Ramon did not enjoy giving this lesson. *I myself had to change. I am probably left-handed, too. But this may save his life someday.*

Several hours later after Garsinda discovered the bruises on young Ramon, she sought out her husband. "You are being too physical. He is only a little boy!"

"Yes, but he is a count's little boy. Did he tell you what happened?"

"No, he did not want to talk."

"He wanted to fight as a left-hander."

Garsinda paused. "You told me you had to make adjustments. I don't remember you saying the transition was violent. Did you have to beat him to convince him?"

"It wasn't a beating. He discovered the consequences and he will not forget the painful lesson he learned today."

Garsinda calmed. "Husband, I think it is also time that our son learns how to read and write. It is never too early, and besides, he is very intelligent."

"That means he will go to the monastery every day."

"And they will teach our son to hold a quill with his right hand."

"We must not say anything to Bishop Hugues or his monks about his preference for his left hand," Garsinda added. "The Bible says 'Jesus sits at God's right side and God's left hand is the hand of judgment.'"

Ramon added, "Another, more frightening passage in Scripture states, 'When the Son of Man comes to His glory, and all the angels with Him, He will separate the people as a shepherd separates his sheep from his goats. He will put the sheep on His right and the goats to His left. Then the King will say to those on His right, you who are blessed by my Father. Then He will say to those on His left, you who are cursed into the eternal fire.'

"We don't want the monks quoting the Bible and making our son feel condemned."

###

Over the next several years, Petithomme was tutored by the monks at Saint Sernin Abbey and learned to use a pen with his right hand. He also trained right-handed using sword and shield, practicing against the sons of knights. Only with his father, did young Ramon train with a sword in each hand. Count Ramon remembered that twice he had survived in battle because he was equally skilled with both his left and right hands.

Garsinda had given birth to a girl, Eleanora, now four years old. With two children, she decided to accept the services of Robine as lady-in-waiting. The young woman, the daughter of Lord Pons of Aurillac, had arrived several days earlier and Garsinda and she quickly became friends. On this cool, but sunny day, the two women conversed as they watched the children play in the chateau garden.

Young Ramon had just finished dagger practice using wooden knives with several knights' sons, and the other boys had departed. After Garsinda ensured he was safely out of range of his sister, she let him swing his sword at imaginary opponents as Eleanora watched. His sister picked up a wooden knife and started to imitate his sword movements. Garsinda was pleased but interrupted her daughter and took her aside. "Eleanora, I am happy you are enthusiastic, but here . . ." She reached under her dress and pulled out a metal dagger. "Dear, the best hold to use is like this." Garsinda held the dagger by the handle so the blade lay along the back of her forearm. "Now when I have my arm at my side, you cannot see the blade. It is hidden behind my arm." Garsinda returned her knife to its hiding place. "Robine, do you have your own dagger?"

The young woman nodded. Then Eleanora held the wooden knife in her right hand as her mother instructed. Garsinda held the little girl's left wrist. "Now, since you have hidden your knife, you will be able to surprise an assailant. She showed her daughter how to escape an aggressor's grip by cutting his wrist and then fleeing. "You will learn more when you are older."

Their practice was interrupted when Ramon entered the garden and announced to his wife that two messengers had arrived. One was from Laon, the city near Paris where King Louis IV resided. The other had been sent by Pere, who was traveling to Narbonne and Gothia to maintain the loyalty of

Ramon's vassals. Robine and a servant took the children as Ramon and Garsinda retreated to the office.

Ramon opened the leather tube containing a scroll from King Louis. He read to Garsinda, translating from the written Latin to Occitan: "Count Ramon Pons, protector of the royal lands, Count of Toulouse, Marquise of Gothia, and Duke of Aquitaine, I hope this letter finds that you and your family through God's blessings are in good health. It is my pleasure to notify you as King of the West Franks I am donating funds to expand the monastery at Saint Pons de Tomieres and purchase land nearby to be cultivated and increase the productivity of the abbey."

"That is wonderful!" Garsinda exclaimed.

Ramon's smile matched her excitement. "The narrative follows with details on delivery of funds before the end of the summer. The king is distributing a decree stating that Saint Pons Abbey is officially under the Crown's protection. He recommends I reinforce the soldiers at Saint Pons and consider what fortifications might be needed." He read further to himself. "I see why."

"The next part of the message warns the Hungarians are on the move again. The East Franks, the Germans, defeated a Hungarian army in Lower Saxony. That is far to the northeast, but the year my father died, when the Hungarians were blocked in the Alps, they changed direction and invaded Toulouse. We defeated them, but I believe only with God's help. Many of their soldiers appeared sick."

"You are more organized now and can expect support from your vassals."

"Yes, Garsinda, I believe you are right, and not just giving me the encouragement of a supportive wife."

Ramon looked back at the letter, the concern leaving his face. "King Louis's wife gave birth to their first child! It is a boy named Charles d'Outremer."

"I am happy for them. Ramon, will you be going to Saint Pons to receive the king's funds and organize the new construction?"

Ramon did not hesitate. "No, Pere or Castellamonte are available." He leaned over and kissed Garsinda. The second message forgotten, they retreated to their bed chambers to be alone.

Ramon awoke disoriented, with fleeting thoughts that it was morning, but the sun was not outside the east window as usual. Then he realized they had enjoyed a deep nap after their lovemaking. He stretched, bumping his wife. Garsinda stirred. "My knight, we should do this more often!"

Ramon retrieved the second letter and when he returned he knocked on the door. "I have our two little soldiers with me."

There was a pause, then Garsinda said, "Come in, I am dressed."

Petithomme and Eleanora ran across the room and jumped into the bed with their mother. Ramon sat on the edge of the bed and opened the second letter. Garsinda asked, "What does Pere have to say?"

Petithomme interrupted his father before he began reading. "Mother, Eleanora has a knife. Girls aren't supposed to fight!"

Garsinda said, "Son, we told you before, you can only sit with us when we are doing business if you remain quiet."

Ramon added, "Petithomme, do you think women can govern?"

"No."

"But your mother makes important decisions, such as building the sewer, correct?"

The boy seemed embarrassed as he glanced at his mother, answering, "Yes, Father."

"Would you want your little sister to be able to defend herself?"

He nodded.

"She isn't trying to be like you. She isn't trying to be a knight, but she must learn the element of surprise as well as technique."

Pettihomme nodded again. Eleanora pulled up her dress to show she had used a kerchief to tie a wooden knife to her thigh.

Her mother and father laughed. Garsinda said, "Children, you can stay only if you are quiet while your father reads."

Ramon read and paraphrased: "Pere says your father sends his love and says all is well in Narbonne and in Gothia. They have heard that King Louis has also issued a grant to the Abbey of San Cugat in Catalonia, which is favored by the Count of Barcelona. That is well and good, but I wonder why the king did not mention that in his letter? Well, it is not important. I can see that by balancing contributions to his vassals, he is trying not to show favoritism. Other news from across the Pyrenees is that Ramiro, King of Leon, has defeated the Arabs near Madrid and recovered the city. Ramiro's Christian allies, however, now oppose him. That opposition has interrupted the Reconquista and stopped Leon's further expansion into the Muslim territories."

Garsinda said, "Just like here. The counties fight amongst themselves and do not unite for a single cause. Children, when you govern, do not be like them, but love each other and support each other, always.

"Do you promise?"

They nodded.

"I am pleased with your answer," and to Ramon she added, "and I am pleased the king has issued grants to both abbeys."

Pere returned from the south a week later. He met Ramon at the chateau for a conference that also included Bishop Hugues, the senior knight Odulf, and engineer Castellamonte. Garsinda was present as usual. Robine, Garsinda's lady-in-waiting, poured wine. Ramon took in the scene, typically reserved only for males. *None of the men are the least bit insulted by Garsinda's presence. Over the years, her dealings with these men have earned their respect and admiration.* Ramon toasted: "To you, the leaders who have made our realm strong and prosperous. Let us hope for continued peace. Sante!"

Pere hesitated to hold up his cup and join in with the toast. Ramon said, "Pere, you look concerned. I understand the long trips to the counties are very demanding and tiring, but the report you sent last week was encouraging."

"Thank you, sire. Since then I have learned of impending threats from the Hungarians."

"I am not surprised," added Ramon. "When they are turned back in one part of Europe, they raid another region. You would hope King Otto would lead the Germans into the Hungarians' homeland and crush them."

Pere continued, "They attack randomly, seemingly foolish, but very cunning, like a troop of foxes. Quick and deceptive. As we encountered here twenty years ago, their armies are comprised of mounted archers who raid and pillage, but do not conquer for land. They return to Hungary with their booty, wait a few years for an area to recover, and then return. There is also news from the Genoese."

"Genoese?" murmured Ramon.

"A Genoese ship, with Ponzio Gambaretto on board, anchored at the mouth of the river at Narbonne. Ramon, Gambaretto sends his regards to you and your family. He was given leave by his captain and rowed up the river to the city to warn us of an imminent invasion by the Hungarians."

An uneasy quiet hung over the group as Pere continued, "Last year King Hugh of Italy was at war with the papal state of Rome. He hired the Hungarians to attack Rome, but they were defeated. The Hungarians returned to Italy this spring and besieged Milan and Pavia. Hugh paid them to leave, but to further appease them, he encouraged them to invade southern Italy. The Hungarians killed thousands. They plundered towns near Rome but could not breach its strong fortifications. They even plundered the Abbey of Montecassino, the first monastery founded by Saint Benedict!"

"I received a letter from King Louis that the Hungarians were defeated in southern Germany," said Ramon.

"Gambaretto said the Hungarians are everywhere, not just Italy," continued Pere. "Since their initial loss in Germany, they returned and won a battle in Bavaria. A raiding party even reached northern Francia and plundered towns on the channel."

"They are a serious threat," Ramon said. "When they invaded Gothia and Toulouse, they burned the outskirts of Nimes, but they could not enter the walled part of the city, nor the fortifications of Narbonne or Carcassonne. I fought them outside of Toulouse, so they wouldn't devastate the farms and countryside."

"Yes, sire, but Gambaretto reported the Hungarian army that recently invaded Italy had over 20,000 horse archers," Pere added. "That is ten times larger than the force we fought years ago."

"Toulouse is safe within its walls, and the towns in Gothia are well fortified. However, Saint Pons does not have walls and only has a small garrison of soldiers," said the bishop.

"Good point, Your Excellency," Ramon answered. He turned to Castellamonte, "I will need you to take a company of crossbowmen to Saint Pons. Recruit unmarried men, if possible, as they may have to garrison in the town for a while. There you will receive the funds King Louis is sending. Use the money to build walls to protect the town and the monastery."

"Yes, sire."

"Pere, I am certain you warned my father-in-law of the threat?" The marshal nodded. "Anything else about the Hungarians?"

"Gambaretto said that when the Hungarians were returning to their homeland with their plunder, the inhabitants of the province of L'Aquila ambushed some of them in the Abruzzo Mountains, recovering much of the stolen goods. Most of the Hungarians, however, escaped."

Ramon curled his lip in thought as Odulf said, "That is valuable information. It reinforces the strategy we must use against them. They were stopped years ago in the Alps. The horse archers cannot maneuver in the mountainous areas. And Count, I will survey the walls of the city to make certain there are no weaknesses."

"Good. I will send a warning to the outlying towns. Pere organize scouts to take the messages."

"Yes, sire. I will also re-train the town's militia in use of the crossbows."

"Very good." He turned to Pere. "You said a Genoese ship anchored off Narbonne. Did you mean a Pisan ship?"

"No, it was Genoese. Gambaretto seemed very proud that the Genoese had recovered their city after it was sacked by the Arabs. They are rebuilding their fleet as well."

Ramon noted that Garsinda had been intently listening. "You have been quiet, Countess," said Ramon.

"I remember what you told me about the Hungarian invasion that occurred before we were married. You positioned scouts far to the east in Gothia, and you discovered the enemy's location, then chose a favorable location to fight. Will you notify the outlying lords to promptly notify you of the enemy's whereabouts?"

"Yes, of course. Years ago, I did locate my own scouts in Gothia. Our relationship with the counties is better now, so I can trust them. It is only luck we received early warning from Gambaretto. I will also ask Maiol to obtain more information from ships that arrive at Narbonne."

"The plans seem very thorough. I agree with Bishop Hugues, my fear is for Saint Pons and I will pray that the walls are ready in time," Garsinda added.

CHAPTER ELEVEN

In the spring of 944 a massive army of Hungarian horse archers surged along the coast of southern Provence. They bypassed Nice, Toulon, and Marseilles, although small parties of the army branched out to steal food and to plunder. The Hungarians progressed westward on Via Domitia, a Roman road, and skirted the prosperous cities of Arles, Nimes, and Avignon.

The Hungarians moved swiftly, which made it difficult for scouts to relay reports in advance. It had been over a year since the first reports of the Hungarian raids. Ramon began to question if the threat of the invasion would materialize. Several days after the invaders passed Marseilles, a messenger arrived in Toulouse. Ramon immediately called Odulf and Pere to his office at the chateau. The scout stood before the leaders. "Viscount Maiol sent me. When I left Narbonne, the Hungarians were camped between Marseilles and Fos sur Mer. They have not attacked any cities and have stolen livestock and food in the outlying areas. Reports from the east have confirmed the same patterns in Provence."

"Do you have an estimate on the number in the army?"

"Over 10,000 horse archers. They have brought spare mounts."

"Any idea of their destination?"

"The King of the Lombards . . ."

"You mean the King of Italy?"

"Yes, sire, he paid the Hungarians a huge sum of gold to invade the Caliphate of Cordoba."

Odulf said, "He is also the Count of Arles and was born in Provence so he may have bribed them to bypass the cities of his former homeland. We shall see what happens now that they are in Gothia."

"If the Hungarians attack Toulouse, our walls should stop them. I have never heard of them using siege machines or catapults. Narbonne has strong fortifications as well. The walls of Carcassonne are so formidable, when the Hungarians see them they will simply turn around and leave," said Pere.

"True." Ramon added, "I do not think they are patient enough to conduct a long-term siege. I pray they will continue to Spain. It would be a fatal error if we fought their huge army in the field."

A few miles west of Saint Pons, Varadolanus embraced Cateline and kissed her goodbye once more before she had to return to Courniou. He watched her trek on the pilgrims' path beside the Salesse River. The tiled roof of the Courniou villa barely showed above the tree line a thousand paces away. He climbed up the north side of the small valley and observed her from his usual vantage point. She entered the gate to the walled compound of the nunnery, and the monk, satisfied, began his three-mile trek back to Saint Pons.

Varadolanus descended to the fertile river bottom and passed a menhir, one of the ancient monoliths left by an unknown people. It marked where the stream tumbled down the valley into the river. It also marked their secret place, and Varadolanus felt the warmth still radiating throughout his body as he thought of Cateline. *It is a balmy spring day, but the cool air by the stream enveloped our bodies and excited the texture of her arms, her legs, and . . .* he became aroused reliving their intimacy. *But our passion burned away the chill.* He stumbled in the tilled soil and returned to the present. *Dear God, years ago, I renounced my vow of chastity to you. Forgive me for not revealing it to my brethren.*

Varadolanus now traversed the land that Saint Pons monastery had purchased with funds provided by King Louis. The monk had volunteered to lead the effort to cultivate and tend the fields, which gave him an excuse to be near Cateline. Stepping over the furrows and verdures of lettuce, Varadolanus recalled turning over the black earth. Other than prayer, the activity was his favorite meditation. When he tilled the soil with his hoe, all the workings of the world played out in his mind through the intricacies of gardening. Then he thought again of Cateline. *It is good she lives in Courniou and I live in Saint Pons. It would be too much distraction if we saw each other every day.*

Far ahead, he detected a flash of movement through the trees lining the bends in the river. He saw it again. A dozen riders moved swiftly through the woods. He crouched in the open field, watching. *They are not soldiers from Saint Pons. Their horses are small, barely larger than ponies, and the riders have bows on their backs—enemy horse archers! I waited too long, they will see me when I run. If I return to the stream and climb the hill, I might get away, but they are heading toward Courniou! I am sure they saw the walls around Saint Pons and Tomieres and went elsewhere to find an easier target.*

The monk stood and worked the earth. *Too late to run. If I turn my back, I will be an easy mark.* The horse archers galloped to a stop thirty paces away from the monk. *They do not look like Saracens. They are the Hungarians we were warned about. I must delay. But for what?* He remembered how to say friend, one of the few words his Hungarian father had taught him. "Barat! Me barat!"

A horse snorted. Varadolanus pulled up a head of lettuce, offered it to them, and said, "I have plenty to share. Do you favor these greeneries or maybe your horses would like a nibble?" He then recalled the word for eat. "Eszik! Eszik!"

One man jumped from his mount, landing agilely in the soft cultivated soil of the field. He was bow-legged and shorter than the monk, but very robust. The other soldiers remained on their horses. Without speaking, he strung an arrow. Varadolanus held out his hand toward the archer and shouted, "Wait!" The monk smiled and placed the head of lettuce on top of his head. He pointed to the lettuce and motioned shooting a bow and then nodded to the Hungarian. The bow-legged man looked back at his cohorts and they laughed with him. *Maybe we can get by without bloodshed.* The archer aimed. The instant he shot, Varadolanus bent his knees. The arrow pierced the leafy sphere, breaking it apart, and dropping pieces on the monk's shoulders. "Szar!" The Hungarians laughed. *I remembered the word for shit! But I am lucky that I guessed correctly he would try to impress his comrades and aim for my face.*

He crowned himself again with lettuce and forced himself to smile. *I always jest when I am nervous, but the habit is saving my life— for a few moments.*

The archer shot again and the monk turned sideways and parried with his hoe. A metallic ring sounded as the metal head of his tool deflected the arrow meant for his chest. To calm himself, he returned to gardening, but he kept a guarded watch out of the corner of his eye, and repeated: *Father, Son, and Holy Spirit, Father, Son, and Holy Spirit . . .*

After a round of laughter, the soldiers on horseback drew their bows and loosed a flight of arrows. Varadolanus twisted, deflected one arrow with the hoe, and dodged another. The other arrows pierced the fringes of his monk's baggy habit, but none of the bolts found his body. Varadolanus ran and shouted, "Thank you! Now I don't need a belt for my tunic!" *Will they take the bait?*

Several riders galloped past him and blocked his escape. A handful dismounted and surrounded the monk, brandishing their swords. *Now I have a chance, they are angry, but proud, and they want to end this hand-to-hand.* Varadolanus whirled the hoe above his head, creating a ring of defense that briefly kept his adversaries at bay. As they paused, the only sound was the hum from the revolving tool. They all attacked at once.

As the men charged inside the rotation of the hoe, the monk whipped the metal edge across one's face, then chopped a deep gash into the wrist of a second. The other three closed in, their weapons slicing toward Varadolanus. He blocked a scimitar with the hoe, stopped another slash by seizing the enemy's sword-wielding hand, and yanked the man's arm into the path of the third soldier's sword. The Hungarian screamed as the blade severed his arm, still held by the monk. The other two attackers slashed again, one cutting at the monk's legs, the other at Varadolanus's head. He stabbed the hoe into the ground. The sword twisted on impact, the flat of the blade knocked the monk to the ground, and the high strike missed. In the same instant, Varadolanus thrust the sword, the unfortunate Hungarian's hand still gripping the weapon, into one adversary and stabbed the end of the broken hoe into the remaining adversary. He could not pull the sword free as another Hungarian scimitar arced toward his head. *Jesus, I am coming!* The assailant unexpectedly collapsed when Cateline smashed his knees from behind with her staff, and with a quick follow-up, broke his neck before he hit the ground. The fight ended as the remaining archers suddenly vaulted onto their horses and fled south into the forest.

Cateline, still breathing hard from exertion and fear, said, "I was in the meadow above the villa picking blackberries, where I saw the Hungarians coming down the valley."

The monk answered, "But why did you come? You could have been killed!"

Suddenly, a troop of cavalry from Saint Pons arrived. Cateline held Varadolanus close ignoring his question. The captain said, "How did you survive against so many?"

"God was with me," Varadolanus answered, "but He left for other matters and sent this angel."

The captain looked puzzled and said, "Earlier today, the Hungarians rode around the village walls looking for a weak point. When they left in the direction of Courniou, we followed, knowing the sisters were in danger."

Cateline said, "Thank you, sir. Thank God you arrived soon enough. A few more seconds and they would have finished us."

The captain glanced at his men as they examined the dead and retrieved their weapons. "You are a fierce pair! How did you do this? Four dead!" Varadolanus was still kneeling. "Brother, can you stand?" The monk nodded. "We will go to Courniou and leave guards there until we search the surroundings. There could be more of the enemy nearby."

Cateline examined his leg. "There is no blood, but your knee is swollen." *How was it possible the sword did not cut through my leg? Did I have a real angel watching over me?* As the monk limped, he put his arm around Cateline's shoulder and used her staff for support. He asked the captain, "Officer, would you bring my hoe, please?"

"Hoe? Where is it?" Varadolanus pointed to the chest of a dead soldier. "My God! You did that?" The monk went down again. "Let's help you onto a horse and take you to Saint Pons. Wait here."

Cateline and Varadolanus were alone. The monk kissed Cateline's hand, looked up at her, and said, "Cateline, my angel, will you marry me?

###

It took several weeks before Varadolanus could walk without assistance from his hoe, fitted with a new wooden pole. On that day, he went to Saint Martin's Church in Tomieres to ask Friar Taenarus to perform marriage rites for Cateline and him. "You can't do this!" Friar Taenarus said. "I mean, I recommend not to do it!"

Varadolanus said, "The Church has no rules against the clergy marrying."

"You are right."

"And I will be departing Tomieres."

"But why leave Saint Pons and give up your abbacy?" said the friar. "Get married and stay here."

"Cateline has been here six years to help the sisters establish the nunnery at Courniou. She has arranged for another woman from Mary's cave to replace her. She wants to return to the mountain. My brothers of Saint Pons monastery are strong in body and spirit, and I am looking forward to a new adventure."

"An adventure in lust?" said the friar.

Varadolanus looked puzzled. "I will not lie to you, Friar Taenarus, and I confess to you and ask for forgiveness. We have been having relations for several years."

"What? Now you are confessing? Why should I agree to conduct the marriage ceremony after such behavior?"

Varadolanus was silent. Taenarus paced back and forth as he looked down, with his finger pressed on his lips. After minutes of pacing, the friar looked at Varadolanus. "No. No, I am wrong. I want to ask for *your* forgiveness, brother. How could I forget? Love is more important than an ecclesiastical career. A lifetime ago, I left the priesthood and married a second time. How can I judge you? But what of Cateline? Did she break her vow of chastity? I will need to talk with her, alone, before I make my decision."

The following day, Cateline sat with the friar in his office at Saint Martin's Church. "Please explain, Sister Cateline, how you and Varadolanus can have a relationship and become married yet continue your role as a bride of Christ."

"Friar, I understand your confusion. Yes, I am a sister, a sister in Christ with the women, but I am not a Catholic nun. We pray and commune together, but I have taken no vows of chastity. I worship Christ at Mary's cave just as you do in Saint Pons de Tomieres."

"Please explain, uh, Sister . . .um . . . Cateline."

"Have you heard the story of Mary Magdalene? How she came to Provence hundreds of years ago and converted many people to the faith?"

"Yes."

"Do you believe it?"

"Well, yes."

"In the Gospel of Mary Magdalene, after Mary quoted words by Jesus, Peter ridiculed her when he said, 'Did He really speak with a woman without our knowledge and not openly? Did He prefer her to us?'"

Taenarus said, "I thought the Gospel of Mary was just a legend. It is not in the Bible."

"Why not?"

Taenarus did not answer.

Cateline said, "Because men, only men, chose which gospels and books to keep. In Mary's gospel, Levi said to Peter, 'Peter, you have always been hot-tempered. Now I see you contending against the woman like the adversaries. But if the Savior made her worthy, who are you indeed to reject her? Surely the Savior knows her very well. That is why He loved her more than us.' Levi also said: 'As He commanded us, we should preach the gospel, not laying down any other rule or other law beyond what the Savior said.'"

"Cateline, I see your argument. Christ did not tell the people to take a vow of chastity nor to reject marriage. You are saying, 'Do not make a rule beyond what Christ said.'" The friar looked worried. "No one must learn any part of this discussion."

Cateline smiled. "So, then, you will marry us?"

###

Ramon surveyed the landscape from the tower, pondering what the Hungarians were planning. *I dislike cowering behind walls, but the best strategy now is to wait. The last report a month ago was that they had crossed the Pyrenees into Spain.* He saw a man urging his horse to gallop along the Via Aquitaine, the road from Narbonne. *Perhaps this rider has my answer.* Within several minutes, there was a knock on the door and the messenger entered. Ramon asked, "What is the news from Narbonne?"

"A message was received by Viscount Maiol from the Count of Barcelona. The Hungarians did not attack Barcelona but continued to Andalusia. They battled with the Muslims and captured a leading general, but they could plunder only a few towns. They went on to central Spain, where it is very dry, and ran out of food and water for their horses, so they ransomed the general and returned east. Three days ago, they bypassed Narbonne and were still headed east."

Ramon released the messenger and sat alone. *What deterred them from their usual pillaging and killing?*

Ramon continued to stay wary and on edge, keeping his defenses ready and troops prepared. Several weeks later Artald, the former Archbishop of Reims arrived, escorted by a contingent of King Louis' knights. After exchanging introductions and pleasantries, Artald said, "My family has been close supporters of the King of the West Franks for generations, as has your family. I crowned Louis myself – yes, it was June 19, 936, and I have been a friend and ally of King Louis since. But he was unable to protect me from my rival clergy, the Count of Vermandois. The count threatened my life and replaced me with his son. I believe Hugh, the Duke of the Franks, was behind the plot. War has shaken the counties and cities in the north. Hugh and Louis themselves have had their own differences, which so far has resulted in skirmishes but not open warfare."

"The unrest here is similar, Your Excellency."

"I am requesting, as per the king's advice, to live in exile under your protection until the powers resolve the bishopric of Reims. You have my promise, and I will confirm to Bishop Hugues, that I will not assume any rank or interfere with his work for the Lord."

"You are welcome to reside here, Archbishop. I will inquire with the Abbot of Saint Sernin about accommodations."

"I am not a young man, Count Ramon, and I am tired from the long ride. May I stay here at the chateau?"

"Yes, of course, Your Excellency. That will give the abbot a few days to prepare your quarters."

"I was hoping to stay here . . . but no matter, thank you, and, oh, yes, I am to inform you that King Louis and Duke Hugh will visit Aquitaine. The king would like to meet you in the city of Nevers within a fortnight."

"I look forward to meeting the king. When I was younger, I traveled to Paris with my uncle and met the former king, Rudolph. I will again be honored to be in the king's attendance."

That afternoon, Ramon called Pere and Odulf to the chateau. He knew he must talk with them before he notified Bishop Hugues, and he wanted Garsinda present as well. "First, I would like to discuss the Hungarian invasion. I cannot explain what deterred them from the anticipated destruction when they crossed our domains."

Odulf said, "the Lombard king was born in Provence, and he was the Count of Arles before his rule in Italy. He paid them to refrain from raiding in Provence. But why didn't they attack Gothia and Toulouse?"

"Possibly he did not want them to abuse Christians," said Garsinda. "The Hungarians did not assault Barcelona."

"Countess, My Lady, with respect, I do not think that can be the reason."

"Why not, Sir Odulf?"

"He employed Hungarians as mercenaries to fight against Rome, the home of the Pope, at least a decade ago. Then several years ago, he used those butchers again to assault Rome, and they threw Pope John X himself into a dungeon."

"Bishop Hugues told me a different story, that the Pope resigned."

"What is the truth about the Pope?" said Ramon. "It depends on the source. If the Lombard king cared about the safety of Christians over Muslims, what leverage did he have to control the Hungarians?"

Pere said, "The reports were that he paid the Hungarians bushels of gold to fight the Arabs in Spain. Did that restrain them?"

"Bishop Hugues would say God has protected us," said Ramon. "That God is on our side because we are being pious, we pray, and we go to Mass. And that we have founded two monasteries and recovered Saint Pons's relics."

The group remained silent for several moments, then Ramon said, "Archbishop Artald arrived today." He cast a knowing glance at Garsinda, who knew of everything that happened at the chateau. The count described the predicament that the archbishop had relayed to him.

"Count, do you think it wise that he is staying here?"

"We are thinking alike, Sir Odulf. Louis may have sent him as a spy. I will make certain he moves soon to Saint Sernin, and I will not accept any more of his excuses to remain at the chateau."

"We should introduce him immediately to Bishop Hugues."

"I agree. Please, Garsinda, will you arrange a meeting?"

Garsinda held dinner in the chateau's hall, which comfortably accommodated the senior knights and their ladies. She opened the window shutters to let in light and fresh air. The spring days had been mild, although inside the hall the stone walls held the previous night's cold. Woolen tapestries lined three of the walls and helped insulate the guests from the chill. The fourth wall was occupied by a large fireplace now in use, adding a pleasant warmth. Relaxing music was supplied by entertainers playing flutes and stringed instruments. Maids brought out soup made of carrots, leeks, onions, garlic, and cabbage. The diners' conspicuous slurps, which showed their fondness for the soup, pleased Garsinda. Next the servants placed before each guest a trencher, a thick cut of bread which served as a plate. The maids then dropped cuts of sizzling beefsteak on the trenchers. The aroma made Ramon's mouth water and the guests waited for him to begin the feast, but he nodded to let the archbishop have the honor. "Please, Bishop Artald, enjoy." Everyone was busy eating and the hall was void of conversation for the next few minutes.

Archbishop Artald was seated next to Bishop Hugues. "I am feeling very welcome! This is a feast of a king!" Like most men, he carried his own knife. He cut his steak to bite-size portions and then speared each piece with his knife. Knights and ladies also used their own knives to eat. The guests pulled off chunks of fresh table bread to have with their meat. The trenchers were typically made from stale bread and after the meal, the sauce-soaked pieces would be offered to the poor.

Artald asked Garsinda, "Delicious steak, Countess. You sweetened the beef with something?"

"Yes, Your Excellency, my cook pounded quince marmalade into the meat to tenderize it and give it a special flavor. I am pleased you like it."

Artald scanned the walls of the hall and turned to Bishop Hugues. "These tapestries are beautiful!"

"The oldest is on that wall." The bishop pointed to a tapestry depicting a man being dragged along a city street by a bull. Although it was a simple two-dimensional scene woven with colorful threads, the images of violence and blood-letting were real enough to be unsettling. "Do you know the story of Saint Sernin, the city's patron saint?"

The bishop told Artald of how Saturninus, a Christian during ancient times, refused to sacrifice to the pagans' bull. They tied him to the animal to be dragged through the streets of Toulouse, and he was martyred.

"Of course, the Monastery of Saint Sernin was founded in the martyr's honor!" added Artald.

The bishop pointed to another wall-hanging, its faded red cloth and threadbare condition hinting its ancient age. Woven into the material was a large gold Occitan cross. "Yes, and that tapestry is the second oldest. It was made for the first Count of Toulouse in Ramon's family, Count Fredelo. It was a gift from Charles the Bald, King of the West Franks."

"Bishop, where were these tapestries made? Were they woven by artisans in Toulouse?"

"No, these two were crafted by monks in Saint Martin's monastery of Tours."

"And I see the other tapestry is a battle scene, with a knight fighting among masses of fallen men and horses. He is fighting on foot with two swords. Is that city in the background Toulouse?"

"No, that is the city of Carcassonne, and the knight is Ramon Pons himself, when he defeated the Hungarians twenty years ago."

Their conversation was interrupted when Garsinda stood and called out, gaining the guests' attention, "Do you like this wine? It is Cahors vintage, my husband's favorite!" At this Ramon stood and held up his cup. "And please visit with our guest, Archbishop Artald. To the archbishop and to the king. Sante!"

"Sante!"

When the main course was finished, the servants brought out more fresh bread and dishes of quince marmalade. For dessert, the guests covered the bread, still warm from the oven, with the sweet preserve and enjoyed it with spiced wine.

Garsinda went to the head of the large table and spoke. "Honored guests, I hope you have enjoyed the dinner! Our cooks made the marmalade and seasoning from quinces grown in our manor orchards. Ramon's great-grandfather, Ramon I, started the orchard from seedlings brought from the quince trees planted in Charlemagne's royal gardens. The growth of those first trees and the continued health and abundance of the current orchards is just one symbol of the close ties and the count's loyalty to the kings of West Francia. To commemorate this noble fruit, I am honored to recite a poem bestowed by our friend Rabbi Samuel of the Judaic Academy in Narbonne. The author of the poem is Shafer ben Utman al-Mushafi, vizier to Caliph Al-Hakam II of Cordoba in Andalusia."

Ramon was transfixed by his wife as she began to deliver verse. *I married the right woman!*

The Quince

It is yellow in color, as if it wore a daffodil tunic,
And it smells like musk, a penetrating smell.

It has the perfume of a loved woman and the same hardness of heart,
But it has the color of the impassioned and scrawny lover.

Its pallor is borrowed from my pallor;
Its smell is my sweetheart's breath.

When it stood fragrant on the bough and the leaves
Had woven for it a covering of brocade,

I gently put up my hand to pluck it and set it
Like a censer in the middle of my room.

It had a cloak of ash-colored down hovering over
Its smooth golden body,

And when it lay naked in my hand, with nothing more than
Its daffodil-colored shift,

It made me think of her I cannot mention, and I feared
The ardor of my breath would shrivel it in my fingers.

MICHAEL A. PONZIO

West Francia and borders with Germany 944 A.D.

CHAPTER TWELVE

In the north of France, King Louis made peace with his rival and advisor Hugh the Great, Duke of the Franks. In a show of cooperation, the two traveled together to Aquitaine. There the vassals were required to reinstate their loyalty to Louis. In Perigueux, Elabus and Maurice gave them their utmost respect, and the king was satisfied that the duchy's loyalty was intact. Louis returned to his capital while Hugh went to Nevers, where Ramon was to renew his declaration of fealty.

When Ramon arrived, he was surprised to discover that Louis had not come with Hugh. The duke met with Ramon at the monastery adjacent to the Cathedral of Nevers. Ramon included Pere in the introductions. The weather was agreeable, and in the parklike setting they found tables where the duke's steward served them wine. The count and Hugh then strolled through the cloister and among the gardens next to the river. Ramon considered Hugh a pleasant man, but sensed his civility was a facade. The duke exclaimed, "A day like today makes one happy to be alive! Behold this scene—the ancient oak trees, the birds singing, and the landscape!" He was gazing at the river. "The view of the Loire Valley from this vantage point is stunning!"

"Yes, Duke, I agree. God has given us another beautiful day."

"Count Ramon, you may be wondering why the king is not here. He has departed for Laon. When in Perigueux, the king's wife, Queen Gerberga, became very sick and so they returned home. Louis sends his apologies and asks that you travel with me to his court in Laon. There he will confirm your position."

Why do I feel uneasy? Is it just Hugh's personality? When Artald told me I must meet with the king, he mentioned it in a casual way. Not like my visit years earlier to King Rudolph's court with my uncle. Yes, Louis is the new king and I should meet him. Ramon answered, "I would be honored to be a guest at the king's court."

The next morning, Ramon and Pere retained half of their troop of knights and sent the rest back to Toulouse. As he was preparing to depart for Laon with Hugh and his escorts, the duke commented, "No need to bring any of your knights, Ramon, the king will provide you with escorts."

The statement troubled Ramon. *How does he think I will return to Toulouse without escorts? Perhaps his tongue slipped? I am suspicious again, yet I have no other options. I am the king's vassal and must go to Laon.* He answered, "That is appreciated, but I will bring them along so my men have the opportunity to enlighten themselves and to experience northern France."

They arrived in the city of Laon five days later. Ramon sat alone in comfortable quarters at Louis' castle, Chateau Gaillot. There was a knock at the door and Ramon was called to the court. A yeoman escorted Ramon to Louis's office chambers. There he joined the king, attended by a scribe. The king sat at an ornately carved table in an armchair upholstered with soft cushions. "Please, Count, share wine with me."

Ramon settled himself across from the king on a comfortable chair as Louis continued. "Count Ramon, you have been very successful governing the southern counties. I have learned of the history of your family line, starting with Count Fredelo, who was appointed by King Charles as the first Count of Toulouse from your family. His descendants have been loyal allies of the King of the Franks. I value your advice and would be pleased if you would join my court."

Ramon was startled, but calmly hid his surprise and asked, "Sire, would you first grant me leave to transfer governorship in Toulouse?"

"Uh . . . well, no. I need your help now. I believe Hugh is trying to rebel again and I need an expert military commander. I have heard of your prowess on the battlefield."

"Sire, wouldn't I be more valuable to you as an ally to keep the southern counties loyal to the crown?"

"Yes, yes, that is important, Count Ramon, but as I said, I expect you to guide us now. I met your second, his name is Pere, no? He is capable to help your wife to govern until you return."

"How long do you need my service, Sire?"

"It depends on the success of my campaign to recover the Duchy of Lorraine."

A week later, Pere returned to Toulouse with Ramon's knights and delivered a message from the royal court. Pere entered the chateau office and handed Garsinda a leather packet. Neither spoke as she struggled to open it although the case had a simple clasp. She let out a sigh of frustration as she broke the seal which was stamped in Latin: Ludovicus Gratia Dei Francoru Rex, Louis King of the Franks by God's Grace. The countess removed a scroll and read the document aloud to Pere: "Countess of Toulouse, the royal court of King of the West Franks, Louis IV, has declared that Ramon Pons will retire his title as Count of Toulouse, Duke of Aquitaine, and Marquis of Gothia. He has joined my court as an advisor. You will act as Regent for your son until further notice."

Fear and anger welled up within Garsinda. She cried, not from grief, not from fear, but from frustration. But her sense of helplessness quickly evaporated. "Why isn't there a letter from Ramon? Pere, did you speak to the count before you left?"

"No, Lady. I asked for him, but I was told he was not available."

"He must be a hostage," said Garsinda. "They think I cannot do something about this!" she shouted. "Well, they are wrong!"

"Yes, My Lady."

Garsinda called a meeting with the leaders of Toulouse to discuss the king's declaration. Pere, Odulf, and Bishop Hugues sat with her in the tower. She chose to meet there because the view over the city gave her a special confidence. The men were silent, waiting for her to begin. "Pere, what can you tell us of Hugh and Louis?"

"Countess, I only met Hugh and King Louis during one short introduction. I did, however, quarter with Hugh's soldiers in Nevers, and our knights that escorted Ramon to Laon quartered with Louis's men. The soldiers talked freely among themselves."

"Go on."

"It is widely known that Louis returned to West Francia from exile in England, with the strong support of Hugh. I discovered, however, that Hugh expected to control Louis as his puppet. Louis has not submitted. There have been a series of disagreements between them, hostile enough to lead to skirmishes. Each time, they come to a truce and then tolerate each other for a time. Then conflict starts again with another round of fighting."

Odulf said, "Did you know that years ago, Hugh refused the crown, so the nobles elected Louis's predecessor, King Rudolph, instead?"

"Yes," said Pere. "Hugh thought if he became king and assumed the insignificant royal domains, he would risk losing control of his vast land holdings."

Odulf added, "You would think he would have been able to combine the domains."

Pere said, "I agree, but Hugh knew the Normans and the East Franks are always waiting for an excuse to claim territory once the king shows any sign of weakness. Hugh did achieve that union in his own way, however. He is not only Duke of the Franks, but he is also the Count of Paris, so he claimed the royal capital when Rudolph died, along with the surrounding royal domains. Louis rules very little land, just Laon and the immediate area."

Odulf and the bishop exclaimed, "What? The king controls only a small domain?"

"Hmm, very complex," said Garsinda. "Then Hugh the Great actually has greater landholdings than King Louis, and the king is resisting and will not act as his puppet."

Odulf said, "My Lady, I can explain, the –"

Pere's eyes rapidly danced between the countess and Odulf and he appeared anxious when Garsinda interrupted. "Sir, I have come to understand very well the complexities of the politics among the counties in the south. I can do the same for the north. Do not patronize me."

"Yes, My Lady."

Garsinda said, "Pere, I want to know the balance of power in the north. Who is allied with whom?"

"Of course, Countess. Power resides among the four nobles: Hugh, Louis, William Longsword of Normandy, and Otto, King of the East Franks. The northerners refer to Otto as King of the Germans."

The bishop added, "The Pope favors King Louis, being a descendent of Charlemagne and the legitimate heir."

"Thank you, Your Excellency, a very important fact," said Garsinda.

Pere continued, "I drank with Hugh's soldiers in the taverns. They let on that Hugh and William Longsword were planning to visit Otto."

"And anything about Louis?"

"Yes, My Lady. The Duke of Lorraine, Giselbert, had just visited the king."

"Lorraine? A duchy. Where is Lorraine? The map on the wall in the office, I pass by it every day. Pere, please go and find where Lorraine is located."

Pere hurried out the door. The bishop excused himself, leaving Odulf and Garsinda alone. She said, "Odulf, I thought you respected me more. The comment you made earlier?"

"I do respect you, Countess. I am very sorry."

"I believe you, Sir Odulf. It is hard to rid oneself of old habits, like those that dismiss the views of women. I have been ordered to rule as Regent by the legitimate king, who is supported by the Church. I plan to govern until my husband returns."

Bishop Hugues returned and took his seat. Pere was breathing hard after running up the steps. "Countess, the Duchy of Lorraine is part of East Francia, under Otto's rule. And I heard Louis's men say that Hugh has claimed that Lorraine belongs to him, through inheritance."

Garsinda stood, then paced across the room. "I believe that Hugh and Longsword are going to ally themselves to Otto. Louis has so few resources, they should be able to control him, so why would they need Otto's help? Perhaps because Lorraine is going in with the king?"

Pere added, "Countess, Louis does not have large land holdings, but he is very wealthy and he has loyal and well-trained troops. They are all professional milites."

Garsinda scanned the seated men. "What clues can we extract from the brief letter?"

"My Lady, may I speak?" asked Odulf. Garsinda nodded. "The letter from Louis lacked details, Ramon did not or could not include a letter, and it was puzzling they denied Pere from talking to the count before he left Nevers. Any one of these facts alone would not be suspicious, but together, they are troubling. The count, however, is a vassal of Louis, and although we are used to minimal contact with the royal court, it is within the king's right to appropriate Ramon's help.

"I recommend you immediately send a letter to the king and ask him outright how long the count will be in his direct service."

"Excellent advice," added Garsinda. "And I will emphasize that I need this information to plan my governorship."

"Also, I advise that you indicate that your messenger will await his response for return to Toulouse," reinforced Odulf.

Pere added, "I will organize a team of fast riders to minimize the time for communications to Laon, and for the return."

"Very good. Bishop, anything else to add?"

He shook his head.

Garsinda continued, "So again, Ramon will fight for the king. Their ally will likely be the Duke of Lorraine. My husband is a formidable leader, but they will be against a coalition of Hugh the Great, the Normans, and Otto. The Pope favors Louis. I am praying that the Pope and God are on good terms.

Odulf and Pere chuckled, but quickly composed themselves when the bishop showed a look of disapproval. Garsinda did not notice, still deeply in planning her strategy.

"And there may be more information we can gain locally. We know the exiled archbishop, who is here at Saint Sernin, was removed with Hugh's influence. I suggest we visit him and learn the truth about why he is here."

Two weeks after Ramon was coerced into serving the king, the pair led Louis's troops to Metz, the capital of Lorraine. Louis's disciplined army of knights, infantry, and archers set up an orderly camp outside the city. After inspecting the bivouac, Ramon and the king met with Duke Giselbert and planned their strategy. Once back at their camp, they convened in the king's tent, where Louis poured Ramon wine and raised his cup. "So far, resistance has been light. A few skirmishes. Count, your strategy at the last town worked well. Otto's garrison fell quickly."

"And to you, King Louis. You have developed a well-trained army."

"Ramon, do we keep pressing east to the Rhine? Basel would be a rich prize. Then beyond? What fortuitous timing that King Otto has exiled his brother, Henry, who has joined us along with his knights, a welcome addition to our forces."

"Yes, I agree we should continue east and evict Otto's garrisons from the towns here to the Rhine. *Louis is flush with victory and overconfident.* "I recommend we stop there. The river is the best defensible barrier.

"Sire, before we move on Basel, I need to know the conditions at Mainz. The last message from the Archbishop of Mainz indicated he was in control of the city and was confident he could hold it. We must make sure it remains securely in our hands before we move east. It controls the best river crossing on our north flank."

"I will send knights to Mainz to evaluate his claims before we march to Basel," said Louis. "What do you think about Giselbert's soldiers here in Metz?"

"They were spirited, but after observing the sloppy condition of their weapons and their unorganized camp, they appear to be more like an undisciplined militia or even a rabble."

"Yes, I agree. I would use them for an initial charge on the battlefield to break the enemy formation. Then our knights could sweep the field."

"Sire, that is a good battle plan, but only if the make-up of the opposing army is all infantry or perhaps a balanced force like yours. The best use of Giselbert's soldiers depends on the type of army we will fight and the location of the engagement."

"Ramon, I made the right decision promoting you to military commander."

Within two days Louis's scouts returned from reconnaissance of Mainz. Louis called Ramon to his tent, where he joined the king, engrossed in conversation with the knight who had led the scouts. "Give us both your report, soldier," said Louis.

"Sire, we were just over a day's ride on the road to Mainz when we encountered Archbishop Hildebert. He said Otto's knights drove them out of Mainz. The archbishop fled with the few men he had left, but Hildebert is sure Otto's knights will pursue them after they secure the city."

"How many men did Hildebert have with him?" said Ramon.

"A few score."

"You said knights attacked them in Mainz," Ramon said. "Did Otto send an army? Was the force made up off infantry or mounted troops?"

"Hildebert said there were at least 80 mounted knights from castles across the Rhine."

Ramon said, "Sir, you have done excellent work."

The count turned to Louis. "We know the nature and size of the enemy. We need their location."

The knight added, "Sir, I sent several of my men to continue to Mainz to determine the whereabouts of Otto's forces. Also, Hildebert should be here in a few hours."

"Very good! Let's prepare for a fight."

Only one of the scouts returned that afternoon, giving a report that the enemy was within two hours of Metz. The remaining scouts had been captured or killed by Otto's knights. Louis organized his army, and Giselbert's forces joined them. Ramon led a vanguard of knights out the east gate of Metz to secure the most strategic location. They rode through level fields, but forests closed in on the road a few miles east of the city. Ramon determined this was the most advantageous place to fight. As he returned he met Louis's forces advancing through the meadows. Louis had positioned Giselbert's men tramping in front of the army, anticipating he would send them forward first in the engagement. Ramon joined the king, who rode beside Henry and his knights. "Sire, we should form our lines before the forest closes in on the road. The fields are not as wide there, and it will hinder the tactics of Otto's knights. They will not be able use their speed to outflank us."

Ramon recommended Louis place his archers and pikemen in the center. Ramon would lead a troop of knights to cover their right flank and Louis would defend their left flank with a contingent of chevaliers. Ramon split Giselbert's infantry to take positions on both wings. The count placed Henry and his knights as reserve forces in the rear.

Within minutes of establishing their lines, a trio of Otto's German knights exited the forest. The small group appeared startled upon encountering a massed army of several thousand, just a few hundred paces away. Two knights reigned in their steeds and monitored Louis's army waiting in the bright sunlight. The other knight returned down the road darkened by tree cover. Their wait lengthened to a quarter hour, long enough to wonder if the Germans were indeed attacking, when suddenly enemy knights burst out of the forest at full gallop. The columns of four fanned out into a line of twenty across and charged the center of Louis's army. More knights followed, and groups organized into second, third, and fourth lines of charging riders. Ramon was pleased. *Good! They think they can mow us down like wheat with their heavy cavalry.*

Louis's archers released their arrows. Only a few knights fell from direct hits, but more lost control and were unsaddled when their horses were wounded. The first and second waves of knights tried to break through the center, but pikemen unhorsed many and Louis's infantry engaged them. Trying to find softer targets, the next waves of German knights changed course to attack Giselbert's ragtag infantry. Ramon and Louis led their mounted knights and intercepted them. Seconds after the opposing knights clashed, Giselbert's infantry entered the melee, pulling riders out of their saddles and overwhelming the enemy with numbers. The remaining enemy knights were cut off from retreat by Henry's forces and taken prisoner. As customary, they would be ransomed.

During the next month, Louis and Ramon secured Mainz and Basel without a battle, then returned to Laon. At the Chateau Galliot, as they studied maps of East Francia, they discussed the status of the garrisons left to defend Lorraine. "Louis, I left a contingent of archers and several officers to provide training for Giselbert's soldiers. That should improve his army's skill and discipline."

"Very good, Ramon, I am confident the duke can hold Lorraine. He was eager to proclaim loyalty to me. When you charged him with monitoring and defending the river crossings, what did the duke choose as his strategy?"

"He is having his men patrol along the river between Basel and Mainz. There are no longer any bridges over the Rhine. If Otto is determined, he could rebuild the decking on the concrete pilings that remain from the old Roman bridge at Mainz. Two centuries ago Charlemagne had wooden spans constructed on the pilings, but the bridge burned only a few years after it was completed."

"I believe the Rhine will be a defensible barrier to secure Lorraine," said the king.

A servant, after gaining permission, entered the room and served them wine.

"To Lorraine!" toasted Louis. Ramon echoed the salute. The men sat and relaxed. "Ramon, you have not mentioned your family lately."

"The campaign to recover Lorraine has taken all my time and occupied my thoughts," answered Ramon.

"Write a letter to your wife. I have prepared a letter for Archbishop Artald and your correspondence can be included in the courier's packet."

Later that evening, Ramon finally had time to compose his thoughts.

Dear Garsinda, Pettihomme, and Eleanora,

I love you and miss you all very much. Son, how is your sword practice going? Daughter, I hope you are learning to be a little lady-in-waiting as well as learning the stealth of the dagger. Garsinda, my love, Louis is a gracious king and we were successful in battles, as well as recovering his family's duchy of Lorraine. I am proud of the victories, but I will ask him if my duty is done and can return home within the month. I am healthy.

Love, Ramon

He let the ink dry and rolled up the scroll, inserting it in a leather mailing tube. *Louis will read this before he sends it, so when I ask him if I can leave he will not be surprised.*

He next morning, Ramon broached the topic over a game of chess. "Sire, we have had great success in Lorraine. The city of Reims has renewed their pledge to the crown. I know other cities will align themselves with you and abandon their allegiance to Hugh. If my task is done, please consider allowing me to return home."

"Ha! Count, you were so distracted by those thoughts, you missed my last moves. Checkmate!

"You have done well, Ramon. Those tales of your defeat of the Saracens and Hungarians are proven true. I believe you are indeed a military genius! I also trust you, Ramon. But I need your help on one more mission."

"What is that, King Louis?"

"Ramon, in private call me Louis. We are now friends and brothers, no?"

"Yes, sire . . . yes, Louis."

"Good. My next venture will not require you to accompany me, but to return to Lorraine and verify that there is order. The milites respect you and will do as you command, as they proved by their excellence in battle.

"I have received two important messages. One from Lorraine. Flushed with the victory we had over Otto's knights, against my orders, Henry and Giselbert crossed the Rhine. They were defeated and Giselbert drowned as he fled back across the Rhine. With Giselbert gone, I need you to make sure Henry still has control of the duchy."

"I will leave tomorrow, um . . . Louis."

"And I will also leave tomorrow for Normandy. My entire life, the Duke of Flanders and I have had a strong alliance. He sent me a message that William Longsword had an accident that was fatal, although you will hear rumors it was an assassination." The king looked down and cleared his throat. "Now I hope to convince the Norman nobles to resume their loyalty to the crown."

Two weeks later Ramon returned from Lorraine, pleased with the measures that Sir Henry had put in place to protect the duchy. However, all was not well elsewhere. A courier had delivered a letter to Queen Gerberga from the nobles of Normandy. They had captured King Louis as he was attempting to influence several nobles in Rouen to pledge allegiance to him. The Norman council now held him as hostage. Louis's wife Gerberga would make the final decision on the negotiation to release the king.

Ramon met with Gerberga. "My Queen, I heard the Normans are proposing to exchange your son for Louis. They know your son is very dear to you, but I recommend you offer Richard, son of William Longsword, who is in your care, instead."

Gerberga's eyebrows arched. "Why would they accept the boy Richard? He has been rejected by most of their nobles?"

"Because there may be enough of them still loyal to the memory of William. He is a descendent of Rollo, the first Duke of Normandy. To our advantage, it could divide their cohesion and the turmoil will help free your husband. All they can do is reject the offer, but I recommend we try."

"Hmm . . . I agree. Offer them Richard for my husband."

Hugh the Great, a close ally of the Normans, insisted that in addition to releasing Louis in trade for Richard, the king must give up Laon as well. To make the trade acceptable, King Otto, though a former enemy, promised he would give King Louis and his family sanctuary in Aachen. Otto, as well as King Edmund of England, were both interested in preserving Louis as the legitimate crown of West Francia, thus strengthening their own positions as legal heirs. Otto, however, took advantage of the situation and entered Lorraine to recover the duchy, then held the city of Reims under siege. Eventually, Louis was freed.

Louis's household was now preparing to evacuate Chateau Galliot. Gerberga bustled about the castle directing the servants. Louis sat in his armchair, staring vacantly. Ramon entered the room, knelt next to him, and placed his arm on the king's shoulder. "Louis, Queen Gerberga is a torrent of energy! It is comforting to have such a dependable spouse in times like this. Hold your head up! King Otto will protect you and your family. Very soon you will regain your authority in West Francia."

Louis did not respond.

"Liege, what can I do for you now?"

"Your skills are what I need to recover my domains, Ramon, and I hoped you could stay to serve the Crown. But I recently learned that Archbishop Artald has returned to Reims and organized the bishops of East and West Francia to support me. The Church pressured Otto to shelter my family. Your gracious act giving the archbishop sanctuary in Toulouse in addition to your wife's generous donation to Artald's diocese compels me to release you. I am not so charitable, but I respect you. Go back to your home but be wary. Although King Otto has granted me protection, that safety does not extend to you. He harbors enmity toward you for destroying many of his best knights. I am sorry I cannot provide an escort."

Ramon took leave of the king and his wife and gathered his armor, weapons, and mount at the stables. Hoping to be inconspicuous, he draped a woolen cape over his armor, pulled up his hood, and rode south. Leaving Laon, just several minutes after the pedestrian and wheeled traffic dissipated, he detected a pair of horsemen following him. They had drawn their swords. *Are these Hugh's men or Otto's assassins? It does not matter. They will not stop me!* He galloped ahead until he was out of their sight around a bend in the road, then wheeled, and charged the men. He unhorsed the first rider, impaling him with his wing spear, and disabled the second assassin after a clash of swords. He left both crumpled in the road. Ramon then hurried south.

He knew the siege of Reims had been lifted, but Hugh's and Otto's soldiers remained in the city, so he headed on the only other road south to Paris. He stopped at an inn outside of the city, to avoid traveling at night. Late that evening the creak of an old door hinge saved his life. He was awakened by the noise as an assassin entered his room. Ramon had the jump on the intruder. He had been sleeping in a chair behind the door and plunged his dagger into the assailant, whose attention was focused on the bed.

From then on, every person Ramon encountered was suspect. When he retrieved his horse at the stable, under the folds of his cape he had his dagger ready. He was constantly under stress and in a state of readiness. Riding south from Paris he continually looked about for threats. On his third night from Laon, he abruptly left the road at an arbitrary location, out of sight of other travelers, and made a fire. He mounded some turf near the fire and covered it with his blanket. He hid nearby in the darkness, and within a short time a pair of cutthroats rushed the blanket. Ramon slipped away undetected.

He knew he must assume a new identity. At Limoges, the monks helped him transform himself. He had arrived at the monastery with a beard and long auburn hair but left clean-shaven and with a monk's dark tonsure. The rest of his journey to Toulouse was completed without incident, and he stole into the city wearing a monk's habit over his armor. From Saint Sernin Monastery, he sent a message to Garsinda.

It was night and the brothers of Saint Sernin had retired. On his cot Ramon detected someone entering the dormitory. He retreated into the corner of the cubicle with dagger ready, but relaxed when he saw Garsinda with Pere, Odulf, and several knights outside the door. The count guided them to the cloister to avoid awakening the monks. He embraced Garsinda and held her for several moments. "I love you," he whispered,

She echoed her affection and stepped back. "Did you receive any of my letters?"

"No, not one. But right now, my concern is that I am being pursued by assassins. He looked at each in the group and said, "Trust only those of us who are here.

"I must stay disguised until I am sure there are no more threats. Now that you know I am safe, go back to the chateau and protect our children." Ramon looked at Pere and Odulf and said, "Closing the gates at night will not be enough. Patrol the walls around the city. There will be strangers coming to destroy our family."

They departed. Ramon had to see for himself that Garsinda returned safely. He retrieved his long staff from under his cot and followed them at a distance through the dark streets. Pere and Odulf walked on each side of Garsinda. A pair of milites walked ahead and two more took up the rearguard as they returned to the chateau. Ramon waited in the shadows of the street as the troupe entered the courtyard. Within a few minutes, he detected movement in the darkness. A pair of men clad in dark tunics were scaling the wall surrounding the chateau courtyard, with one man supporting another atop his shoulders. Ramon silently approached them and used his oak staff to sweep the legs of the supporter. The intruders collapsed in a pile on the stone pavement. One recovered quickly, drew his sword and slashed down at Ramon. The count blocked upward with his staff, and instantly knew his error by the angle he parried, when the sword chopped through his wooden weapon. The dense oak absorbed most of the energy however, and Ramon avoided being cut. Meanwhile, the second assassin recovered, and Ramon holding a pair of short sticks, now confronted two sword wielding adversaries.

He knew it would be difficult to parry the swords, so he went on the offensive. Ramon stepped into his opponents and intercepted the sword blades arcing towards him. He directed the recoil to smash their hands, breaking their grips and disarming them. He finished with devastating blows to knock them unconscious. When Ramon saw Odulf exit the chateau courtyard and approach with several milites, he disappeared down the dark street.

Over the next several weeks, more assassins materialized in Toulouse. Several tried to enter the city gates and were captured or killed by the milites on guard, and the few that slipped into the city were hunted down by the count. Interrogations revealed that they had been sent by Hugh, Duke of the Franks. After months of being absent on campaign in the north, followed by three or four months living disguised in Toulouse, Ramon had been removed from the public eye, with no explanation of his fate. Rumors spread that he was dead. The stream of assassins finally subsided several months after he had returned from Laon.

The Normans, the Franks, and the Germans skirmished and competed for allies in northern Europe. King Louis gained support from Otto and recovered his capital city of Laon and regained Lorraine and Burgundy. Aquitaine, Toulouse, and the rest of the south was relatively peaceful and Ramon welcomed the return to an undisturbed life with his family.

One summer morning, Ramon and Garsinda surveyed the fields and pastures of their manor north of the city, as they waited for the stable hands to bring them their riding mares. Eleonora and Pettihomme were eager to find their ponies. The girl shouted, using one of the Basque words she had learned from her mother, "Where is my *pottoka?*" She chased

Pettihomme into the stables to find their black and white dappled ponies. The petite horses had been culled from feral herds that roamed the Pyrenees Mountains not far to the south. The ponies' gentle demeaner made them ideal mounts for the children.

Away from the public and with no one in sight, Garsinda gently kissed her husband. "Ramon, I cherish the times our family is together."

"We should be thankful for every day," said Ramon. "With the recent death of King Louis, his thirteen year old son Lothar is now king. He will be dominated by Hugh, Duke of the Franks, who is still powerful. Gerberga, Lothar's mother and the regent, is clever, but she is without an army. Her only effective defense has been to warn Hugh that Lothar is the legitimate king, having been sanctioned by the Pope and the German monarch, Otto."

Garsinda added, "If Hugh eliminates opposition in the north, I pray this does not mean he will have the resources to turn his aggressions toward us."

"Before he sent assassins. This time it would be war. And through family tradition, I owe my fealty to the King of the Franks, Lothar. I will fight Hugh."

They were both still, as if absorbed in the implications of Ramon's last statement. Then Garsinda uttered, "Oh no, what bad fortune! Coming now through the manor gate are riders, I fear with a dreary message."

A pair of knights arrived and reined their horses. They dismounted, bowed tersely, and handed a leather tube to Ramon. "Sire, this arrived today from Queen Gerberga."

He dismissed the knights and removed a rolled message from the tube. They read the document together. "Gerberga is shrewd!" exclaimed Garsinda. "She protected Lothar by turning over parts of Burgundy and Lorraine to Hugh."

"She is politically astute. I predict, when Lothar comes of age, she will help him recover the duchies," added Ramon.

"It seems like it was just yesterday that I returned from the north and was a fugitive in my own city, but it has been over a year. Gerberga's talent reminds me of your abilities, love. Garsinda, your influence and timing were perfect, convincing Archbishop Artald to contact Otto and to give Louis sanctuary. It saved both of us and freed me."

She frowned. "It was not all due to my negotiating skills. The funds I donated to his church were significant."

"Yes, but that is part of negotiation, knowing when. Money can be meaningless if used at the wrong time or in the wrong way."

"Husband, how soon will you be returning to your annual rounds to visit the vassal counties? We will miss you."

Ramon held his wife's hand. "I have assigned Pere instead and he has instructions to train senior knights for the duty. Being away so long has made me realize how much I love my family. I will leave more of the governing to my cousins that I have placed in the vassal counties. They will report to me once or twice per year, rather than me riding constantly from county to county to ensure their loyalty. It will require me to travel less often."

Garsinda's faced beamed with joy. "How wonderful!"

"My cousin Maurice Pons will govern Aquitaine in the event Elabus fails. Ison Pons of Fos will govern Gothia. My first cousin will govern Rouergue under the supervision of his father Ermengol. It will all be kept within the Pons family."

Ramon noted his wife was suddenly grim. She muttered, "The world is full of fathers, sons, brothers . . . of family members . . .opposing each other, and killing each other for power."

"That is what I will ensure does not happen," said Ramon. "by staying close to my cousins and my vassals. Several times per year I will host a sumptuous gathering in Toulouse, inviting the vassals to celebrate the unity of our realm and to make sure I understand their needs. Thus we can promptly address grievances and not allow them to fester."

Garsinda brightened. "You once told me that some of them *might* be cousins. Perhaps it is only a coincidence some of them are named Pons? How can you trust them if the relationship is that questionable?"

"That is it! *I wish* they were my cousins, so I treat them as my cousins, and they reciprocate."

Garsinda paused, drew close, examined his eyes and sniffed. "No, it does not appear you were drinking before we left the chateau." She sighed in acquiescence, then with a smile and renewed enthusiasm, "Yes, stay with your vision, husband!"

Garsinda and Ramon treasured the moment as they watched Pettihomme help Eleanora mount her skewbald pony. It was a sunny day in late June and the fields of their manor were lush and verdant. Under a blue sky they rode across fields of purple as the fragrance of lavender chased them on the summer breeze.

MICHAEL A. PONZIO

ABOUT THE AUTHOR

Since childhood, Mike Ponzio has read books about ancient Rome. He traded books and stories with his father, Joseph E. Ponzio, and they discussed the origins of the family surname. Mike traveled around the Mediterranean to Europe, Asia, and Africa, visiting many of the locations he would later write about. He continues to travel and writes stories which he imagines may have taken place during the lives of ancient ancestors.

Mike met his wife, Anne Davis, in 1975 at a University of Florida karate class. Since that time both have taught Cuong Nhu Martial Arts. With John Burns, they wrote and published six instructional books on martial arts weapons. Mike retired in 2015, after working as an environmental engineer for thirty-seven years. Anne and Mike have raised four sons. They are all engineer graduates, following in the footsteps of their Davis and Ponzio grandfathers.

The author's previous novels listed below make up the *Lover of the Sea* series. As in *Ramon Pons: Count of Toulouse*, the title characters are historical.

- *Pontius Aquila: Eagle of the Republic*
- *Pontius Pilatus: Dark Passage to Heaven*
- *St. Pontianus: Bishop of Rome*

For more information use the link to
Amazon's Michael A. Ponzio Author Page
https://www. **amazon.com/author/michael_a_ponzio**

Or the author's website:
Ancestry Novels: Pontius, Ponzio, Pons, and Ponce
https://**mikemarianoponzio.wixsite.com/pontius-ponzio-pons**

AUTHOR's REQUEST

Please write a brief review *of Ramon Pons: Count of Toulouse*
on Amazonbooks.com

Comments or questions are welcome:
mikemarianoponzio@gmail.com

Ancestry Novels- A New Sub Genre of Historical Fiction

Have you ever wanted to live in another time in history? And if so, did you imagine what it would be like to take the place of an ancestor? My lifelong experience reading books on history combined with my love for family has inspired me to bring these visions alive, by writing a series of "Ancestry Novels".

It began over ten years ago. My father, Joseph Ponzio, also read books on history as a hobby. We traded books and discussed the possibility of being related to ancient Romans. I went one step further and wrote novellas for my father about our 'ancient ancestors'. The first story was about an Etruscan, Pontias Larth, whose only historical record was that his name was engraved on a tomb in 474 B.C.. I wrote another story about Pontius Cominius, a scout in the Roman army. He was mentioned by the Roman historian Livy in his narrative on the sack of Rome by the Gauls in 390 B.C. The source of the third novella was relatively generous, being a few pages of historical record, that described the defeat of the Roman legions by General Pontius Gaius at Caudine Forks.

I suggest two criteria when writing "Ancestry Novels". The main character must be documented in history. And there must be a possibility the historical person is related to your family based on surname. The documentation in history can be as little as the name inscribed on a tomb or as much as several pages in the historical record. Sparse historical records are preferred, because when the character is well documented, the author's experience is lessened and there are fewer chances to develop characters and stories.

Write the novels you want to read but that no one has written. Experience the story and live the dream as one of your ancestors. Use the personality of a relative for the a main character and include memories of family experiences. Memorialize a favorite departed pet by adding it to the novel. Use the results of family

DNA tests to add previously unidentified ethnicities and localities to the stories.

I have published three ancestry novels that take place during ancient Rome. The first novel is about Pontius Aquila, a tribune elected by the common people. He infuriated Julius Caesar when he refused to stand with the other officials as the dictator's chariot passed by during a parade in Rome. The second novel takes place 100 years after Aquila. Emperor Tiberius Caesar ordered Pontius Pilate to return to Rome from his post in Judea, because of a complaint that the governor had used excessive force to put down a rebellion. In the third novel, Saint Pontianus, Bishop of Rome, must deal with the persecution by Roman authorities and fight street battles with the followers of the anti-pope, Hippolytus. When the novels are read chronologically, connections are revealed as to the relation of the characters across generations, however, the stories stand on their own and each book can be read alone.

The fourth novel occurs during the Middle Ages. *Ramon Pons: Count of Toulouse,* chronicles the ruler of a region in the south of France in 924 A.D.. Ramon Pons longs to fulfill his dying father's request to build a monastery in honor of their ancestor, Saint Pons of Cimiez, but he must serve his people first. He is obligated to marry and produce an heir, put down rebellions by vassals, and protect his domains against Saracens and Hungarians.

Ramon Pons   Bibliography

1. Adamson, Melitta, Weiss, ed., Regional Cuisines of Medieval Europe: A Book of Essays, New York, Routledge, 2003.
2. Aline Durand, Philippe Leveau. Farming in Mediterranean and France and rural Settlement in the Late Roman and Early Medieval Periods: The Contribution from Archaeology and Environmental Sciences in the Last Twenty Years. Barcelo Miquel et Sigaut Francois. The Making of Feudal ´ Agricultures, BRILL, pp.177-253, 2004, The transformation of the Roman World, 90-04-11722- 9.
3. Avignon France history, www.triposo.com/loc/Avignon/history/background March 4, 2017
4. Barbichon, M – Par, P., Ed., Dictionnairie Complet De Tos Les Lieux de la France, Freres, Tetot   Libraries, Paris, 1831.
5. Bias Against Left-handed People, wikipedia.org/wiki/Bias_against_ lefthanded_people#Favorable_perceptions
6. Compton, Michael, Medieval Sailing, A Wikipedia Compilation,
7. Dunbabin, Jean, France in the Making 843-1180, Oxford, Oxford university Press, 2000.
8. Farmer, Sharon and Rosenwein, Barbara, H. ed., Monks & nuns, Saints & Outcasts, Cornell University Press, Ithaca and London, 2000.
9. Fossier, Robert, ed., The Cambridge Illustrated History of the Middle Ages, Vol. 2, Edinburgh, Cambridge University Press.
10. Guichenon, Samual. Historie genealogique de la yale maison de Sovoie, justifiee par titres, Fondations de Monesteres, Chex Jean-Michele Briolo, Turin, 1777.
11. Hallam, Henry, View of the State of Europe During the Middle Ages, Vol. 1, W.J. Widdleton Publisher, New York, 1866.
12. Hare, August, J.C., Paris, Macmillan and Company, New York, 1896.
13. Hazlitt, William, barrister of the middle temple, The Classical Gazetteer: A Dictionary of Ancient Geography, Sacred and Profane, London, Whittaker and Company, 1851.
14. Hungarian Raid in Spain, wikivisually.com/wiki/Hungarian_raid_in_Spain_ (942).
15. Key, Charles, August, The First Crusade: The Accounts of Eye-Witnesses and Participants, London, Humphrey Milford, Oxford Press, 1921.
16. Knight, Charles, Geography or First Division of the English Encyclopedia, Vol III, London, Bradbury, Evans, and Co., 1867.
17. Lacroix, Paul, Manners, Customs, and Dress during the Middle Ages and during the Renaissance Period, New York, Skyhorse Publishing Inc., 2013. PLewis, Archibald, R., Development of Southern French and Catalan Society, 718-1050, University of Texas Press, Austin, Texas.

18. List of Ancient Watermills, en.wikipedia.org/wiki/List_of_ancient_watermills, 12-5-2016.
19. Louis IV. www.britannica.com/biography/Louis-IV-king-of-France IV
20. Loveland, John Douglas Errington, The Romance of Nice, Plymouth, William Brendon and Son, 1912.
21. Middle Ages Fruit. www.lordsandladies.org/middle-ages-food-fruit.htm
22. Omniglot.com/language/phrases/Occitan, / www.omniglot.com/language/phrases/occitan.php, August 2017.
23. Philippe Lauer (ed.), Les Annales de Flodoard. Collection des textes pour servir à l'étude et à l'enseignement de l'histoire 39. Paris: Picard, 1905. by Flodoard, of Reims, 894-966; Lauer, Philippe, 1874-1953.
24. Projects MedLands-Toulouse http://fmg.ac/Projects/MedLands/TOULOUSE.htm, Nov. 2017.
25. Remensnyder, Amy, Goodrich, Remembering Kings Past: Monastic Foundations in Medieval Southern France, Ithaca and London, Cornell Press, 1995.
26. Reynolds, Terry, S., Stronger Than A Hundred Men: A History of the Vertical Watermill, The John Hopkins University Press, Baltimore, 1983.
27. Rose, Elise, Whitlock, Cathedral and Cloisters of the South of France, Vol. 1, G. P. Putnam's Sons the Knickerbocker Press, New York and London, 1906.
28. Russell, Ben, The Economics of the Roman Stone Trade, Oxford, Oxford University Press, 2013.
29. Scribes Scribbling, scribescribbling.wordpress.com/2013/03/26/ink-ingredients-modern-and-medieval/
30. Siege of Paris, thefreelancehistorywriter.com/2015/04/17/the-siege-of-paris-of-885-886/ Sept. 5, 2016.
31. Sismondi, Simonda, Jean-Charels-Leonard, The French Under the Merovingians, London, W & T Piper, Paternoste Row, 850.Sahuc, Joseph, L'art Roman à Saint-Pons-de-Thomières, Societe Anonyme de L'Imprimerie Generale du Midi, Montpelier, 1908.
32. Spence, Lewis, A Dictionary of Medieval Romance and Romance Writers, London, George Routledge and Sons, LMTD, New York, E., P, Dutton and Company, 1913.
33. Taylor, Bayard, The History of Nations-Germany, revised by Sidney Fay, Collier & Son, New York, 1906.
34. The Flower of wheat: Bread in the Middle Ages. http://www.engr.psu.edu/mtah/articles/flower_of_wheat.htm
35. The Story of Quince. /prospectbooks.co.uk/wp-content/uploads/2014/09/Quinces_extract.pdf
36. Toch, Michael, The Economic History of European Jews: Late Antiquity and Early Middle Ages, Boston, Brill, 2013.
37. Were left-handed knights forced to switch to their right hand? www.reddit.com/r/AskHistorians/comments/1g6dh0/were_lefthanded_knights_forced_to_switch_to_their/

Made in the USA
Lexington, KY
16 November 2019

57093578R00127